CHESAPEAKE CRIMES

THEY HAD IT COMIN'

IN THE SAME SERIES

CHESAPEAKE CRIMES

THEY HAD IT COMIN'

Twenty tales of revenge and murder

**Edited by Donna Andrews,
Barb Goffman, and Marcia Talley**

With a foreword by Katherine Neville

WILDSIDE PRESS

Chesapeake Crimes: *They Had It Comin'*

Coordinating Editors
Donna Andrews
Barb Goffman
Marcia Talley

Editorial Panel
Erin N. Bush
Megan Plyler
Mary Augusta Thomas

This edition is published in 2010
by Wildside Press, LLC.
www.wildsidebooks.com

CONTENTS

FOREWORD

by Katherine Neville

Not many of us would admit, even to ourselves, that we had actually *wished* for something awful to befall anybody we knew. On the other hand, if we've ever felt exploited by an acquaintance, or undervalued in a job that we felt trapped in—if we've experienced an unappreciative boss, a backstabbing co-worker, a jealous rival, a manipulative friend, a faithless lover, an intrusive neighbor, or even a controlling homeowners' association board . . . well, you get the picture.

Each of us has doubtless gone a round or two with someone whom we secretly felt deserved more than a small dose of Divine Justice. This probably explains why most of us can't help but smile upon hearing that somebody who "done us wrong" has, at long last, gotten his "just desserts." In extreme cases (that is, if you're anything like me) you might even have gone so far, in the past, as to uncork a small split of champagne!

I suspect there'll be plenty of bubbly flowing as you relish reading about twenty of literature's most deserving villains, who get their comeuppance in *Chesapeake Crimes: They Had It Comin'*.

The surprising range of these tales is wide and deep, from motive to method, from historical to futuristic-fantastic. The following smattering will, I hope, tingle your taste buds for more:

- Against the shared background of the Civil War, Karen Cantwell and Audrey Liebross tackle everything from slavery and mistaken identity to espionage and visionary prescience.
- When it comes to the time-tested crime of passion, Trish Carrico, Mary Ann Corrigan, Carla Coupe, C. Ellett Logan, Ann McMillan, and Helen Schwartz, all deal with infidelity in a variety of creative ways, including: a Japanese canal, a selection of gourmet appetizers, a lacy brassiere, a load of concrete, a computer hack-in, and a stake through the heart.
- After the twenty years I spent in the working world, a particular favorite theme of my own has always been bumping off maleficent bosses and other controlling authority figures. Meriah Crawford, Sasscer Hill, Mary El-

len Hughes, B.V. Lawson, Bonner Menking, and Shelley Shearer manage to even the score with a corrupt sheriff, a venomous stable-owner, a couple of arrogant employers who are bilking others, a threatening new neighbor, and a manipulative homeowners' association board president.

• Falling for the wrong person (for example, a rapist-murderer, a child molester, or your own psychiatric patient) is a topic handled with very different, yet astonishing, twist endings by Smita H. Jain, Barb Goffman, and Debbi Mack.

• The book world itself is tackled by Donna Andrews and G.M. Malliet, when an envious aspiring author and a crazed literary fan run amok in literary land.

• And, last but not least, Lisa M. Tillman leaves us guessing: Who really "had it comin'" in the end: the unwitting killer? Or the accidental victim?

Chesapeake Crimes: They Had It Comin' is a tour de force, displaying an unusual variety of plot complexity and a colorful cast of characters. It is certain to stay on the shelves, pleasing readers, for a very long time.

THE PLAN

by Donna Andrews

As soon as Darius Wentworth heard that the Chesapeake Chapter of Sisters in Crime was accepting submissions for the fourth volume of its popular anthology series, he took a sheet of paper and began drawing up his action plan.

Darius was a firm believer in action plans. As he was fond of saying during chapter lunches, the moment he completed a well-crafted action plan, he felt as if his project was off to a successful start—indeed, more than halfway done.

Unfortunately, among his few failed projects were his efforts to place stories in the previous three volumes of *Chesapeake Crimes*. He had read those volumes with an increasing sense of frustration. Not that the stories the editors had chosen were bad—far from it. The anthologies were a worthy setting in which his own small gems could shine—if only the editors could be brought to see it that way.

He would have been tempted to cry prejudice—after all, he was one of the chapter's few "brothers in crime." But since submissions were done blindly, so that the editorial panel did not know the authors' names until after they made their selections, reverse sexism could hardly account for his repeated rejection. With the first volume, he chalked it up to the aberrant taste of the three members of the editorial panel. But since the chapter recruited a different editorial panel for each volume, his second and third rejections rankled more.

Subtle interrogation of the editors at several chapter gatherings revealed no profound distaste for his style or subject matter. "It was very close," they'd say. "We had such a lot of good material, and ultimately a few good stories just didn't make the cut."

In other words, his stories weren't quite good enough. Darius brooded over that for a while. He considered dropping out of the chapter. But when he heard the announcement of the fourth anthology, inspiration struck.

At the top of his action plan, Darius listed all the authors with stories in the three previous anthologies, marking a star beside the names of those who had been included twice. There was even one annoyingly successful writer with a story in all three anthologies.

Darius studied the list for a while and then crossed off the names of those authors who were at all well known—writers whose names could reasonably be expected to help sell the anthologies. And he added a few other names—chapter members who hadn't yet had stories in *Chesapeake Crimes* but who had placed stories in other publications.

He reviewed his list and nodded with satisfaction.

"The competition," he said.

His action plan was simple. The submission deadline was four months away. Between now and then, he needed to complete the best story he was capable of writing and eliminate enough of the competition to ensure that his story was chosen. A minimum of six, he decided, though if the opportunity arose, eight or nine might be safer.

His first target was an easy one. By eavesdropping after a chapter meeting, he learned that the next gathering of her writers' group would be held in a restaurant in Georgetown the following week. While researching one of his stories, Darius had learned how to break into and hotwire cars. When the critique group broke up and his target began her stroll to the Foggy Bottom Metro station, Darius was waiting with a stolen Nissan Maxima. Another sad hit-and-run accident in the District of Columbia.

He found the moment of silence at the next chapter meeting profoundly moving. And his first success was all the more satisfying since the critique group she'd been attending on the night of her death was one that had previously spurned his offer to join them. Perhaps after they had recovered from their loss, he would approach them again.

His second target was an elderly chapter member who was well known for dropping, breaking, spilling, or losing something during almost every meeting. She also took digoxin for a heart condition and usually remembered midway through lunch that she hadn't yet taken it. How easy to divert her purse long enough to steal half a dozen digoxin tablets from the medicine bottle she carried, and even easier, after a brief trip to the men's room, to slip the powdered tablets into her after-lunch coffee. Luckily her symptoms did not begin until after she'd left the meeting.

Darius contributed generously toward the donation to the American Heart Fund that the chapter made in her memory.

After that his project stalled. Not the writing project—he'd already completed his story, a hard-boiled noir tale in the finest tradition of Hammett and Chandler, and turned it in to the editorial committee. But his efforts to get the drop on the others on his target list were failing. He was almost spotted while attempting to sabotage one writer's car in the parking garage of her condo. His repeated attempts to reproduce his successful hit and run were stymied by the onset of cold weather and an inexplicable increase in wariness on the part of his targets. And most of his targets usually arranged to sit with the same small group of friends at every meeting, making it virtually impossible to accomplish another poisoning.

With only a few weeks left in his window of opportunity, and only one more chapter meeting, Darius was beginning to feel discouraged. Then fate intervened. The chapter member who served as luncheon coordinator announced that she was forced to resign for health reasons. Darius immediately volunteered to take her place.

As the meeting drew near, he studied the checks and menu selections he received from members. He was delighted to see that most of his targets would be attending the next meeting. Better yet, most of them had ordered the salmon. So had a few other members, but Darius resigned himself to losing a few innocent bystanders to achieve his goal.

He brushed up on his poisons and decided to use a concentrated dry extract of oleander—notoriously the world's most poisonous plant. A nighttime raid on a neighbor's greenhouse produced sufficient plant material for his purposes, and Darius arrived at the meeting in possession of enough powdered oleander to slaughter the entire chapter several times over.

He had observed at previous meetings that while the chapter members were finishing their salad course, the waiters would begin staging the entrées on a large sideboard in the hallway outside the room. A well-timed trip to the men's room enabled Darius to pass by the steaming plates and sprinkle his powder generously over all the salmon dishes.

Even Darius found the ensuing chaos unsettling. Particularly when he realized that among the thirteen chapter members who had succumbed to the salmon was one of the more helpful and sympathetic chapter officers.

And the next few months were difficult. All other chapter business came to a dead halt during the murder investigation. Darius wasn't singled out particularly by the police, but like all the chapter members, he had to endure his share of police attention. And he wasn't by any means the only chapter member to breathe a sigh of relief when the police arrested a disgruntled waiter with a history of mental illness and a hobby of writing threatening letters to local, state, and federal government officials.

"Of course he'll never see the inside of a jail cell," the chapter secretary said at the next month's lunch meeting. "I understand he'll be involuntarily committed."

"We're still petitioning to be allowed to make a victim's impact statement," said the chapter president—formerly the vice president, but the president had, unfortunately, been among the salmon fanciers. "And I certainly hope all of you can arrange to come. We want to make a strong showing."

All of them nodded vigorously. Of course all of them consisted of a single table of only eight diners. While chapter membership was up, thanks to the publicity Sisters in Crime had received, attendance at the lunches was still way down.

"And I have one more sad announcement," the president said. "It's about the anthology. We lost so many of the writers who submitted or were planning to submit that we just don't think we could get enough submissions to make a go of it. And even if we did—well, most people don't realize it, because she is—was—so self-effacing, but the lion's share of the hard work involved was done by . . ."

And here the president broke down and could barely sob out the name of the hard-working member in question. Darius didn't know her well—could barely call her face to mind—but he put on an expression of grave sorrow and joined the murmured chorus of sentimental nonsense.

Under the circumstances, he decided it would be imprudent to seem too upset about the demise of the anthology. Better to echo everyone else in saying that of course it would be completely inappropriate to push forward with the anthology at such a difficult period for the chapter—and hope that the passage of time would change their minds.

Ah, well, he thought. They probably would have rejected me again anyway. He concentrated on looking sad and on noting, just in case it became useful in the future, what entrée selections the remaining diners had made.

At the end of the meeting, while most of the members were saying goodbye and exchanging tearful hugs, the president drew Darius aside.

"I just wanted to say that the story you submitted was wonderful," she said. "And the editors loved it, too. It was definitely the best one we'd received. I know it's small comfort at a time like this, but if we'd been able to do volume four, we definitely would have used your story."

Donna Andrews had a short story, "Night Shades," in Chesapeake Crimes I, *and is delighted to return to the fold with "The Plan." Not that she has been slacking off in the intervening years*—Swan for the Money, *the eleventh book in her Meg Langslow series, hit the* New York Times *extended bestseller list, and she has published short stories in* Wolfsbane and Mistletoe *(edited by Charlaine Harris and Toni L.P. Kelner, Ace),* Unusual Suspects *(edited by Dana Stabenow, Ace), and* Ellery Queen's Mystery Magazine. *Donna has assured her fellow editors that no actual chapter members were harmed in the making of this story. For more information, see her website: www.donnaandrews.com.*

THE RECOLLECTIONS OF ROSABELLE RAINES

by Karen Cantwell

Rosabelle Raines had lived at least a thousand lives, and much to her dismay, she could recall them all.

Lying on the cold, winter ground, Rosabelle rubbed her aching eyes while she recovered from the most recent incident. Some wisps of her fine, ebony hair had slipped from its silk netting, falling over her face.

"Rosa," whispered her sister, Flora. "Are you with me?"

Drained of energy, Rosabelle moaned, but would be unable to speak for a minute or more.

"Does this happen often?" The man she heard speaking appeared as a blur at the end of her tunneled vision. He seemed to hover miles away, but in reality his warm face was nearly touching hers. She could smell his breath—a touch of ale, she thought, and possibly some corned beef. She detested corned beef.

"She . . . she has . . . fainting spells." Flora offered a worried, tentative explanation. Weaker in spirit than Rosabelle, she was badly affected by her sister's spells. They gave Flora such distress that she would suffer stomach maladies for many days after.

"We should get her to a doctor," the man urged.

"No!" Rosabelle shouted, her voice returning just in time. Rosabelle found herself sitting upright, and the man responsible for her condition was no longer a distant blur. Pleasing to her eyes, he was fair of skin and possessed a head of enviously thick hair the color of summer wheat. In his left hand he clutched a newspaper and a stovepipe hat made of fine silk that belied his humble station. Perhaps the hat was a tribute to the late President Lincoln. Rosabelle might not care for his corned beef breath, but she would consider a person of good spirit if he revered a man the likes of Mr. Lincoln. Not a popular sentiment for a woman from the South, Rosabelle knew, but she did not often subscribe to opinions just because they were popular.

"I have no need for a doctor, sir. A brisk walk in the fresh air and some tea at our destination will be the only medicine I need." She brushed a strand of hair out of her eyes. "Flora, could you help me to my feet please?" Rosabelle placed a hand in the shallow snow to give her some leverage, while holding her other up for her sister's assistance.

"Here, let me help." Eli Witherspoon, the young man who had touched Rosabelle's hand by way of introduction just moments earlier, was about to touch her again by placing his own hand under her back as support in her attempt to stand.

Signaling him to keep his distance, Rosabelle rebuffed his offer promptly. "No! You have done enough." Stuttering a moment on her words, she quickly corrected herself. "What I mean to say is you are too kind. Truly, sir, your assistance is unnecessary. We have a system, my sister and I." With a minor struggle, Rosabelle was on her feet. She quickly tucked the wayward strands back into her snood, attempting to regain some appearance of dignity. "See? I am upright." Rosabelle gave a slight curtsy to Mr. Witherspoon while brushing snow from her sapphire velvet cape, then placed her hands back in her muff for warmth. Only then did she notice the newspaper the young man held.

"Interesting article is it not?" Rosabelle asked.

He looked at the paper with an odd expression as if it had materialized out of nowhere. "Ah. Well . . ." He cleared his throat. "I have not read this paper yet." He fidgeted in a nervous manner, shoving the paper under his arm.

"You should!" Flora exclaimed, her eyes brightening. "Rosa and I read it earlier today—a fascinating story about a lady spy! What was her name, Rosa?"

"Abigail. Abigail Dawes," Rosabelle answered, studying the distracted Mr. Witherspoon intently.

"That is the name!" Flora said. "A lady spy for the South. Evidently she is a master of disguise. It is very intriguing. She escaped from jail some three weeks ago now. Gives me goose pimples all over my arms."

Mr. Witherspoon pulled a watch from his breast pocket to check the time. "That . . . is . . . yes. Interesting. Well, excuse me for my abruptness, but . . ."

"No." Rosa put her hand up as if to stop his words mid-air. "Excuse us, sir. Come, Flora, we will be late for our engagement with the Waters family."

Rosabelle rushed away, her long hooped skirt pushing the snow along like a plow, while Flora, trailing desperately behind her, looked back at Eli Witherspoon, giving him an apologetic smile.

Flora's interest in Mr. Witherspoon was not lost on Rosabelle, but she did not have time to be concerned with such trivial matters. Not since her recollection.

"Rosa," Flora wheezed, finally reaching her sister. "You were so rude to Mr. Witherspoon."

"Me, rude? Did you see how strangely he was behaving?"

"Maybe you intimidated him. You have that effect on people. Oh! I very much wanted to speak with him longer."

"Sister," Rosabelle said, stopping abruptly and pointing down the road from where they had come. "Look. Your Mr. Witherspoon has disappeared into thin air." Indeed there was no sign of the man.

Rosabelle continued on. "And did you hear him say he had not yet read the newspaper?"

"Well—"

"Yet it was crinkled and worn and turned to the Abigail Dawes article, several pages in."

"But—"

"Flora, something is afoot with that man, and before the day is done, he will either kill or be killed. If you have an interest in this Mr. Eli Witherspoon, come with me now and devise a way to determine which it will be and hopefully stop this crime before it occurs."

Full of vigor and intention, Rosabelle turned on her heel and quickly crossed King Street just as a horse and buggy passed. Flora jogged to catch up.

"These dreams of yours!" Flora panted as she trotted closely behind her sister, her blonde locks bouncing. "Why must you have them? Mr. Witherspoon seems to be gentle and kind. Surely you are wrong."

"Flora," Rosabelle corrected, blue eyes flashing. "I have told you before—these are not dreams. They are recollections. Memories of my other lives."

"How could you possibly know this?"

"How do I know the air is free to breathe? How do I know to smile when I see snow fall from the sky or to cry when a baby dies? I just know. I know."

"Bah! Other lives. You speak such blasphemy! We live only one life on this earth then, God willing, an eternity with Him. How can you think otherwise?" Flora pressed a hand to her bodice. "Dear, my stomach turns. I am feeling ill."

"Remember before the war, when Father entertained those importers from Japan? They called themselves Buddhists—they believe we maintain a cycle on Earth of birth, life, death, and then re-birth. It is not an uncommon belief, this idea that we are reborn to new bodies after we die. Much of the world believes the same."

"Pagans!" Flora was fanning herself.

"Flora, you don't even know what a pagan is," Rosabelle responded, rolling her eyes. She was easily annoyed by her sister's fears. Flora did not fare well with anything outside of the ordinary and expected. And indeed, Rosabelle's recollections were neither ordinary nor expected.

"Well I know the people of this town would consider you a witch and have you burned at the stake," Flora huffed, obviously proud of her foreboding comment.

"I should hope the day of witch burning is past us, but you speak correctly regarding local sentiment. If word of this got out, I could be shunned or, even worse, put in an asylum for the ill of mind."

Flora shook her head. "It scares me so, Rosa."

"Listen to me—we keep this secret between us, and no one will suffer. Now tell me," she said, changing the subject, "when did you meet Mr. Witherspoon?"

"Last Sunday at church. You would know that if you had been there."

"I was there."

"Inside God's house, not outside, contemplating your many wild and sinful lives."

Exasperated, Rosabelle heaved a healthy sigh. Flora could be so trying. "Let us stay with the topic at hand, shall we? Who introduced you?"

"Amelia Patton," her sister replied. "Eli Witherspoon is her cousin, come to Alexandria to work at her father's shipping company. He studied at the University of Virginia," Flora stated with a hint of awe in her voice.

Rosabelle stopped walking for a moment. "Amelia Patton? Is he living in the Patton home?"

"I think so. Why?"

Ignoring Flora's question, Rosabelle resumed her determined trek. "About my recollection—it began when Mr. Witherspoon touched my hand. I saw two men. Both wore tattered garb made of wool. Their hair was long and unkempt, with some strands in braids; their faces bearded. One man was fair-haired and pale while the other had dark hair and eyes black as coal. This darker man was tending a field of some sort, but it was on a hill. The fair-haired man rode up on a horse and dismounted. They talked and shook hands. When the dark man turned back to continue his work, the fair man drew a large knife and stabbed him in the back." Rosabelle shivered with the memory.

"Rosa, I don't understand how you connect your dream—your recollection—with Mr. Witherspoon. Are you saying the fair man is Eli Witherspoon?"

Rosabelle shook her head. "I am not sure. What I do know is this: every time I have a recollection, the person who touched me is involved in an incident almost identical to the recollection."

The strange episodes began nearly a year earlier, just after their mother passed on. Since their father had died before her while fighting for the South, they had become orphans of sorts, even though Rosabelle was twenty and Flora, eighteen. Without husbands to care for them, they were forced to move from Norfolk to Alexandria to live with their Aunt Martha and Uncle Ephraim. Even though Martha and Ephraim Raines had been warm and inviting in every way possible, losing both of their parents and leaving the only home they had ever known proved tragically painful for both girls. It was during that emotional time that Rosabelle experienced her first recollection.

They always occurred in the same way. A person would touch her, by way of introduction, possibly, or just in passing. At that moment Rosabelle would find herself in another world, watching a scene unfold before her. When Mrs. Kincaid put her hands on Rosabelle's shoulder during a quilting party, for example, she had seen a woman drown in the middle of the sea while a ship went down in flames nearby. Later that day, Mrs. Kincaid drowned in the Potomac when she slipped off a pier and was swept away by the heavy current.

Each time Rosabelle had a recollection, she would relay the story to Flora with amazing detail. Within a day's time, a similar event would always occur, and always involving the person who had touched Rosabelle, initiating the memory.

The latest recollection involved four-year-old Edwin Hutchins. Rosabelle had agreed to care for him while his mother walked to market for some fish. Full of a little boy's energy, his blond curls bounced when he bounced. He took Rosabelle's hand with his own chubby little fingers and smiled up at her. Immediately Rosabelle was beneath a tree dressed in the most exquisite finery, mounted on a spectacular steed. An armored man rode past her, but she paid little attention to him. Instead she was calling a name. William. She was calling and calling, and she felt fear. Then a young boy's voice rang out. It came from above her. She looked into the tree. In its highest branches was a beautiful boy with red hair and blue eyes who smiled down at her. He moved as if to make his way down the branches, but his foot slipped. Before she could hear the scream from her own mouth, he was on the ground, mangled. Dead.

Still unaccustomed to her recollections, and not convinced that the related incidents weren't just coincidental, Rosabelle neglected any action. She told Flora, but she did not say a word of her vision to poor

Edwin's mother, who found her son the next day in a mangled heap on the ground beneath their tall oak tree.

Gift or curse, Rosabelle no longer cared. She had vowed that day never to dismiss a recollection again. She would stop this eventual murder. The problem was, she had no idea if the handsome Eli Witherspoon would be the murderer or his victim.

▐ ▐ ▐

Rosabelle turned the corner to a quieter street lined with tall, handsome brick homes.

"Rosa, you've turned on the wrong street." Flora pointed in the opposite direction. "The Waters family lives that way."

"They will have to wait. What we need is more information about Mr. Witherspoon."

"Where would we possibly find any such information?" Flora asked, losing her breath in a desperate attempt to keep pace with Rosabelle.

"Where else but in a room full of women?" Rosabelle smiled while stopping in front of the finest of the brick townhouses, at 220 Prince Street.

Rosabelle climbed the five brick steps to the artfully carved walnut door, seized the brass, pineapple door knocker, and rapped smartly three times. By the time the door opened, Flora had made her way next to Rosabelle and the two of them were greeted by a small Negro woman who would not look directly at either of them.

"Good day, miss." Rosabelle offered the young woman a friendly smile. "We are here for a meeting of the Alexandria Women's League. Please tell your mistress that Rosabelle and Flora Raines have arrived."

A large voice boomed from behind the servant, followed by the sudden appearance of the elaborately jeweled woman who belonged to the voice. Mrs. Harriet Franklin was large in body, personality, wealth, and reputation. Rooms seemed to shrink when she filled them. Her billowing, silk and lace skirt only accentuated her wide girth, and Rosabelle was certain Mrs. Franklin intended it exactly so. Mrs. Franklin loved the spotlight.

"Miss Raines!" Mrs. Franklin bellowed. "Such social graces are not necessary when addressing my Negroes," she laughed. "They may not be slaves any longer, but their station remains the same. What a surprise to see you. We thought you had another engagement."

"Yes, but your lovely neighbor and our esteemed friend Miss Amelia Patton convinced us we should change our plans. Is she here yet?"

"I'm afraid not. Any moment I should imagine though. Lucy, take their capes and bonnets, then get back to help with the preparations. There is much to do; I will not stand for slacking today."

"Yes'm." The girl curtsied to her demanding employer. Lucy took Flora's wrap and muff as they were handed to her, then reached for Rosabelle's. Rosabelle smiled again at the shy Lucy, who looked more toward the floor than toward Rosabelle while attempting to take charge of her overgarments. During the exchange, Rosabelle grazed Lucy's cold, dry hand. Before she could catch her breath, she was in another time. Looking around, she knew she was having another recollection.

But there was something oddly familiar about this memory. She was crouched behind a massive bush that pricked her skin, and the air was cold and damp. She heard the sound of a horse's hooves on hard ground and a man calling another man's name. Crawling on hands and knees to peer around the bushes, Rosabelle gasped. It was the fair man on the horse and the dark man tending the fields. This was the same recollection as the one she experienced when introduced to Eli Witherspoon, with the exception that everything seemed enhanced a hundred fold. Sounds were clearer, colors brighter, and she felt . . . emotion.

She looked down at her own body. Dressed in peasant rags, Rosabelle had the hands of a small girl of eight or nine. She was breathing shallow, erratic gulps of air. She was afraid of this thin-skinned, blond man, but she did not know why. As before, the dark-haired man greeted his visitor, words were exchanged and hands were shook. Rosabelle's fear grew, knowing the end of this story and feeling hopeless to stop it. Once again, when the dark man turned around, the fair man drew his blade and sank it deep into the farmer's back. Rosabelle covered her eyes hard and screamed. When she opened her eyes, she was on the floor in the Franklins's foyer, with Mrs. Franklin waving a foul-smelling vial under her nose.

As usually happened after her recollections, Rosabelle was unable to speak. She would remain mute for a minute or two. Flora twittered on to the many women who had gathered around.

"She has these fainting spells. I am so sorry to be a burden like this, as is Rosa. So sorry. She will be fine. If someone can help me raise her from the floor . . ."

"The sofa in the parlor," Mrs. Franklin exclaimed. "She can recover there." Turning to one of the young women, she added, "Anna dear, fetch Dr. Gordon."

Rosabelle shook her head violently while scanning the room for Lucy.

"You are so kind Mrs. Franklin," Flora said. "But Rosa does not want . . . I mean . . . she has already seen the doctor. These are just mild fainting spells due to . . . low nutrition you see. A cup of tea and an orange or a pear will bring her around just beautifully. Thank you. And some space, I should think, if you please."

With the aid of Marjorie Baker, one of the other guests, Flora successfully moved Rosabelle to the parlor sofa where she found her voice to thank Marjorie for her help and kindness.

"Of course, of course. Let us adjourn to the library—we will continue our meeting there—and leave Rosabelle and Flora some air." Mrs. Franklin herded the dozen women and their voluptuous hooped skirts out of the room, closing the tall double doors behind her.

Rosabelle had been rubbing her head more for the drama than for the purpose of relieving an ache, but once the doors closed, she grabbed Flora's arm.

"Sister! You will not believe what I just witnessed."

Flora tugged her arm away and pressed her index fingers to her own temples.

"Rosa, these dreams of yours—they come too often! They wear me down. Can you not control them?"

"No more than I can control the seasons. Flora, I need you now. Please listen."

"Fine. What did you see this time?"

"It was the same recollection."

"The same as what?"

"Eli Witherspoon. When I touched Lucy's hand, I witnessed the entire murder again."

"Lucy? Who is Lucy?"

"Mrs. Franklin's maid."

"You mean the Negro girl?"

"Yes."

"I don't understand."

"Lucy must be one of the two men in my recollection. Lucy and Eli Witherspoon."

"Well," Flora sniffed. "That seems very odd."

Rosabelle fell back on the sofa laughing.

"What?" Flora asked.

"Is not all of this to be classified as odd, sister?"

Flora, who remained serious for just a moment, finally found the humor in it and laughed as well, which pleased Rosabelle. She desperately needed her sister to accept her condition, as she was the only person in whom Rosabelle could confide completely.

The two sisters sat smiling silently on the sofa for a moment, soaking in the absurdity of their new reality.

"Do you suppose then," Flora said finally, "that Lucy is going to murder Eli Witherspoon?"

"Or is he to murder her? That is precisely what I need to determine. This recollection was different. More detail, and I was acutely aware that this time I was a young girl. Do not ask me how I know this, but the dark man—he was my father. Also I felt true fear when the other man rode up on his horse. Feeling fear when Lucy touched me—does this mean that Lucy is the murderer and Mr. Witherspoon the victim? I don't know. I just don't know."

"Do you suppose we should do something?" Flora asked.

"At the very least, for the moment, I would like to put my eyes on Lucy."

A loud rapping at the front door, followed by a flurry of activity and female chattering, compelled Rosabelle and Flora to leave their temporary sanctuary.

Opening the double doors of the parlor, they found the women had not yet moved to the library. Instead they were huddling around Mrs. Franklin who read aloud from a note in her hand.

"Miss Amelia Patton sends her regrets. She is ill and thus will be unable to attend today's meeting."

Mrs. Franklin put a hand to her heart. "Poor dear. She has not been looking well these last two days."

"I think she has worried herself sick," piped in Marjorie Baker, who stood next to Flora.

"Worried herself about what?" Rosabelle asked.

"That cousin of hers, Eli Witherspoon. Rumor has it he will be the next to die," Marjorie responded more quietly for deeper effect.

"It is true," clucked Mrs. Franklin in her strong, superior tone. "But I must say though, that the young man most likely brought it all upon himself with his questionable ways."

Rosabelle put two comforting hands on Flora's shoulders.

"What are you talking about?" Flora's voice trembled. "Who would want to kill Mr. Witherspoon?"

"The Southern Avenger of course," Marjorie said.

"The Southern what?" Rosabelle asked, soaking in every bit of information thrown her way. It was a stroke of luck for her that this conversation should arise now. She could weed through the truths and untruths later, but the current situation required her to take in everything.

"The Southern Avenger is what they are calling him. He's killed five men already. All of them Northern sympathizers and traitors who put slaves before the needs of the South. Rumor has been that Eli Witherspoon will be next."

"Why?" Rosabelle asked.

Mrs. Franklin lowered her voice and squinted her eyes. "He was a slave sympathizer during the war. He helped many escape from their owners."

Some of the women, obviously unaware of this rumor, grew wide-eyed and covered open mouths with their hands. Others, who must have been privy to the scandalous gossip, nodded knowingly yet disapprovingly.

One of those women was Anna Cameron. Seeing Rosabelle's confusion, Anna took great satisfaction in sharing her own prized information. Moving her face close to Rosabelle's, she whispered. "The word is that he loved a Negro girl who was killed transporting escaped slaves to the North during the war. Can you imagine? A man of fine, southern breeding keeping with Negroes? If you ask me, he has it coming."

"I think we should let God be the judge of that," Rosabelle said. "Unless the Lord has passed responsibility for judgment on to you, Anna." The room became silent as a tomb. "Now, has anyone seen this Southern Avenger?"

The women looked around at each other, then many shook their heads.

"So it is not a matter of any known fact that this killer is a man and not a woman?"

More heads were shaking to answer no.

Rosabelle felt as if she was getting somewhere. "Mrs. Franklin, tell me please, when did Lucy first come into your employ?"

"Early last week . . ." the hostess answered more quietly than usual.

"Do you remember the exact day?"

"Why, let's see . . . let me think . . . what exactly does this all have to do with Mr. Witherspoon?"

"The day, Mrs. Franklin. Please, it could be important."

Mrs. Franklin stared into the distance while counting on her fingers. She tapped her forehead once, which must have worked some miracle, because then she offered an answer.

"Tuesday. I think," she said.

"Are you sure?"

"Well . . . yes. Yes, I am sure. I remember. She came to our back door Tuesday morning looking for work after the Pattons had turned her down. I had just come in need as we will be entertaining a house full of visitors from England soon. I learned of the visitors on Monday evening. Yes. It was Tuesday."

Rosabelle was making progress. "So she had been trying to obtain employ in the Patton household? Where Mr. Witherspoon now resides?"

"Yes."

"And does anyone know when the last murder occurred?"

"Oh! I know that one!" The recently married Sarah Pike shot her hand into the air like a schoolgirl bidding anxiously to answer a teacher's question. "My husband knew of this man. They found him dead in his Manassas farmhouse . . . last Monday afternoon!"

Rosabelle grabbed Flora's arm and dragged her down the hall, leaving the group of befuddled women to whisper among themselves. Rosabelle heard Mrs. Franklin mumble something about "that odd girl."

"I am so confused, Rosa," Flora sputtered. "Tell me, please. What is happening?"

"Remember that newspaper story about Abigail Dawes, who was a spy for the South?"

"Yes! We were just speaking to Mr. Witherspoon about her."

"And her favorite disguise was . . ."

"A Negro woman!" Flora stopped just short of the door that opened to the back alley behind the Franklin home. A fresh chill around the area made Rosabelle suspect that someone had just exited through that door.

"Yes. A Negro woman. I think Lucy is Abigail Dawes in disguise."

Flora's eyes grew wide. She pressed a hand to her mouth, stifling a scream.

"Flora, I need you to be strong and do something important for me."

"What?"

"Leave the meeting now. Say you are feeling ill. Run to the police house around the corner and bring them here. I will try to find Lucy and stall her. Make haste!"

"But—"

"Don't argue. Go!"

After Flora scooted off, frazzled but determined, Rosabelle opened the door to the alleyway and poked her head out looking for any sign of Lucy. Nothing. The steps had long been cleared of snow, leaving no chance of tell-tale footprints. She had not given much thought to what action she should take next. Should she search the house, and perhaps find the woman in one of the rooms inside? Or should she look more closely outside? While she stood motionless with indecision, she heard a cracking sound from under the steps. Her heart started beating furiously. Possibly the woman was right below her, hiding.

Rosabelle's respiration grew fast along with her beating heart, and the air filled with her visible breath.

"Miss Raines!" Mrs. Franklin called from the parlor. "Whatever are you doing?"

"Please do not mind me," Rosabelle answered while her fingers turned white from the cold. "I'm stepping outside for a bit of fresh air. I will return in just a moment. Do continue your meeting!"

Rosabelle stepped out onto the landing and closed the door behind her, preempting any argument from Mrs. Franklin about the silly nature of her choice to stand outside in the frigid weather without her cloak. Hoping that it would not be much longer before Flora arrived with the police, Rosabelle decided to venture down the four steep stairs to the muddy ground below. Indeed, once there, she could see faint footprints leading around to the under portion of the staircase. Taking a deep breath and making a silent prayer, she called out.

"I know you're there, Abigail Dawes."

She heard a rustling beneath the stairs.

"Stay away from me if you want to live, Miss Rosabelle Raines. I do not have time for the likes of you," a woman's voice growled.

Fear racing through her veins, Rosabelle took two steps back. She was considering her next course of action when the door above flew open and Flora appeared.

"Rosa! There you are!"

A round and rather squat uniformed policeman squeezed past Flora. At the same time, the small but agile Abigail Dawes sprang out from under the stairs, visibly intent on making a quick getaway. Stopping for just a moment and glaring at Rosabelle, she did not pretend now to avoid eye contact. Her face had been scrubbed clean of whatever she had used to darken it, revealing alabaster skin. Her angry, green eyes bore into Rosabelle's, and Rosabelle shivered not from the cold, but from the chill of hatred that radiated from the woman.

When the policeman started barreling down the stairs, Rosabelle feared Abigail would get away. With no forethought, she lunged toward the woman, hoping to grab some part of her dress and hold her back. Abigail Dawes had other plans. Before she knew it, Rosabelle was caught helpless with a knife blade tight against her throat. Abigail Dawes was a master of battle as well as disguise. She had whipped Rosabelle's arm fiercely tight behind her back while positioning the deadly weapon.

The policeman stalled his approach while two more appeared in the doorway above. They attempted some verbal negotiations, which had no effect at all on the determined Abigail. The woman began pulling Rosabelle backward, moving ever closer to the busy street at the end of the row of townhouses.

"Stay right where you are men, or I will kill her right here, right now."

"It is me that you want, Miss Dawes," said a calm, resolute voice behind them. "Leave this woman be."

Rosabelle had only heard that man's voice once, but she knew it to be the voice of Eli Witherspoon.

Abigail whipped around, carrying Rosabelle along for the ride. The forceful movement caused the blade to open her skin, and Rosabelle could feel warm blood trickle down her throat.

"Let her go," Witherspoon pleaded. "I offer myself as a replacement hostage, but please let this woman go." He was so close to them that Rosabelle could see the sweat beading his temple.

Rosabelle knew Abigail was a rat in a trap, and she feared this added to her own danger. She eyed the holstered pistol under Witherspoon's morning coat. Abigail was sharp, so certainly she saw it as well.

"Do you think me a fool, Eli Witherspoon?" Abigail hissed, still twisting Rosabelle to and fro as she looked from Witherspoon to the police and back again.

"I think you are wise enough not to bring harm to this innocent woman."

The twisting stopped. Time seemed to stand still. Rosabelle could barely breathe and felt her world going dark.

Without warning, Abigail loosened her grip on Rosabelle and shoved her into Witherspoon, causing them both to lose balance and fall to the ground. Rosabelle screamed in pain as her arm seemed to snap from the force.

Rosabelle had only a peripheral view of Abigail Dawes fleeing into the street, but during her fall, she heard the loud clatter of hooves on brick, the shrill warning cry of a man, and the screams of onlookers. It was a ghastly sound that Rosabelle imagined she might never forget as long as she lived. On the ground, tangled in the arms of Eli Witherspoon, she was granted relief from witnessing the horses of a carriage trample the avenging woman. Mr. Witherspoon, strong and kind, shielded Rosabelle, making every assurance that once she was able to stand and walk, she would not be forced to view the grisly scene.

Rosabelle would later be told while recovering at home that Abigail did not survive the accident. Over the next few days, Mr. Witherspoon made several visits to the Raines home to check on Rosabelle, whose arm was mending from a severe break acquired during her fall.

Rosabelle worried that Flora would be jealous, but such was not the case. In fact Flora always smiled when Mr. Witherspoon appeared at the door and then excused herself from their company in order to allow them the time to be alone.

"Rosa," Flora confided to her sister one day, "Eli Witherspoon is not the man for me. I think he suits you far better."

On quiet walks, he revealed to her his own early suspicions that Abigail Dawes, the Southern Avenger, and the new servant, Lucy, were one and the same. In fact, he told her, he had asked his cousin Amelia not to attend the gathering at the Franklin home for that very reason.

He told her as well of his life before coming to Alexandria. The stories had been true. Mr. Witherspoon had felt great romantic love for a Negro girl named Bess. They had worked together setting slaves free and transporting them to havens in the North. He believed that all men were God's men, regardless of color, and he would never owe allegiance to a people who would enslave another. When Bess died, he went into hiding until after the war, continuing his work as he was safely able.

It was obvious to everyone that young Mr. Witherspoon had more than just a polite interest in Miss Rosabelle Raines, and that she gladly returned the interest. Before her she found a compassionate man of staunch integrity, who understood that being different was not a bad thing.

"How did you know?" Eli Witherspoon inquired on one of their walks.

"Know what?" she asked with reserve.

"That Abigail Dawes was hiding disguised in the Franklin home."

"I didn't really know anything. She just . . . acted strangely."

"Strangely?"

"Suspicious . . . I guess. She was acting oddly and . . . I just became curious. That's it. I was curious."

He laughed lightly while sliding Rosabelle a sly glance.

"It still seems to me," he teased, "that you know more than you are telling me."

"What in the world could a woman like me know?"

Rosabelle's attempt to act coy was ineffective. "My guess is, Miss Raines, that you are no ordinary woman."

She smiled and guided their discussion toward her companion's new employ in the business of shipping.

One day, Rosabelle knew—one day she could share her own secret with Mr. Eli Witherspoon, and that he would not judge her, think her a witch, or jail her in an asylum.

One day she could tell him all, and he would embrace her for who she was, and he would love her. That was what Rosabelle knew in her heart.

And time would prove that Rosabelle Raines knew correctly.

———

Karen Cantwell spends her time juggling the love for her family with her love for writing. She lives in Reston, Virginia, where she manages her husband's optometric practice while sometimes (but not always) finding the time to feed her cats and clean her house. Luckily her kids will feed the cats when she forgets. Read more of Karen's writings at www.karencantwell.com.

DEATH NEAR THE RIM OF HEAVEN

by Trish Carrico

It wasn't until Thursday that Anna realized what was happening.

They'd landed in Osaka late on Sunday and caught the train that shuttled between the Osaka airport and downtown Kyoto. They boarded separately and sat a few rows apart—as if they were strangers. She sometimes thought George's attempts to pretend they weren't together were almost comical. Anna doubted that the few bleary-eyed businessmen in their car would have noticed them, but George insisted on the arrangement.

As the train pulled out of the station, the uniformed cleaning ladies who'd been freshening the car as they arrived bowed in unison. It was an action—an attitude—Anna knew well.

She'd met George at an industry event she wouldn't have attended but for John who ran the office. It was essential, he said, "to keep up to speed." John was ten years younger and had half her experience, but she couldn't defy him and refuse to go. She channeled her feelings into worrying about what to wear, how to fix her hair. At the last minute she'd thrown something on, pulled a comb through her auburn curls, and went.

And there she met George. He stopped her with a smile.

Normally she didn't like jewelry on a man, and he sported an elaborate college ring where a wedding band might otherwise be, and a diamond pinkie ring—along with a gold watch, cuff links, and tie clip. But it all suited him. Him and his smile.

They had sex that night at her apartment. "You're like a virgin," he said, pleased. Smiling.

She wasn't a virgin, in fact. Just out of practice. Afterward they sat on her balcony looking across the river to the city where he had an office and an apartment. And—she was to find out later—a wife.

⌐ ⌐ ⌐

Monday morning as Anna waited in the underground mall attached to the train station—waited for George to appear—she watched the people of Kyoto go about their lives: young women in frilly clothes studying the screens of their cell phones as they hurried through; businessmen striding past with starched collars and French cuffs sticking out of their tightly buttoned suit jackets; matronly women with colorful fabric shopping bags on their arms navigating the hallways of the mall in tiny, mincing steps. The only non-Japanese face: her own, reflected in a mirrored pillar.

Anna checked her watch. Ever since George encountered a business acquaintance during their trip to Atlantic City, they had stayed in separate hotels. He was at the hotel above the railway station; she, at an older, western-tourist type two blocks away. She couldn't ring his room. She knew he wouldn't like that. Besides, she didn't know how to use the telephone here. That's one of the reasons why, when George suggested the trip, she'd hesitated. Though she liked what she knew of Japan, she worried she wouldn't enjoy a place where she couldn't read the signs and didn't even know how to ask for help.

"I'll take care of everything," he had said, as he always did when his mind was made up.

She checked her watch again. What if something had happened to him? What if—

"This isn't where I said we'd meet," George said in an agitated whisper.

Anna looked up into his less than happy face. "But—"

"The outside steps, I said. Near the tourist office. Come on." He turned and started off while she followed.

╭ ╭ ╭

On Tuesday George decided they should visit some of the shrines and temples perched high on the hills ringing the city. For each site, this entailed walking up and then down a steep, narrow street lined with shops and open-sided stalls selling trinkets, religious objects, and photo souvenirs. Flags and banners fluttered in front of candy stores and tea houses eager to attract passers-by. At the first temple, George pushed his way through the stream of Japanese visitors—elderly couples, mothers with tiny babies, high-school students in their uniforms. Anna lagged behind, caught in the crowd, feeling isolated and embarrassed by George's rude behavior.

She looked up the street. *Where was he?* A stab of panic. *Where could he have gotten to?* She anxiously scanned the street, and after a few frantic moments saw George waiting for her. Not smiling, but waiting.

After visiting another temple, they strolled off the grounds to find themselves not on a path downhill but in a cemetery, an otherworldly graveyard of small square plots covered with narrow stone markers of varying heights. Some had niches for candles or vases for flowers. The graveyard was so densely packed that every inch was either plot or pathway. There was not a tree, a bush, or a blade of grass; nothing growing or alive.

"Efficient, aren't they?" George opined. "Maximum utilization of space."

"We should go back the way we came and find our way out." She moved to start back on the walkway.

"No. This is interesting." He jutted out his chin, then made a show of examining a large family plot.

She shouldn't have said anything. He'd likely dawdle in the airless, oppressive city of the dead until she was quite uncomfortable—just to show her who's boss.

Anna pressed her teeth against her lower lip and winced. The lip was still sore where he'd bitten it the afternoon before, bitten it as he crushed himself against her in her hotel room.

They lingered there, in the sad silence that filled the graveyard, until—as she knew he would—George demanded that they leave.

r r r

Late Wednesday afternoon the rain let up enough that they could visit the royal gardens. They wandered for a while, then watched the gardeners use plume-topped reeds to brush leaves and other debris from the moss garden's surface.

"Shows how much it rains here, when you've got moss instead of grass." George adjusted his cap against the drizzle. He refused to carry an umbrella.

Earlier, touring old Kyoto, they'd been caught in a downpour and took cover under the short roof of a shop. Suddenly an elderly man— the shopkeeper, she assumed—appeared with two plastic umbrellas in hand. While she gratefully accepted the pink one, to the consternation of the old man, George declined the yellow one. When George tried to pay for her umbrella, the man waved away the yen and disappeared inside. George spied what looked like a mail slot in the store's front and pushed the money through. Honor satisfied, he grabbed her arm and pulled her toward the main street. Taking a fleeting look back, Anna saw the shopkeeper peeking out his window, probably wondering at the strange ways of westerners.

r r r

Thursday brought them to the final temple in what the guidebook called The Rim of Heaven. George leaned forward, studying the information card in the temple.

"Ha!" he half-laughed.

"What does it say?" she asked.

He gestured at the immense statue of Buddha. "This is supposed to be the Winking Buddha." George moved around the side of the statue to study the eyes. "It does have a certain slyness to it."

Anna didn't see anything sly about the statue's expression. To her it seemed less inward looking than the other Buddhas they'd seen, but that was all.

On their way back down, past the clutter of shops and tea houses, George abruptly stopped at an open-sided stall that sold religious objects, including small copies of the Winking Buddha. They stood under the stall's awning while the stallkeeper wrapped the inexpensive statue as carefully as if it were real gold. But George was getting impatient.

"That's fine. That's fine," he said, waving a fistful of yen at the man. But the stall man's calm, blank face never changed, and he did not hurry. Finally he topped all the paper wrappings with an ornate seal.

George didn't hide his irritation. "That took awhile," he said as the stall man handed him a white shopping bag containing the well-packaged Buddha.

"Here." George thrust the shopping bag at her. "It's for you."

"For me?" George had given her a few things but nothing ever like a souvenir of a trip together. Maybe it was the kinship he seemed to feel with the Winking Buddha: whenever she looked at the statue, she was to think of him.

"Keep it," he said to the stall man who was trying to give George his change. "Let's go." He hurried her away, leaving the stall man standing there holding the money.

┏ ┏ ┏

A heavy mist had started to fall. Not unpleasant but damp. They headed toward their hotels, walking on the path that ran alongside the old canal. A geisha—or a woman very like one, without the makeup—passed by them going in the opposite direction. She wore long gloves that went all the way up to her elbows.

George stared at the woman, even turning his head to keep looking at her. Anna looked resolutely ahead. She'd caught him doing this a couple of times recently, and each time it made her feel as if she'd suddenly become invisible.

They had been walking by the part of the canal with shops and restaurants, but then the path had come into a more-wooded area.

George stopped at one of the narrow foot bridges that crossed the canal.

"There's been a change in plans. I have to go back to the states, to the city."

"When?"

"Tomorrow. I'll give you some money and you can stay and shop—"

"By myself?"

"Japan's one of the safest countries in the world—"

"Why do you have to go back?"

George looked down at her. "My wife called. She needs me."

The rain began to come down harder, splattering on the bridge and the path.

"How can you just leave me here?"

"You don't understand. It's over. It's your choice whether you go back or stay here. You're on your own." He turned away from her and walked onto the foot bridge.

Her choice. *What* choice? Anna's mouth trembled with words she couldn't say. She would have done—had done—anything he wanted because he said—he swore—he wanted her. Needed her.

The bag with the brass Buddha hung heavily on her arm. The ache in her arm matched the pain in her chest.

She reached down into the bag, clutched the Buddha to her, then threw it at him. It struck the back of George's head with a sickening *thunk*. He fell sideways into the canal as the Buddha sank from sight.

"Uh!" She gasped, then froze. She had wanted him to feel her pain but . . .

The only sound was the rain. She slowly looked around. No one in sight. Trembling, she started walking along the path, not looking over the edge of the canal, not looking back, stopping only to stuff the shopping bag into a trash can. As soon as she could, she left the canal path for a regular street and worked her way back to her hotel.

And there—too afraid to think—she waited for whatever would happen next.

 ◆   ◆   ◆

At eight o'clock the next morning there was a knock at her door. It was the young man from the desk who spoke English. With him were two young policemen who evidently didn't speak the language, as the desk clerk did all the talking.

"Police need to talk to western ladies, especially USA," the clerk explained. "There has been accident, western man, USA."

Of course they wanted to talk to her, there were so few westerners in town. Earlier in the week she'd hoped that wrapped together in their otherness, she and George would find a closeness they never shared in the city. Frightened as she was, the memory still made her chest ache.

The two young officers escorted her to the nearby police station and to their chief's office. As she entered the room she came face to face with the stall man who'd sold them the Buddha. The chief, a middle-aged man, asked in English for her passport, looked quickly at it and her, then opened the green trash bag on his desk. From it he produced a sodden package.

Anna felt her face go numb. The stall's insignia still secured the wrappings on the statue.

The chief pointed to the package and addressed the stall man in Japanese, seeming to ask for confirmation. *"Hai?"*

"Hai." The stall man nodded, barely glancing at the package.

The chief gave Anna a sidelong look and asked the stall man another question. Anna knew it was about her.

The stall man stared at her, his face the same calm blank she remembered. Then he slowly shook his head, *"Ie."*

"Ie?" The chief of police drew back.

"Ie," the stall man repeated.

The chief jerked his right hand up and issued orders to his assistants, orders that included the name of George's hotel. Then he straightened up and bowed to Anna. "Sorry to inconvenience you," he said and handed back her passport. *"Sayonara."*

"Ari-Arigato," she stammered.

One of the young policemen opened the office door for her, then seconds later, walked briskly past her and out through the revolving door of the station house.

As Anna moved forward, she realized the numbness in her face had spread over her whole body, down even to her legs. She made it through the revolving door and looked back to see the stall man staring at her. And in the fractured light and the reflections on the glass, she saw his left eyelid slowly lower in a wink.

———

Trish Carrico was born in a mill town in New England into a Russian-Scots-Irish family. She studied theater in college and grad school and worked in poverty programs, in government employment agencies, and for federal contractors. She has had feature articles published in the Washington Post *and the* New York Times. *She has lived in and around D.C. for most of her life and has been married for thirty-nine years to a man who reminds her of Fred Astaire.*

DELICIOUS DEATH

by Mary Ann Corrigan

Eleanor Saslow had never envisioned using food as a weapon until the night the Dicksons came to dinner. She'd barely known Donovan Dickson twenty years before when her college roommate married him. Tonight, within minutes of his arrival, he made her short list of "Men Most Likely to Improve the World—by Their Demise."

She served the appetizers in the living room and bent over to set down a plate of bite-sized quiches on the coffee table.

"Sweet ass," Donovan muttered from his seat on the sofa behind her.

She straightened as if shot in the rear with a dart, turned, and glared at him. Her husband, Bruce, fiddling with the CD player, hadn't heard the remark.

Paige Dickson must have heard but chose to ignore it. She sat on the sofa next to her husband and ran her hands along her silk skirt, ironing out non-existent creases.

Donovan smiled up at Eleanor. "You look terrific in those pants. Paige has given up on clothes that cling—for a good reason." He squeezed his wife's upper arm. "Flab, Paige, I can feel it. Ask Eleanor to take you to her gym."

Paige flushed and crossed her arms.

Eleanor felt her own face grow hot with anger. "We've all put on a few pounds since college." She gave Donovan's paunch a meaningful look.

In return he gave her breasts a meaningful stare. "Some people add the padding in the right places. Twenty years ago, you were downright bony."

True, and Paige had been voluptuous, vivacious, and confident. Now she sat hunched beside her husband as if to protect herself from his next taunt. The extra pounds didn't do anything for her below the neck, but above it, they plumped out any wrinkles she might have acquired. She still had a gorgeous face.

"You look great, Paige," Eleanor said. "I love your scarf and shoes."

Her friend smiled with tight lips. "They're Gucci."

"That's Italian for ridiculously expensive." Donovan winked.

He was good for something after all—financing his wife's shopping sprees. Perhaps that's why she put up with him.

Bruce's jaw clenched. "Paige doesn't need expensive clothes. She'd look beautiful in anything."

Paige responded with a megawatt smile.

For a moment Eleanor felt like a wren overshadowed by a bluebird, exactly as she used to feel in college when Paige walked into the room. But after two decades, the wren had some things the bluebird lacked: a successful career, two children, and a husband who wasn't a jerk.

"You hear that, Paige?" Donovan nudged his wife. "Bruce thinks I should cut your clothing allowance."

He launched into anecdotes about the California law firm he'd just quit in favor of a D.C. lobbying firm.

Eleanor fled into the kitchen and stayed there until she put the dinner on the table.

Donovan's eyes lit up when he saw the centerpiece, Eleanor's paella. "A gourmet feast! It looks like a work of art. Kudos to the chef."

Eleanor muttered, "Thank you," not yet ready to forgive him for ogling her and insulting his wife, but still pleased by the compliment. She'd created a collage of different colors in the paella pan—saffron rice studded with green peas and diced red pepper, circles of brown chorizo contrasting with curls of pink shrimp.

"Hmm. Tastes as good as it looks," Donovan said after one bite. "Why can't you cook like this, Paige? All I ever get at home is roast chicken and green-bean casserole."

Paige pressed her lips together. "You told me you like chicken and string beans."

"I did—twenty years ago, but tastes change." His tone implied that more than his food tastes had changed.

Eleanor felt suddenly embarrassed about her elaborate dish. "I don't cook like this all the time. It's a special meal for a special occasion." The foursome's first get-together since the Dicksons moved from L.A. to D.C.

Bruce shook his head. "Not true. She makes a terrific dinner every night."

Eleanor had taken up gourmet cooking to please Bruce the foodie. And now Donovan had turned her skill into a weapon against her friend. She hated him for that and would find a way to punish him. The next time the Dicksons came to dinner, Eleanor would show her solidarity with Paige. She'd prepare the kind of food Donovan had just belittled: roast chicken and a green-bean casserole made with cream-of-something soup and topped with canned onion crisps. She'd have to find a substitute, though, for the crisps. The only time she'd served that casserole, Bruce had called the onion topping "freeze-dried bird turd."

But suppose her meal tasted far better than what Donovan ate at home? Paige might think Eleanor was trying to show her up, and the whole idea would backfire. No, Eleanor would have to find another way to cook Donovan's goose.

During dinner Donovan requested frequent champagne refills and still had some left in his glass when Bruce passed around after-dinner drinks in snifters.

Donovan lifted his half-empty champagne flute and used it as a prism through which he viewed his wife. "Ever notice, Bruce, how women are like drinks? Some of them are champagne. They start out full of life but turn flat. The fizz goes out of them."

Everyone loses pizzazz as they age, but nothing had prepared Eleanor for the change in the formerly lively Paige, now sitting with hands folded and rigid in her lap. Donovan had sucked the life out of her.

Donovan set the flute down and raised his brandy snifter. "Now for the cognac. The really good stuff only comes into its own after years of seasoning. It ages well and just keeps getting better." He tipped his glass in a toast to Eleanor.

As Eleanor watched the tears well in Paige's eyes, she decided what to serve the next time the Dicksons came to dinner—individual ramekins of Coquilles St. Jacques, Donovan's portion to be laced with something indigestible.

Later, after the Dicksons left, Bruce loaded the dishwasher. "Until tonight I didn't realize you were the apple of Donovan's eye."

Eleanor set a pile of dessert dishes onto the counter with a clatter. "Donovan's just trying to drive a wedge between us and Paige. He remembers how close the three of us were in college."

At their Midwest university, they'd formed a drama club triumvirate and won national awards for their productions: Paige the lead actress in every play, Bruce the business and publicity man, Eleanor the set designer and stage manager. In the crowning production of their senior year, Donovan had sat in the audience, taking a rare night off from his law-school studies. He'd come to applaud his younger sister, who had a bit part in the play, and ended up falling for the show's star. Paige had fallen for him, too, married him right after graduation, and moved with him to L.A. Over the years, Donovan's job had taken them up the West Coast and down again—Seattle, San Jose, and back to L.A. Meanwhile the Saslows put down roots on the other side of the continent.

Eleanor helped Bruce load the plates into the dishwasher. "I can't believe she's still married to him. I wish we'd made more of an effort to stay in touch with her. Maybe with our support, she'd have gotten rid of him long ago. She could have pursued her acting career instead of picking up and moving every few years."

Bruce shrugged. "We were busy ourselves. The twins were a handful."

"But now we have our chance." She imitated the voice of a wicked witch. "We'll spike his next 'gourmet feast' with an untraceable poison."

Bruce laughed. "It better be colorless, odorless, and tasteless, or you'd never spoil one of your dishes by adding it." He scrubbed the paella pan as if he wanted to eradicate the memory of tonight's dinner. "Remember when I asked you why she was marrying him?"

"How could I forget?" Eleanor recalled everything about Paige's wedding, the day that altered the course of her own life and Bruce's as much as it had Paige's.

She and Bruce had been the last to leave the reception. They'd moved from one table to another, emptying the remains of the wine bottles into their glasses and becoming more melancholy with each sip. Eleanor was losing her best friend, and Bruce the woman of his dreams.

He had poured the dregs from the last bottle. "What does she see in him?"

Something only a man would ask. Eleanor ran her fingers up and down the stem of her glass. "Do the words handsome, rich, and suave mean anything to you, Bruce?"

"Actually, no. Smart means something to me."

"Okay. Let's work with that. Some people would consider Donovan the smart choice. Law degree. Job in Southern California, not far from Hollywood, Paige's mecca. Good lifetime earning potential. Her parents have put a lot of pressure on her to marry him."

"Practically an arranged marriage. It's medieval." The grumblings of a man infatuated by a woman he could never snare.

Both tipsy, they took a cab to the apartment Eleanor had shared with Paige and two other girls in their senior year. Bruce had planned to walk to his own place half a mile away. He bent down to plant a friendly good-night kiss on her lips. She responded. She'd always liked him. Their tongues intertwined, and before long, they were on the bed ripping off each other's clothes.

Two months later, they faced an arranged marriage of their own—arranged by a combination of biology, alcohol, and their own moral values. She refused to consider abortion, and he insisted they get married. They both doted on the twins born six months after the elopement. The organizational skills Eleanor developed through stage managing had served her well as she juggled the girls' schedules and ran her event-planning business. With her knack for projecting herself into the future and forestalling crises, she envisioned the day when the twins would move away and leave their parents without a single common interest. She set about fixing that problem. Next to his daughters, Bruce had three passions: football, fishing, and food. Eleanor couldn't even feign an interest in the sports. Food, though, was something she could get into.

During slow times in her work as an event planner, she signed up for gourmet cooking classes, though she'd have preferred to take art lessons. Summer vacations meant camp for the girls, fishing trips for Bruce with his buddies, and culinary school for her. By the time the girls went off to college, Bruce wouldn't have traded a dinner at home for a meal in Washington's finest restaurant.

A month after the dinner party, Eleanor had a meeting near the Virginia suburb where the Dicksons had bought a house. When the meeting ended in mid-afternoon, she called Paige, who invited her to stop by.

Paige made instant coffee. The two women exchanged stories about the twenty years they'd spent apart. Eleanor talked about raising the twins and starting a business. Paige talked Hollywood. While still in her twenties, she had snared a few small roles but landed on the cutting room floor more often than not. Because of Donovan's transfer to Seattle ten years ago, she'd passed up a substantial role in a movie that looked like a sleeper but turned into a hit. Now in her forties, she had no hope of an acting career and no idea what else to do with her life.

Eleanor glanced at her watch as Paige put the coffee cups in the dishwasher. "It's already past four. I'd better get on my way or the Beltway traffic will be unbearable." The usual forty-five-minute trip to her house in Maryland would take twice as long in rush hour.

"Why don't you stay for dinner? You said Bruce was out of town, and Donovan told me he was meeting a client for dinner. It'll just be the two of us." Paige opened the freezer and pulled out a package. "Filet mignon. Even I can't mess up that."

Eleanor eyed the two-inch-thick steaks Paige unwrapped. They'd take quite a while to defrost. Unless Paige planned to nuke them first. Eleanor shuddered. "Why don't you save those for another day? I could go to the store and pick up something fresh." She stopped short of offering to cook the meal. Paige might take the offer as an insult to her cooking.

"I have plenty of food here. I'll just pop these in the oven. They'll be done in two hours or so." Paige shoved the steaks into the oven without waiting for it to preheat. Then she reached into the pantry for a box of potato flakes. "Look. Mashed potatoes. And I have a bag of mixed vegetables in the freezer. Carrots, cauliflower, and green beans, all in one package. An easy side dish."

Easy to make. Hard to swallow. Orange, white, and green chunks, different shapes but with the same taste and texture. Eleanor resigned herself to a dinner that her husband would have shoved away in disgust. The point was to visit with Paige, not to eat well.

The phone rang. Paige took the call, hung up after a minute, and announced, "That was Donovan. He'll be home for dinner after all. I'll grab another steak from the freezer."

How to make any meal worse—add Donovan to the menu. Eleanor pulled her cell phone from her purse, made a pretense of checking her voice mail, and then announced that an event she'd arranged for later in the week had run into a snag. She'd have to leave and fix the problem.

Paige frowned. "But I've already put another filet in the oven."

"Sorry." Eleanor gave her a peck on the cheek. "Why don't you give mine to Donovan?"

A few weeks later, the Dicksons invited the Saslows to dinner at a top Washington restaurant. Fortunately two other couples were included in the invitation. Donovan played the perfect host, aside from one allusion to Paige's mediocre cooking as the reason for eating out rather than at home. Paige laughed off the barb, apparently still capable of putting on a good act if the audience was large enough.

After that dinner, Bruce prodded Eleanor into inviting the Dicksons again and suggested a casual meal at the summer house they rented on Lake Anna, ninety minutes from Washington.

Eleanor's desire for revenge against the man who treated her friend badly had softened a bit over time but hadn't disappeared. She no longer thought about giving Donovan gastric distress, just food he wouldn't enjoy. Three months before, the first time she invited the Dicksons to dinner, she'd asked Paige if there were any foods either of them didn't eat. "Donovan hates broccoli. And he never touches nuts," Paige had said.

So Eleanor planned a meal that would taste good to everyone except him—an appetizer of pita chips and broccoli dip with crushed almonds, broccoli soup as the next course, followed by stir-fried beef with broccoli. She could find only one dessert recipe with the necessary ingredient— caramelized coconut milk tapioca with broccoli puree, chocolate sorbet, and a candied broccoli floret. Sounded ghastly. Instead, she would make pecan pie. If he refused to eat broccoli or nuts, he'd go home hungry.

Bruce grinned when she told him what she was serving and why. "Not exactly the undetectable poison you wanted for him but still a form of torture. Why don't we have dinner on the pontoon boat? Then he can't scrounge around in the kitchen for a broccoli substitute."

Eleanor hesitated. The pontoon boat, a.k.a. the booze barge, could seat a dozen people but wasn't large enough for her to escape the loathsome Donovan. At least in the house she could retreat into the kitchen. "No, I'd have to change the menu. I can't stir-fry on the boat."

"Let's at least have drinks and the appetizer on the lake."

Eleanor agreed.

The clear June afternoon was perfect for boating. She brought two insulated totes aboard the barge, one to keep the beer and wine chilled, the other to keep the dip warm. After they motored to the middle of the lake, she served the dip, its main ingredient unrecognizable in the macerated blend.

Donovan scooped a large glob onto a pita chip, chewed it, and then scooped again and again.

He smacked his lips. "This is the best dip I ever tasted. What's in it?"

Uh-oh. Eleanor had done too good a job of masking the vegetable's strong flavor.

Bruce grinned. "It's broccoli!"

Donovan's hand, holding another dip-laden chip, stopped on its way to his mouth. He examined the greenish-beige blob.

"You're a sorceress, Eleanor! So is Paige, but in a different way. She can turn a piece of prime beef into shoe leather just by looking at it. You wave a spoon and transform a vegetable I hate into food for the gods." He gobbled the chip and reached for another. "What's . . . what's the crunchy stuff?"

Eleanor peered at him. His face looked rosy, as if he'd just had a vigorous workout instead of exercising only his jaw. "Crunchy? Could be the water chestnuts or the almonds."

"Almo—" Donovan turned puce. He clutched his throat and gasped for air. "I can't—"

"What's wrong?" Bruce pounded Donovan's back.

"Eh . . . eh . . . pe . . . pen."

Bruce stopped pounding. "A pen? He wants to write something?" He turned to Paige.

Paige opened her mouth, but nothing came out.

Eleanor remembered a banquet where a woman with symptoms similar to Donovan's had pulled a cylinder from her purse—an EpiPen. The woman, allergic to peanuts, had self-injected a serum to counteract the allergen. "Is he allergic to anything, Paige?"

Her friend nodded. "All kinds of nuts. I thought you knew. The almonds . . ."

How would Eleanor know? She'd heard only that he didn't eat nuts, nothing about an allergy. "Do you have an EpiPen?"

Paige cupped her face in her hands like the figure in *The Scream*. "In my purse, but it's back at your house. Hurry!"

Eleanor sprang toward the wheel that controlled the boat's direction and turned it. The unwieldy craft responded in slow motion. With the wind against them, the three-horsepower engine could take half an hour to reach shore.

She glanced at Donovan. His lips had turned blue. "Try to keep his air passage open, Bruce." She wiped away tears. The idea that her food might kill someone appalled her. How could she have joked about poisoning Donovan?

Above the low hum of the motor, she could hear Donovan wheezing, the worst sound she'd ever heard . . . until the wheezing stopped.

Paige screamed. "He's not breathing. Do something, Bruce!"

Bruce started CPR.

"Does anyone have a cell phone?" Eleanor asked. "If we call 911, maybe the police could send out a fast boat or even a helicopter."

Bruce shook his head. "Mine's back at the house. Check his pockets, Paige."

Paige reached into her husband's trouser pocket and extracted a cell phone. "I'm not sure how to use this. It's one of those fancy ones with the alphabetic keyboard."

"Give it here." Eleanor held out her hand.

Paige studied the gizmo as she took a step toward Eleanor. She tripped over the tote containing the drinks and sprawled on the deck. On the way down, she let go of the phone. It plopped into the water.

"Oh, no!" Paige scrambled up. "Should I jump in? Maybe I can grab it."

"No!" Eleanor yelled. That would just slow them down. "Wave your arms and try to attract the attention of another boater."

After fifteen minutes, someone in a motorboat responded to Paige's signaling, and a man climbed aboard to assist Bruce. Neither of them could bring Donovan back to life. The other man had a cell phone and called 911. The EMTs were waiting on the dock for them.

For the next few hours, Bruce comforted Paige and Eleanor through the ordeal of dealing with the police, the doctor, and the medical examiner. Then the three of them returned to the lake house and sat like shell-shock victims in the living room.

Bruce caught his wife's eye. "We could all do with a stiff drink and some food."

Eleanor went into the kitchen and opened the refrigerator. The sliced beef was marinating in a teriyaki sauce, next to it a plastic bag full of broccoli florets. Maybe she'd stir-fry the beef later but not the vegetable. Would she ever eat broccoli again without thinking of Donovan?

Stiff drink first, worry about food later. She closed the fridge door and leaned her back against it.

Paige's white leather purse sat like a tombstone on the kitchen counter. Here lies the purse that might have saved Donovan. If only it had made it onto the barge. And here, next to the purse on the counter, lies the recipe card labeled "Broccoli Dip." If only Paige had read the ingredients . . .

A chill crept over Eleanor. Had Paige noticed the ingredients and deliberately left the purse with the EpiPen behind?

A scene from college theatricals flashed into Eleanor's memory—Paige playing a klutz, tripping over her feet on cue. She'd reprised that role on the boat today. Her stunt made tossing the phone overboard look like an accident. No cell phone, no 911 call, no medical help for Donovan until it was too late.

Paige had improvised the perfect crime, letting someone else kill her husband for her.

Eleanor just might have to propose a toast to that performance. She filled three cut-crystal tumblers with ice, poured two fingers of Southern Comfort in each, and loaded them on a tray. This would be the last drink she'd have with the "friend" who'd used her as a surrogate killer. Her boat moccasins made no sound on the wood floor as she crossed the dining room. She heard whispers from the living room.

With her voice trained for the stage, Paige enunciated clearly even when speaking quietly. "I'm so happy, Bruce. We're together at last."

Bruce's low tones didn't carry as well, but Eleanor caught the drift from a couple of words: "always loved you . . . a dream come true . . . divorce."

The tray nearly slipped from Eleanor's grasp. She crept closer and saw her husband and her best friend kissing.

Rage coursed through her. She'd spent twenty years with a man who loved someone else. He'd never gotten over an adolescent infatuation. Now, in his midlife crisis or second adolescence, his wife didn't matter to him. Had he ever cared for her, ever appreciated her?

The tray shook in Eleanor's tight grip. One glass tipped over and shattered on the floor.

Bruce and Paige sprang apart.

Guilt and anguish mingled on Bruce's face. "Oh God, I'm so sorry,

Eleanor. I didn't want you to find out this way."

Sorry about how she'd found out, but not sorry about destroying his family. How would the twins react when their father left their mother for another woman? They'd either turn against him or walk on eggshells to avoid taking sides. He wasn't thinking of his children, of course, only himself.

Paige took possession of Eleanor's husband by slipping her arm under his elbow. "We're not doing this to hurt you, Eleanor. We really care for you, but Bruce and I want to be together."

A spur-of-the-moment decision? Not likely. In a flash of intuition, Eleanor saw it all. Paige had set the stage months ago when she played the downtrodden wife to rouse Bruce's protective instincts. She craved adulation. When her husband no longer gave it, she decided to replace him. She'd have divorced Donovan as soon as she was sure of Bruce's devotion, but then a better opportunity arose—a way to get rid of her husband with less trouble and a bigger payoff. Divorce would have given her half of his assets at most. Now she'd get everything. And a new worshipper at her shrine.

Eleanor set the tray down on the sideboard and turned back to the kitchen, the room where she did most of her thinking.

"Are you okay, Eleanor?" Bruce asked. "Where are you going?"

"To deal with this mess." Her open-palmed gesture included the glass on the floor, her husband, and her former best friend.

Eleanor rummaged in the broom closet. Would sharing her suspicions with the police bring the culprit to justice? No one could prove Paige had read the recipe. No law required her to carry an antidote for her husband's allergy. How would Bruce respond if Eleanor brought in the police? He was so besotted that he might turn on her and report what she'd said about poisoning Donovan's food. Paige might claim she'd told Eleanor about Donovan's allergy. Charges, countercharges, and one undisputed fact—Eleanor had prepared and served the fatal food.

She returned to the living room with a whisk broom, dustpan, and garbage bag, resigned to sweeping Donovan's death into oblivion as fast as she swept away the broken glass.

Bruce grabbed the broom. "Let me do this." He stooped and brushed the shards into the dustpan.

Maybe he was afraid of what Eleanor would do with jagged glass. Or maybe he was just behaving as usual, the decent man who always helped around the house.

They'd helped each other over the years, but how much had they loved each other? With the twins grown and on their own, she and Bruce were leading separate lives, together only at the dinner table and in bed. Not much heat left in bedroom and way too much in the kitchen.

No more elaborate dinners. Hallelujah. From now on, Eleanor would make simple French bistro-type meals, ready in minutes. An omelet, grilled fish, Salade Niçoise. It usually took her fifteen hours a week to plan, shop for, and cook for a foodie. Until now she'd lacked the leisure to pursue her own interests. Now she'd have the time to design sets for the community theater, make collages, or take up oil painting. Her artistic designs would go on a canvas instead of a plate, and no one would eat them.

What kind of life would Paige and Bruce have together? Eleanor picked up one of the crystal tumblers from the tray, and stared into it like a fortune teller—no, like a stage manager visualizing a scene.

Those two would get their comeuppance. Paige would never put in any time in the kitchen, too busy at the shopping mall spending Donovan's money. If Bruce didn't get the kind of food he craved, he'd turn into Donovan the Second, even more critical than his predecessor. Donovan the First had merely whined about his wife's cooking. Bruce would make nasty remarks. Eleanor imagined what he'd say about Paige's freezer-to-oven meat, instant mashed potatoes, and frozen mixed vegetables: "Charcoal briquettes, library paste, and vege-kibble."

He'd better not indulge his wit too much, though, not while married to a woman who'd killed her first husband.

Poor Bruce wouldn't even enjoy his last meal.

Eleanor grabbed the garbage bag with the glass shards from Bruce, fetched her purse from the living room, and opened the front door.

"You're taking the trash out?" Bruce took a step toward her before Paige stopped him.

Eleanor smiled. "No, Bruce, I'm leaving the trash with you."

———

Mary Ann Corrigan, an instructional designer for online courses, has taught writing, detective fiction, and drama at Georgetown University and other colleges. Her short story "Chimera" appeared in Chesapeake Crimes 3. *She has also contributed nonfiction to five anthologies.* The Murder Racquet, *her unpublished mystery featuring a tennis-playing private investigator, was a finalist in the 2008 St. Martin's Press Malice Domestic Competition. Unlike her main character in "Delicious Death," she does not enjoy cooking, preferring instead to spend her time on tennis, bridge, and crosswords.*

HIS FAVORITE GIRL

by Carla Coupe

Louisa Bea glanced at her Timex and walked faster, turning into the narrow alley that ran behind Mr. Wong's Fine Grocery and Gifte Shoppe. Breathing through her mouth—the trash pickup was overdue again—she looked up and her steps slowed. Next to the Dumpster, Jimmy Perkins and Buster O'Keefe were talking. Well, Jimmy was talking.

Jimmy.

She tucked a strand of wiry, red hair back under the little net cap all the Olde Country Inn waitresses wore. Deborah Ann Perkins, who used to be just Debby before she gained the title of hostess and started wearing a tight black dress to work, said they gave the Inn a period look. But then again, Debby could wear her blonde hair loose now, instead of twisted up under stiff, white mesh. Louisa Bea thought the caps made the waitresses look like the Mennonites who took all the blue ribbons at the county fair.

Smoothing her starched apron, she crossed the alley in time to hear Jimmy say, "That should shut her up."

Buster nodded and scratched his permanent stubble. "F'r keeps."

"Afternoon, Jimmy." Louisa Bea smiled at him the way she always did, ever since she was in the seventh grade and he was in the eighth. Maybe he wouldn't notice her heavy orthopedic shoes or her frumpy, candy-pink uniform. She resisted the urge to fiddle with her hair again and nodded. "Buster."

The tanned skin around Jimmy's eyes crinkled as he returned her smile.

"Oh, hey, Louisa Bea." He flicked the ash from his Marlboro—Jimmy never smoked anything else—onto the asphalt and took another drag, his nostrils flaring.

Shoulders hunched, Buster mumbled something; it could have been her name.

"What're you two doing here?" She watched Jimmy exhale, smoke streaming from his nose and mouth. "Mr. Wong won't like it."

"We, uh," Buster began, but Jimmy shook his head, and Buster shut up. Buster always shut up when Jimmy told him to.

"Just transacting a little business." Jimmy tossed the end of his cigarette into an oily puddle, where it flared and then went out. He leaned over and wrapped his arm around her shoulders. "Buster's helping me arrange a little surprise for the old lady. You won't say nothing to her, will you?" He squeezed her shoulders.

Buster made a noise like he was swallowing a belch, but Louisa Bea had more interesting things to think about than Buster's digestion.

Jimmy's clothes and skin smelled bitter from smoke. His warmth seeped across her breast and hip, and her belly tightened. She wanted him more than anything, wanted him to hold her, smile at her forever.

"A surprise for Debby?" The name tasted sour on her tongue. Debby with the long legs and the smooth hair. Debby who'd convinced Estelle Hartley to make *her* hostess at the Inn instead of Louisa Bea, even though Louisa Bea had been there longer and worked harder. Debby who went home every night to share a big bed with Jimmy in their second-hand double-wide.

"Yeah." Jimmy rubbed his cheek against her temple, messing up her hair, but Louisa Bea didn't care. "You wouldn't want to spoil it, would you? Me and Buster have worked real hard to plan everything."

"Course not, Jimmy."

Him and Buster. Louisa Bea never understood why Jimmy let Buster hang around all the time. Everyone knew the only thing Buster was good at was whaling on noisy drunks down at the roadhouse. But he only hit guys. Around women he acted all gallant. If he'd had a cloak, he'd have put it down on every puddle in the street. Rumor said he did a booming side business hocking your Aunt Sally's pearl necklace or Grandpa's gold watch, or finding you a TV or stereo on the cheap. Sometimes she'd see him standing outside the back door of the Inn, like he was waiting for somebody, but whenever she opened the door and asked him what he wanted, he just lifted one broad shoulder and walked away.

Somebody once said Buster'd killed a man on a bet, but Louisa Bea wasn't sure she believed that. She wasn't sure she didn't believe it, though. You never could tell with Buster.

"Good." Jimmy gave her shoulders another squeeze before he stepped away. "You're the best, Louisa Bea. You know," he winked, "you're always going to be my favorite girl."

She almost doubted him for a second, when she remembered Debby. But Jimmy wouldn't lie, not to her, so it must be true. *She* was Jimmy Perkins' favorite.

Her feet seemed to barely touch the sidewalk as she walked down the street and around the corner to work.

▰ ▰ ▰

"What's wrong with you, girl?"

With a start, Louisa Bea turned from the window. "Nothing."

Debby ran her hands down her black dress and frowned. "You've been mooning around all night. It's like you've gone and got yourself a boyfriend." She stopped, and her frown deepened. "You haven't, have you?"

Louisa Bea couldn't tell Debby what Jimmy had said. Not yet, at least. "No."

"I know!" Her face suddenly brightening, Debby turned back to the office. "It must be that Buster O'Keefe. He's always hanging around outside, waiting for you to get off work."

"It's not . . ."

But Debby disappeared, the door marked "Private" slamming closed behind her.

Louisa Bea glanced back at the window. Was that why Buster stood outside the back door? Because he wanted to be her boyfriend?

She shook her head. Even if Buster wanted her, she'd given her heart to Jimmy years ago. She'd give Jimmy everything else, too, if he asked. When he asked.

She was his favorite girl, after all.

Louisa Bea'd have no problem believing that, except for Debby.

Well, Jimmy had said he had a surprise for Debby. Louisa Bea dunked the rag she used to wipe the tables into the sink and wrung it out. What were Jimmy's words? Something about Debby being quiet. No, about Debby shutting up. She closed her eyes, remembering the way Jimmy had stood there in the alley, a cigarette dangling from his fingers, a lazy curl of smoke circling the top of his thigh.

The echo of his voice. "That should shut her up."

Then Buster had said, "For keeps."

Louisa Bea opened her eyes. Jimmy Perkins had spoken the truth. *She* was his favorite. That meant he loved her. Hadn't he as good as said that he was going to kill Debby so they could be together?

┏ ┏ ┏

She waited all week for Debby to die.

Every afternoon when Louisa Bea walked into the Inn, disappointment twisted in her chest. There Debby stood, elegant in black, golden hair shining, right behind the hostess station. But Jimmy knew how much Louisa Bea wanted him; he wouldn't keep her waiting any longer than necessary. She just had to be patient, and Debby wouldn't be around anymore.

Sometimes she wondered how Jimmy would do it. Would he wrap his hands around Debby's neck and choke her until her tanned face turned as blue as her eye shadow? Or hit her on the head and dump her body in the trash-filled creek down at the bottom of town? Maybe he'd get her good and drunk and when she fell asleep he'd stick her head in the oven and turn on the gas.

She liked thinking of ways Debby could die.

Every night Buster hung around, waiting in the alley until Louisa Bea got off work, following her to the little clapboard house her grandparents had left her. Buster's attentions bothered her at first, until she realized they must be Jimmy's doing. Jimmy just wanted to keep her safe until *he* could be the one to escort her home every night. So Louisa Bea would sneak out a glass of milk and a piece or two of sour cherry pie for Buster, and let him walk beside her on the narrow sidewalk all the way to her front porch. She wanted Jimmy to know how much she appreciated his concern.

Friday morning, Louisa Bea crept into Madame Edna's Dress Shop and asked the price of the lacy, black underpants and bra displayed in the window. The cost took her breath away, but she couldn't wear her old cotton panties with the stretched-out leg holes on her first night with Jimmy. She paid for them with cash, counting out bill after bill, and watched as Madame Edna wrapped them in pink tissue paper as gently as if they were antique, glass Christmas ornaments.

When she saw Debby at work that night, Louisa Bea was glad she hadn't worn her new lingerie. She'd wear them tomorrow, on Saturday, because surely Jimmy would be hers by then.

r r r

The underwire from the bra dug into the soft flesh beneath her armpit and the lace panties scratched her thighs as she walked to work, but Louisa Bea didn't mind. Not until she saw Debby standing at the hostess station, smiling broadly.

"Look what Jimmy bought me for our anniversary." Debby held out her hand, tilting it back and forth so the light caught the diamond in the ring and sent flashes around the room. "I've told him for *ages* I wanted a diamond, and he surprised me with it last night." She sighed, her smile softening as she looked at the ring. "Such a romantic boy. He tied a red ribbon around it and put it on my pillow . . ."

Louisa Bea stared at Debby's hand. A ring. A diamond ring.

At that moment her heart cracked and broke, exactly the way the light splintered when it hit Debby's diamond.

Jimmy *lied* to her. She wasn't his favorite girl after all.

Louisa Bea didn't break down and cry. She didn't scream at Debby and run out of the Inn, although she would've liked to. She just bowed her head.

"It's very pretty."

If she was a little quieter that night, a little slower to chat with the regulars, no one seemed to notice.

No one but Buster.

During her break, she carried out a big piece of apple pie and a glass of milk, then waited while he balanced the glass on the lid of a trashcan and took a bite of pie.

"Did you know about Debby's diamond ring?" She watched him closely in the dazzling spill of light from the back stoop.

He took another bite and nodded.

"I guess Jimmy asked you to find it for her."

Another bite, another nod.

"I thought he was gonna kill her."

Buster stared at her, the fork loaded with a fat piece of apple stopped halfway to his mouth.

Louisa Bea took a deep breath, her fingers tugging at the underwire poking her ribs. Buster's eyes widened, and he set down the fork and the plate with his half-eaten pie on the trashcan lid next to the milk. His lips were shiny, his breathing rough. For the first time in her life, Louisa Bea saw desire in a man's eyes.

She knew exactly what to do.

Stepping forward, she put her hand on his arm, his greasy, plaid wool jacket scratchy against her palm. "He lied to me, Buster. Jimmy *lied*. He told me *I* was his favorite girl, but I'm not." Her voice caught, she curled her fingers around his heavy biceps. "I'm nobody's favorite."

Buster stared at her fingers and made a sound like a motorcycle starting up.

Louisa Bea leaned forward so that her breast, encased in the black lace bra under her crisp, pink uniform, just brushed Buster's chest. "What'd you say?"

Face so dark she wondered if he was having a stroke, Buster opened his mouth. "Mine. *My* favorite."

"I am?" Louisa Bea pressed a little closer and tried to ignore Buster's sour breath. The faint tang of cinnamon from the pie made that easier. "Then you'll help me, won't you?"

▰ ▰ ▰

When she returned from her break, Buster's rumbled "sure" echoing in her head, Louisa Bea smiled at Debby and even admired her diamond ring. Maybe one day Louisa Bea would have a ring even better than Debby's. After all, Buster had found one diamond ring. Surely he could find another, bigger one. And Buster, who had always followed Jimmy's orders, wanted to help *her* instead, although she had to wait until after work before she could explain to him exactly what that help would be.

Her heart light, her step brisk, Louisa Bea finished her shift. Buster waited to walk her home as usual. Only this time she led him to the alley behind Mr. Wong's store. It seemed fitting to reveal her plan in the place where Jimmy had lied to her and broken her heart.

She faced Buster, looked up into his pale gray eyes. He tilted his head and gently ran his callused finger down her forearm to her wrist. Louisa Bea shivered, only partly from disgust.

"I want to kill Jimmy."

Buster stared at her.

"And Debby," she added. With Debby dead, the hostess position would be open again. Estelle would *have* to give it to her this time.

Buster continued to stare.

Louisa Bea sighed. Really, how much clearer could she be?

But Buster wasn't good with words. So she cupped her hands around his shoulders and pressed her breasts against his chest. His body shook, an earthquake shuddering deep inside. She rubbed against him, just a little because the underwire poked her, and then slid her hands up to his face and touched her fingers to his lips. The promise of a kiss, maybe, but she hoped she wouldn't have to go *that* far.

She didn't.

＊　＊　＊

Fortunately Buster knew a thing or two about killing people.

Sitting together on the rough wooden bench in the old school-bus shelter at the end of town, they could see the lights in Jimmy's trailer. It sat all alone in a corner of the field that Jimmy's daddy had left him before he died. Louisa Bea listened to Buster's suggestions, his smelly jacket draped over her shoulders against the evening chill. If those suggestions were expressed in a handful of one- or two-syllable words, what did it matter? It was the thought that counted.

And the result.

Buster told her that Jimmy and Debby never locked the door of their double-wide and that Debby hated sleeping with the bedroom windows open. And that the big propane tank in the side yard had just been filled.

Buster, absurdly worried that she not be caught, wanted her to wait outside.

"No way," she said, so he insisted she wear his big leather gloves. After all, his fingerprints were already all over the house, even on the knobs of the stove. Hers weren't.

No one—not even his mama—would call Buster sweet, but his courtesy, his almost-reverence for her, touched Louisa Bea. He'd agreed to help her, he'd come up with a plan, he'd treated her like a lady. For all this, Buster deserved a reward. She leaned over and brushed her dry lips over the stubble on his cheek. Not too horrible. Actually, she was surprised at how not horrible it was.

Buster gazed at her the way she'd seen beaten dogs look at someone who held out a hand, offering a pat: hope and want and fear all mixed up together. Louisa Bea sat up straight, power tingling in her fingertips. *She* was the one person who could change that look in Buster's eyes. She could feed his hope and his want, or she could starve them.

"Buster."

He tilted his head, wary.

"You know what I'm wearing under my dress?"

Buster froze. His throat worked, a sound like the start of a NASCAR race filled the shelter as he slowly shook his head.

"I've got on a bra. And panties. Want to know what they're made of?"

Buster blinked. His chin dipped in a shallow nod.

Breathless, Louisa Bea suddenly understood why girls like Debby teased boys.

Leaning forward, she whispered, "Black lace."

Buster's hands shook. She sat back with a smile.

They waited until the lights in the trailer went out, then sat another hour to make sure Jimmy and Debby were asleep and not just fooling around in bed. Louisa Bea let Buster wrap his arm around her shoulders and pull her close. The night air was cold, after all, and she appreciated Buster's warmth, if not his smell of stale sweat and old dog.

Finally Buster decided it was safe to approach the trailer. Louisa Bea followed him across the cracked concrete drive and up the softly creaking wooden steps. The door opened into the living room, the looming shapes of sofa and television faintly picked out by the lights on a VCR. Buster turned to the left, into the kitchen, brighter still from the microwave's clock.

He blew out the pilot light and turned all four burners on full. Louisa Bea padded back through the living room, drawn by the soft snores coming from Jimmy and Debby's bedroom. She stood for a moment peering into the dark room. Then she turned and joined Buster at the front door, wrinkling her nose. The strong smell of gas made her queasy.

Buster led her outside into the fresh air, and they returned to the bus shelter.

Louisa Bea settled on the bench and leaned into Buster's warmth. "How long do you think it'll take?"

"'Bout an hour."

They sat, waiting, until the hour was up. Buster insisted on going alone to check on Jimmy and Debby. Louisa Bea closed her eyes and inhaled slowly, imagining how they looked on the big bed in their double-wide, eyes open, hearts stopped. Then she practiced her story for the police, about how Buster and Jimmy had argued last night and how Buster'd said he'd kill Jimmy. That kind of thing happened a lot in their part of town.

She smiled when Buster returned and said "dead." He didn't whisper so much as rumble, like the sound of far-off thunder in the mountains.

Dawn faintly washed the horizon by the time they returned to her little house, and Louisa Bea left Buster in the kitchen while she climbed the narrow stairs to her bedroom and changed into her nightgown and robe. Although she enjoyed the fantasy of black-lace lingerie, the reality wasn't nearly as comfortable as well-washed cotton flannel.

Buster looked oddly out of place standing in her neat kitchen, his big body taking up most of the room, but she sidled around him and sat in her usual chair.

"For heaven's sake, take a seat," she said. Waiting until he pulled out the other chair and perched gingerly on the gingham cushion, she clasped her hands.

A sudden worry made her lean forward. "You didn't turn off *all* the burners, did you? The police'll check that one's still on." Or maybe the fire department would be the first out there. Louisa Bea didn't care. Either would do.

"Nah. Might blow, though." Buster's hand crept across the table and touched hers. His fingers were twice the size of Louisa Bea's and rough with calluses. "If there's a spark."

She nodded, letting him trace a pattern on the back of her hand. "That's okay, too."

"Got a lighter. Y'want me to—"

"No!" She reached out, took his hand in both of hers. How early could she call the police? "No, it's not safe for you to go back again. You did good, Buster. Now go on home and—"

"Here." He shifted and pulled something out of his shirt pocket. "'S yours." He pressed it into her hand.

A ring. A diamond ring. Debby's diamond ring.

When her fingers closed over the ring, Louisa Bea smiled at Buster. Perhaps she should reconsider her plan. It would be nice to have a boyfriend. She'd come home after being hostess at the Olde Country Inn, take off her tight black dress, and show Buster her lacy lingerie. Maybe even wear the diamond ring when no one else could see it. Buster would listen when she asked him to bathe more often and to wear nicer clothes.

And if he didn't behave, she could always make that phone call.

––––––

Carla Coupe is a member of both Sisters in Crime and Mystery Writers of America. She has had two short stories nominated for the Agatha Award: "Rear View Murder" in Chesapeake Crimes II *and "Dangerous Crossing," which appeared in* Chesapeake Crimes 3. *When she isn't writing, you can find her in her garden or belly dancing. For further information, go to www.carlacoupe.com.*

CLEANING FISH

by Meriah Crawford

Jake had expected to find himself digging ditches or washing cars or some such work when he got out on parole, but this wasn't half bad. He whisked a brush down the Thoroughbred gelding's hindquarters, both of them enjoying the shade from the barn's broad overhang and the cool breezes coming from the lake. After he finished, there was a pair of dapple-gray Percheron mares and a palomino gelding who needed grooming. Then, after lunch, Jake would clean tack and do some minor repairs in the equipment shed. Whatever Otho and Anna Waggoner, the farm's owners, asked him to do.

The Waggoners let Jake live in a small, drafty apartment over the barn. In his spare time, he read science-fiction novels or fished in the lake. Sometimes, on Sundays, Anna would drive him into town to see a movie or do some shopping. Otho was even teaching him how to ride, which he'd longed to do since he was a boy, watching old *Bonanza* and *Gunsmoke* reruns after school. Jake's mount was nearly always the Thoroughbred—a gentle, high-stepping bay named Buchanan that he'd come to love in the few weeks he'd been riding. If he didn't look too far into the future or, more importantly, too far into the past, life seemed pretty sweet.

r   r   r

Jake dropped the brush into the plastic bin that held the grooming tools and fished out a hoof pick. A hawk cried in the distance. Buchanan swished his tail to warn off a few flies. And then, as Jake cradled Buchanan's near foreleg, cleaning out the gelding's hoof, he saw Otho walking toward the barn with his rolling gait. Beside him was Sheriff Rove, a retired Army sergeant in his early fifties who'd been the one to arrest Jake more than five years earlier. The sheriff and Otho were chatting—something about the high school soccer team and then the corn crop.

"Best damned corn yield I ever seen," the sheriff said. "Alls we need is another good rain or two and the boys over to the extension office'll owe me a pair of Jacksons."

Otho nodded and uttered a noncommittal, "That right?"

"Yes, indeed," the sheriff said. "Boys bet me we'd be leaner 'n last year. Sum-bitches oughta know better 'n to set up against me."

"Huh," Otho said. His face was still pleasant enough, but Jake knew

Otho didn't much approve of cussing or gambling.

The bay, noticing Jake was distracted, pulled his hoof free and stamped it, narrowly missing Jake's boot.

"Watch your feet, son," Otho called in his gravelly voice. "God only gave you the two, and you'll be needing both of 'em."

"Yes, sir," Jake answered, moving to the side a half step and reaching for the hoof again.

"Leave it," the sheriff said as he came to a stop a couple feet from the horse's head. "We're gonna have us a little chat."

Jake hesitated, and the gelding reached his head forward to nuzzle at the sheriff's hand. Rove smacked the horse sharply on the nose and stepped back, sneering, as the horse threw his head up and whinnied shrilly.

Otho, a tight look on his face, soothed Buchanan, then took the hoof pick from Jake and patted him on the shoulder. "I'll finish up with him while you're talking," he said, giving Jake a serious look and a nod.

The day before, Otho had given Jake a talk about not letting people make him angry. The man delivering sacks of feed that morning had gone to high school with Jake and knew his story. The guy, Sammy, called Jake low-life junkie scum and wouldn't let him sign the delivery slip. By the time Otho came out to see what was wrong, Jake was getting ready to swing.

"You let him make you angry enough to violate your parole, and who wins?" Otho asked Jake, after he'd sent Sammy on his way and told him not to ever come back. "Who does the time?"

Jake knew Otho was right, but he had more than five years worth of bitterness and regret twisting in his belly like a ball of molten pitch, and it was aching to come out. The sheriff was just about the perfect target, too. He was the only other man on this Earth who knew for sure that Jake had been innocent.

Jake followed the sheriff, who came to a stop in the shade of the massive pin oak that stood a few feet from the barn.

"You been busy since you got out of prison, boy," Rove said, hitching up his gun belt and leaning against the tree.

Jake watched a spider crawl onto the sheriff's shoulder and wished it would bite. "Busy?" he asked.

"Folks down around the high school been telling me 'bout you being up to your old tricks."

Jake shoved his hands deep in his pockets and rocked back on his heels. "Which tricks would those be, Sheriff?"

Rove smiled. "You know what tricks I mean, son. Tryin' to get their kiddies hooked on summa that crack co-caine." He scratched roughly at the stubble on his jowls. "Can't imagine Judge Bardon'll like that one bit."

"I don't go anywhere near that school anymore," Jake said quietly.

"Hell, boy, I know that. But my cousin seen you there, sure enough." He chuckled and shook his head like it was the craziest thing he'd ever heard.

Jake's fists clenched in his pockets, and his jaw tightened. The rage washed over him, and, for just a brief moment, it felt so good, so right.

The sheriff saw and smirked. "I got some packages need to be delivered on down to Surry," he said. "Every week, on Sundays. You're going to pick 'em up from Bobby"—Deputy Foley—"and deliver them to the addresses he give you. You get caught, you're on your own."

"And why would I do that?"

"It's that or prison, boy. Choose." The sheriff stepped away from the tree and hooked his thumbs in his gear belt.

Jake turned his back and stood staring at the blue of the lake, trying to think of some way out, knowing there wasn't one. And then, out of nowhere, Jake heard a dull *thunk*. He spun around in time to see Sheriff Rove tip forward, falling smack on his face in the dirt.

Just back of where the sheriff had been standing, Otho stood holding a shovel, looking grim. He nodded and spit in the general direction of the former sheriff of Ashland County.

"My boy," Otho said hoarsely and stopped for a moment. "My boy was just like you, Jake. Only he got in a fight when he was in prison, and we got him back in a *goddamn* box." Otho's hands gripped the shovel so hard they began to shake.

After a moment, Otho shook his head, returning to the present. "I'll go get the wheelbarrow out of the shed. You go on over to the far side of the fence there, near where that old Farmall tractor sets, and start digging." Otho held the shovel out to Jake, and Jake took it.

Still stunned into silence, Jake did as Otho directed. He found the earth firm but willing enough to the shovel. While he dug, he watched Otho tip the barrow forward on its nose, and gently but smoothly, with the skill and strength of a man accustomed to hard physical labor, ease the sheriff into it. Otho rested for a moment, stretching his back and gazing into the distance. There were tiny puffs of smoke that showed where a tractor was pulling a hay rake through the field on River Road. Sheriff Rove sat with his back against the vertical bed of the wheelbarrow, looking as good as alive from a distance. Jake focused harder on his digging.

A few minutes later, he heard the creak of the wheel as the barrow bumped over tree roots and pine cones on its way across the yard.

Otho parked his load a few feet away. He pulled a second shovel from beside the body and started digging alongside Jake.

"Easy, easy," Otho said. "Not so fast. Slow, steady digging'll get you there faster in the end."

Jake eased up a bit and found himself settling into the work, almost forgetting the body that was slumped just a few feet away. The buzzing and movement of a few flies drew his attention from time to time, but he set himself to focus on the small rocks, the reddish soil, and the roots that snapped and pulled from the ground.

Jake started lengthening the hole, and Otho shook his head. "No need to lay him out like he was family. We'll just curl him up in a little square of a hole. He'll be cozy enough."

They worked steadily for a time. It wasn't the sort of thing you could leave unfinished, out in the open air. There was a feeling of breath being held and a need to maintain silence.

Finally Otho stepped back and surveyed the pit. It was about four by three, and nearly four feet deep. He nodded, satisfied, and leaned his shovel against the fence, giving Jake a hand out of the hole. Otho began moving toward the wheelbarrow, and Jake said, "You want me to . . ."

Otho shook his head. "A man should always clean his own fish," he said and grasped the handles. He rolled the barrow to the edge and gently tipped it forward, spilling Sheriff Rove into the hole. Rove sprawled awkwardly—face down, with his legs splayed out and his feet up against the side. Otho set the barrow down again and slid into the hole, shifting Rove so he lay curled on his side. He climbed out again and nodded to Jake. They each took a shovel and began filling the hole in.

Jake winced as the first few shovelfuls of dirt smacked onto the sheriff's flank, but grew accustomed to it quickly enough. The dread that'd filled him since he first heard Rove's voice that day began, slowly, to ease. He wiped sweat from his face and let his muscles work, enjoying the strain of it in a distant sort of way.

With a few inches of dirt covering the bottom of the hole and its contents, Jake and Otho both froze when they heard a muffled, tinny rendition of "Dixie." They looked at each other wide-eyed for a moment, and then Jake said, "Cell phone."

"*Dang* it," Otho said and moved toward the hole and the still-ringing phone.

Jake put a hand out, stopping him. "Let me."

Otho hesitated, then nodded, and Jake slid in. He nearly fell, then stepped on the sheriff's ankle and had to stand very still for a moment until his stomach settled. Finally the cell stopped ringing, and the silence pressed down. Jake brushed the dirt back from the sheriff's waist and patted the belt until he found it. Jake flipped the phone open and pressed the power button, waiting until the screen went dark. He glanced up at Otho. "Leave it here?"

Otho shrugged. "Wipe it clean, then drop it."

That done, Otho offered Jake a hand, and he climbed out again, stepping carefully around the body. Jake saw a grim, gray look on Otho's face for the first time, and he set to filling the hole in again with renewed energy. For the old man's sake, even more than his own, he wanted it done.

It was still early afternoon when they tamped the last shovel of dirt firmly into place. They hauled a load of fence posts over and laid them on the spot so it didn't look disturbed, then cleaned the shovels and hosed out the wheelbarrow.

Both men stood for a moment, looking toward the tree near the barn, then Otho patted Jake on the shoulder and said, "Come on up to the house. Lunch'll do us some good."

᠆ ᠆ ᠆

It was four days later when one of the deputies found Sheriff Rove's pickup truck parked off an old logging road on state land. His rifle was gone, and they figured he'd been out doing a little off-season deer hunting and gotten lost. It had rained hard over the previous two days so there were no tracks of any kind. Though they had no idea which way he'd gone, a small group of deputies, Boy Scouts, and a mountain-climbing club from Charlottesville searched for nearly ten days before giving up.

After three weeks of wearing dark colors and a grim look, and eating casseroles brought by her neighbors, Mrs. Rove put on a peach and lime-green sundress, packed up, and went home to Missouri.

Two months later, when the first frost coated the ground and the water trough had a thin crust of ice at dawn, Otho helped Jake carry his two boxes of possessions up to the main house and moved him into the back bedroom. The small room, with a view of rolling hills off in the distance, held a low bookcase containing westerns, old mysteries, and a short row of track-and-field trophies with engraved plates that read "Seth Waggoner."

When spring came, Jake and Otho went out on the lake in a small boat. They rowed to about the middle and dropped overboard a rifle wrapped in burlap and weighted down with rocks. After a moment's silence, they made their way to Otho's secret fishing spot, and each caught two fine bass for supper. When they got back to the house, Otho handed Jake the fish to clean and joined Anna on the front porch to watch the sun as it set behind the barn.

———

Meriah Crawford is a private investigator and college instructor living in central Virginia. She has an MFA from the University of Southern Maine's Stonecoast MFA program. Details about her other publications and activities can be found on her website: www.mlcrawford.com.

VOLUNTEER OF THE YEAR

by Barb Goffman

"Ladies and gentlemen, the Buckaroo Ball is pleased to honor this year's volunteer of the year, Gaylene Banks."

As the applause began, I took a deep breath and made my way to the microphone. The hot stage lights burned so brightly I couldn't see anyone in the audience. But I knew my husband, Gavin, sat at the honorees' table front and center, likely nursing his second gin and tonic. Heck, maybe his third.

My heart began beating erratically as I started to speak. I didn't know if it was anxiety or my cardiac arrhythmia acting up.

Calm down, Gaylene. It's only nerves. Everything's going to work out just fine.

I inhaled deeply once again, soon got into a rhythm, and the speech flew by. Mother would have been proud if she'd lived to see this day. I was poised and elegant. Not a hair on my silver head slipped from its place. My white pearl necklace and button earrings added the perfect touch to my stylish black dress. Granted, I'd dressed up more than nearly all the other women, who favored casual, southwestern attire. But all eyes were on *me*, not them.

Like a good Buckaroo, I hit all the right notes in my speech. The importance of working in the community. Of protecting children. Of giving back. I touted the Buckaroo Ball. How it's the biggest annual charity event in New Mexico. I thanked everyone in the audience who had given their time and money to help the Buckaroo Ball Committee aid the at-risk children of Santa Fe County. And I gave a nod to my husband, who had supported me all these years, enabling me to volunteer full time—and then some—to help abused children, long before the Buckaroo Ball Committee came into existence.

I'd debated whether to mention Gavin in my speech. I'd worked so hard to keep him apart from my volunteer life. But in the end I realized I couldn't avoid it, not without raising eyebrows. And that just wouldn't do.

An hour later, Gavin twirled me around the dance floor. He was larger than life, his black Stetson casting a shadow over his twinkling blue eyes. He smelled a bit like his favorite horse, as usual, no matter how much he showered.

"Congratulations, Gaylene," Bitsy Allen called as she two-stepped nearby. "They couldn't have picked a better person to honor. And it's wonderful to finally meet your husband. He's a doll."

"Why thank you, pretty lady." Gavin tipped his hat. "Perhaps later this evening, you'd give me the honor of a dance."

"You got it, sugar," Bitsy said.

Yes, everybody always loved Gavin. He knew how to turn on the charm.

It was Gavin who spurred me to get involved in children's causes forty-five years ago. At the time, we'd been married just a couple years. I'd come home a day early from visiting Mother and Daddy in Dallas. Gavin surely was surprised to see me. He hustled little Tommy Greenley out of our den, pretending everything was normal, calling after Tommy to keep working on his batting swing. Tommy looked scared. Wouldn't meet my eyes. Gavin had been coaching Tommy's Little League team, but that wasn't baseball going on in the den.

I left Gavin that night, but I couldn't make it stick. In the 1960s, you didn't talk about things like that. And you didn't leave your husband. So I moved back home a few days later, after Gavin promised to quit coaching. To quit having anything to do with kids. To focus all his time on the ranch. I moved into the spare bedroom, began volunteering with children's causes to make myself feel better, and settled into a quiet, celibate existence.

That was probably my mistake, I realize now. Gavin needed some release. And I'd denied him.

"Gaylene, honey, where's your mind?" Gavin drew me closer than I ever let him in private. "You haven't heard a word I said."

I smiled up at him, shrugged my shoulders. He'd been my dream come true when we met in 1961. I was an eighteen-year-old freshman at Southern Methodist University, ready for my happily ever after. A husband, a home, a family. Gavin was in his senior year. A football star. We had a six-month, whirlwind courtship before we wed. I dropped out of school, we moved to a house outside Santa Fe, and Gavin began working on his family's cattle ranch.

Mother flew out a few times the first year of our marriage, helping me make our house a home while Gavin worked long hours. We even decorated a nursery that looked out on a large pasture dotted with cottonwood trees. But it sat empty.

Thank God.

The song finally ended. I made my way to an empty table while Gavin headed to the bar.

"There she is, our volunteer of the year," Freddy Crawford said as he and his wife joined me. "I don't think I've ever seen a prettier gal, except for my Miranda here, of course." He pecked his wife on the cheek as she sat down.

She laughed and patted my hand. "Honey, it's good to see your husband supporting you at one of these functions. He's missed so many over the years, we were beginning to wonder if he was a spy or something, leading a secret life somewhere else."

"A secret life?" I laughed back.

Miranda leaned forward, her jasmine perfume tickling my nose. "You know, it wasn't till he started volunteering at the YMCA some months back that I knew Gavin shared any of your interests in children's causes. He's been such a help with the afternoon tutoring and the sports programs."

I forced myself to smile. It was Miranda who'd first mentioned Gavin's volunteering to me a few weeks ago during one of our charity luncheons. Then Deborah Paterson piped in that the Boy Scouts were grateful for all of Gavin's support, too—time and money.

How I hadn't known about his renewed extra-curricular activities, I don't know. Maybe I hadn't wanted to know. In the beginning, Gavin seemed to live up to his promise, burying himself in helping run his daddy's ranch. After a while, I'd busied myself so much with my charities that I'd stopped paying attention to what Gavin was doing.

But after listening to Miranda and Deborah, I couldn't stay blind anymore.

I spotted Gavin heading our way and jumped up. "Time to cha-cha. Gavin is just a dancing fool." I hurried over and drew him out on the floor.

"Since when do you like to dance so much?" he asked about ten minutes later, stepping in time with me to a Texas waltz.

"Since you're here in public with me, making a good appearance."

When the song ended, Gavin wanted to take another breather, but I pressed for one more dance. The band had started a real fast one. Gavin might have been in his late sixties and a bit pudgy, but he still could tear up the floor. So much so that we attracted a small audience, which spurred Gavin to keep going for three more numbers.

By the time we took a break, he was sweating something fierce. "Gavin, honey, you don't look so good. You go sit down. I'll get you some water."

"Scotch," he said as he fanned his face with his hat.

I sidled up to the empty end of the bar, set my purse on the counter, and ordered Gavin's drink. The music caught my attention, and I turned around, taking in the room. Everyone looked so wonderful. Bitsy spotted me and waved. Lord, was she fixing to come over here?

"Here you go, ma'am." The bartender set down Gavin's scotch.

"Can I also get a Long Island iced tea, please?"

While the bartender went off to make the seven-liquor drink, I put my cell phone to my ear, pretending I was on a call. I didn't want anyone, especially Bitsy, to bother me. She's nice, but boy, could she talk.

I waited a few seconds and glanced over my shoulder. Good. No Bitsy. Never one to have idle hands, I began fiddling in my purse. When my drink finally arrived, I snapped my purse shut, switched off the phone, and headed back to our table, still swirling Gavin's scotch.

"Here you go. One scotch." I beamed at him while he gulped it down. "Whoa, that's kind of fast, honey. You want another?"

"You're being awful nice to me tonight, Gaylene."

"It's my night. I want everything to go just right."

I got him another scotch, which he downed, too. A few minutes later, Gavin leaned over. "I think I'm gonna be sick."

I sprang up. "Well don't do it here in the middle of the room."

I yanked him to his feet and walked him to the men's room, his breathing shallow. He headed in, and I entered the ladies' room. Calm, as if nothing unusual was going on.

"Congratulations again, Gaylene." Bitsy sat next to me at the vanity while I touched up my face. "That sure is a pretty color lipstick. And I loved your speech tonight. I'm always in awe of you and everything you do for children. There doesn't seem to be any task you're not willing to take on."

I smiled. "Thank you, Bitsy. You're so very sweet."

A commotion nearly overwhelmed me when I left the ladies' room.

"Gaylene! There you are!" Freddy Crawford grabbed my arms. "We've called the paramedics. Gavin passed out in the bathroom."

"Oh my Lord." Forsaking my sense of propriety, I barged into the men's room. Tyler Harrison was giving Gavin CPR. How lucky that a doctor was in the restroom when Gavin collapsed.

"Tyler, what's going on?" I knelt next to Gavin, who now smelled more like vomit than horse. "Will he be all right? What happened?"

Tyler kept pushing on Gavin's chest, his face grim. "How much did he have to drink tonight?"

"Um, I'm not sure. Two or three gin and tonics at the beginning of the night. Then at some point he switched to scotch. Might have had a couple bourbons, too."

"He always drink that much?"

"Yes. But he's never had any trouble before."

"Any history of heart problems?"

"No. You think it's his heart?" I pressed my hand to my own, feeling it beat rapidly in my chest. "Oh, no! His daddy died of a heart attack."

I slumped back against the wall while Freddy hurried the rest of the men out of the room. Then he sat down beside me and took my hand.

Tyler put his ear to Gavin's lips, his fingers to Gavin's neck. Shook his head. When he resumed chest compressions a moment later, Tyler looked defeated. Gavin was pale. I didn't sense any life left in him.

Tears filled my eyes while Freddy patted my hand. "He's gonna be all right. You'll see." The bathroom door banged open as the paramedics sped in, followed by some firefighters and a police officer. I swallowed hard. The room suddenly felt very crowded.

"You've got an overweight man, late sixties to early seventies, apparent heart attack," Tyler said while they took over Gavin's care. "I've done CPR for the last five minutes or so."

"He's sixty-nine," I said, my voice squeaking.

"He collapsed here," Tyler went on. "Vomited first. Looks like he drank too much tonight and overdid it on the dance floor."

"No pulse," the red-haired paramedic said. A fireman hooked Gavin up to a heart monitor, while the redhead took over the CPR. The other paramedic interrupted a few times to shock Gavin. Then someone shoved a tube attached to a ventilation bag down Gavin's throat. Someone else started an IV. I tried to back away.

"We've got to hurry," the redhead said as he and his partner loaded Gavin on a stretcher.

I struggled to my feet to follow the paramedics as they rushed out of the restroom with Gavin, but I staggered. Freddy, bless him, steadied me.

"You okay?" he asked.

I exhaled a deep breath. "Yes. I think so."

"You're gonna have to run to go with the ambulance, Gaylene," Freddy said. "Miranda and I can take you to the hospital. Why don't you let us do that?"

I nodded. "Thank you, Freddy. A ride would be good." My breath became a bit ragged as I fought off tears. "I'd just like a minute to myself first."

"Of course. Tyler and I'll wait outside."

Freddy and Tyler left the restroom, leaving me all alone. I headed to one of the stalls. Thankfully it was clean. I'd always heard horror stories about men's rooms.

I reached into my purse and pulled out the baggie I had packed that afternoon. Just a trace of my crushed heart pills remained inside. I tossed the baggie into the toilet and flushed twice, making sure the evidence floated away.

My tears started flowing then. Tears of relief. And sadness. I wiped my cheek with the back of my hand.

Yes, it was my special night. And Bitsy was right. I'd do anything to keep children safe.

Anything.

———

Barb Goffman is an Agatha Award-nominated short-story author. Barb's short stories have appeared in volumes two, three, and (now) four of the Chesapeake Crimes *anthology series, as well as in* The Gift of Murder *anthology (edited by John Floyd, Wolfmont Press, 2009). Barb is program chair of the Malice Domestic mystery conference and was the 2007 and 2008 president of the Chesapeake Chapter of Sisters in Crime, through which she's met many wonderful people who've helped her plot murder, as well as a few she'd consider knocking off herself—on paper, of course. You can learn more about her at www. barbgoffman.com.*

VENOMOUS

by Sasscer Hill

"I just *love* this perfume!" Kate sniffed her wrist then waved it under my nose.

I tried not to grimace. The hideously overpriced Predator smelled like a dime-store special. Unfortunately Kate had presented me with a bottle of the stuff the previous week for my sixtieth birthday.

"Sure you don't want a little spritz, Janet?" Kate held up the bubble-gum-pink atomizer.

"No. Thank you." She has a good heart, I reminded myself. "My bottle's right here in my purse. Why don't we watch the race?"

I led her to the fence separating Laurel Park's concrete apron from the dirt racetrack and leaned my elbows on the top rail. We'd come to watch Kate's gelding, Pinkerton, in the fifth. Across the mile-oval the starting gate crew loaded Kate's horse and the rest of the field. I watched with interest.

The year before, I'd bought a yearling filly named Platinum Pearl. As the months flew by, I'd become impatient for her to start. Yes, I appreciated my trainer, Leonard Cushman, taking his time with Pearl. But wasn't he being too careful? Other youngsters had started months ago.

In the distance, a bell clanged. The horses burst from the gate and charged up the backside, the fuchsia silks worn by Pinkerton's jockey lying mid-pack. Next to me, Kate hopped up and down, her mauve, designer glasses bouncing, her tightly permed, gray hair motionless.

"Come on, Pinkerton!" she cried.

Her horse might finish second or third, but the *Daily Racing Form* predicted the chestnut, Love the Money, would leave this field in his dust.

Coming around the final turn, Love the Money made his move. His golden-red coat and prominent white blaze reminded me of my Pearl. He opened up by two lengths.

A man on my left yelled, "That's it, it's over. Yeah!"

Almost to the wire, just in front of me, Love the Money took a bad step, staggered, and went down. The crowd gasped. The announcer cried, "Love the Money has stumbled, and now Grail takes the lead, followed by Zinger and . . ."

I didn't listen, dimly aware of Pinkerton finishing third or fourth. Sickened, I stared at Love the Money's thrashing legs. He tried so hard to rise but collapsed back onto the dirt.

On my right, Kate gave a small moan.

The jockey, who'd been thrown clear, scrambled back to the injured horse, grabbed the bridle, and held the animal's head as if to keep the chestnut from getting up.

Love the Money's right, front leg curved at a peculiar angle. An almost painful gratitude toward Leonard hit me. Bless him for being so careful with Pearl. This was awful.

"God damn it, Tapply, you said that leg was fine. Look at him out there!"

I glanced at the two men on my left, one of them the fellow who'd proclaimed the outcome "over" when Love the Money made his move. A big man, maybe fifty-five, the eyes behind his tortoiseshell glasses were an unusual gold-brown color. His knuckles whitened as he gripped his program.

The other man I recognized as Roy Tapply, a young trainer. He had the entire barn across from Leonard's on Laurel's backstretch. I didn't like Tapply. He had this cocky way about him—his upper lip perpetually curled in a half-sneer. His walk reminded me of a rooster's strut. And now he was rolling his eyes.

"You're the one said you didn't want to be eaten up by day rates, Richardson," Tapply said. "That the horse has to earn his keep."

I glanced at my *Form*. Raymond Richardson, Love the Money's owner.

Richardson pulled off his glasses, rubbed the bridge of his nose, then stared at Tapply before shaking his head. "I can't afford to do this anymore. We're done." Sliding his glasses back into place, Richardson turned and walked rapidly away across pavement littered with discarded bet tickets, popcorn, and empty paper cups.

Kate and I exchanged a look.

With a smug smile, Tapply called after Richardson. "I'll send you a bill." Then he turned and sauntered toward the grandstand.

Wasn't he the arrogant so-and-so?

A gasping sound drew my attention. A sturdy, brunette woman stood a few feet away, mouth open, staring at the track. Following her gaze, I cringed.

The horse ambulance had driven up, stopping so the trailer's ramp would drop close to the fallen animal. As the driver and an assistant climbed from the truck's cab, the Maryland state veterinarian jogged toward them. I hadn't met him but knew everyone called him Doc Dorset.

"At least he'll get some painkillers now," Kate said to the dark-haired woman.

The brunette turned her head. Though she was probably in her mid-thirties, the lines around her blue eyes suggested a life harder than Kate's and mine.

"You see that right front?" the woman asked. "He's gonna get a lot more than painkillers, trust me."

"Is it broken?" My voice wavered.

"I think he's blown the flexor tendon and all his suspensory apparatus."

I'd learned enough since buying Pearl to know this was bad, real bad.

"You don't think he'll make it?"

"With that injury?" Bitterness filled her voice.

I stepped past Kate and placed a hand on the brunette's arm. "You know the horse?"

"I bred him. Raised him for the first two years of his life." Her sigh smelled of peppermints and cigarettes.

"I'm sorry." I extended my hand. "Janet Simpson." I gestured at Kate. "My friend, Kate Perkins."

The woman paused, then forced a smile. "Carol Merkel." She sighed. "It's a hard business. You have to sell them if you're going to stay afloat."

"At least you sold him to someone with a good trainer," Kate said.

"Actually, I didn't." Carol's gaze shifted to the huge pink diamond on Kate's finger. "Tapply's a leading trainer—which only means he'll do anything to win."

"Isn't that what he's supposed to do?" I asked.

"Yes, but Tapply uses drugs to increase his chances," Carol said, her voice lowered. "Tapply's like a snake in a nest of baby birds." Her expression darkened. "There are substances strong enough to kill the pain of an injury and a few trainers inhumane enough to use them. If a horse has the will to win, like Love the Money, and he can't feel the pain . . . Well, you see the result." Her hands clenched into fists at her sides.

I turned back to the track, feeling awful. Somehow the two men and the vet had loaded the horse into the van. The trailer's ramp was already up.

Nearby, the jockey and Doc Dorset ducked under the rail and onto the pavement. The vet's voice drifted back as they walked away, "I can't control these things. Regulations just aren't strict enough . . ."

Carol stared after the two men, then turned to me. "Something like this crushes you. But it's a business, and you have to move on."

I didn't think I could "move on," but I nodded.

"I'm getting out of here," Carol said and walked away from us.

"That was abrupt," Kate said, "Why don't we go up to the Jockey Club and get a little drink?"

"How about a big drink?"

It wouldn't help, of course. There wasn't enough liquor in Maryland to erase the image of Love the Money struggling on the dirt.

⌐   ⌐   ⌐

The next day, I stood at the rail with Leonard, hoping the early morning sun could banish the gloom I felt when I heard that Love the Money had been euthanized shortly after leaving the track. The day only grew darker when Love the Money's owner, Richardson, walked behind us, heading toward the stables. I didn't need any reminders.

Platinum Pearl blew by, golden, almost a blur in the moist morning air. My senses sharpened, and my spirits lifted. As Pearl flew under the wire, Leonard thumbed his stopwatch. A twitch lifted the corner of his mouth.

"This filly's gonna be all right."

"What was her time?" Eagerness sharpened my voice.

Leonard squinted at the watch. "Fast." He slid it into his pocket. "Don't need people knowing how fast."

I trailed behind Leonard's brisk walk, knowing he wanted to check Pearl as soon as she returned to his barn. The man could read a horse like a billboard. All the small details and nuances I couldn't fathom.

Walking by Tapply's barn, I spotted the young trainer on the sandy path outside his stalls. He maintained his swagger even while carrying a large box. Near him a young, Hispanic groom with long black braids raked straw from the aisle. She shrank against the wall as Tapply approached.

When he set his box on a bench, she resumed her work in earnest until Tapply grasped the end of her rake, stopping her movements. He slid a finger under her chin, tilted her head up, and murmured something. She squirmed and backed away, one hand tight on her waist pack.

Leaning over to fuss with a shoelace, I kept the pair in my peripheral vision.

Tapply chuckled, then picked up his box and moved along the shed-row. The girl glared at his back, saw me watching, and quickly looked away. Tapply withdrew a key, started to unlock a metal door, then stopped.

"What the hell," he muttered, then turned on the young woman.

"Why is this door unlocked?"

Voice trembling, she said, "I don' know."

He waved his hand at her in a manner suggesting she was useless, flicked on a light in the storeroom, went inside, and shut the door.

Abandoning my shoelace ruse, I rose to leave, but a strangled cry stopped me. I stared at the storeroom. Had it come from there? I heard two distant thumps, then a muffled crash. I hurried toward the sounds, but a hard-looking Mexican with sharp-edged sideburns appeared from Tapply's office and blocked my path.

"What you want, lady?"

"I heard a scream. In that room." I pointed toward the closed door.

"This barn's private. Why don' you mind your own business?"

Behind him, the Latina had stopped raking, and he whirled on her, letting loose a stream of angry Spanish. She paled and bent back to her work, raking furiously.

I glared at the man. "Never mind." I didn't like the way he and Tapply treated their groom. Be nice if a tornado materialized, sucked them up, and dumped them in Oz. "No ruby slippers for you," I muttered.

ⲅ　ⲅ　ⲅ

The smell of coffee, hash browns, bacon, and burritos saturated the air in the noisy, crowded backstretch cafeteria, known as the kitchen, where I sat with Leonard later. People who'd been at work since five a.m. filled the chairs and tables, hungry for breakfast.

I swallowed a last bite of my grilled ham-and-cheese and dabbed my mouth with a napkin.

"What's wrong?" Leonard asked.

"I can't stop thinking about that horse yesterday. Does Tapply use illegal drugs?"

Leonard set his coffee down, his stare penetrating and serious. "Shh. If he does, you didn't learn it from me. You don't want Tapply hearing you talk about him. Leave it alone. For Pearl's sake."

"What are you saying? He'd hurt Pearl to get back at me?"

"Stuff happens, Janet."

That sounded paranoid. Still I glanced nervously around the room, recognizing the black braids of Tapply's young groom near the condiment counter. At the far end of the dining area, Carol Merkel sat at a table with a tray and a sandwich. Doc Dorset stood at the cash register taking money from his wallet.

Leonard leaned forward, the elbows of his worn tweed jacket pressing onto the table. "Fortunately there aren't too many scumbags like Tapply around. He cheats us all—trainers, owners like you, breeders, and the betting public."

And kills horses.

Leonard seemed to be reading my thoughts. "The anti-drug laws are tightening, Janet. People like Tapply usually get what's coming to them."

"I hope so."

▗ ▗ ▗

The backstretch seemed deserted when I left the kitchen and walked past Tapply's barn toward my car.

A scream, sharp and high pitched, sliced through the air. I whirled toward the sound.

The groom with braids stood motionless outside Tapply's storeroom, its door wide open. I pounded across the tarmac, through puddles and bits of manure, heedless of my Coach running shoes and my protesting joints. I stopped abruptly.

A large snake reared up inside the storeroom, its upper body shiny and bright beneath a light in the ceiling. The rest of him coiled darkly behind on the cement floor. The creature rose higher and swayed before us, its open mouth and black eyes dwarfed by a widely flaring hood.

It looked like a cobra! At Laurel racetrack?

The young groom drew a breath for another scream.

I forced my voice to remain low. "No! Don't move!"

A pitchfork leaned nearby. I grabbed the handle and launched it tines-first at the snake. A dead-on hit, it toppled the serpent backwards. I grabbed the groom's arm, jerked her out of the way, and slammed the door closed.

The young woman's knees gave out, and she slid to the ground.

"Señor Tapply! *Esta muerto!*" Her voice broke.

"Roy Tapply's in there? Dead?"

Her face as pale as the snake's underbelly, she nodded.

Tapply would just have to stay in there. I wasn't about to open that door!

As I helped the groom to her feet, I realized she was older than I'd thought, with frown lines etched into her face. I spoke quietly. "I'm Janet. What's your name?"

"Carmen." She looked away from me and whispered, "I no think he do this . . ."

"Who? Do what?" I asked.

But Carmen drew into herself and wouldn't answer.

Forcing shaky hands into my bag, I found my phone and dialed 911. Lord. I'd wanted Tapply to get what he had coming. But not this.

The track security truck arrived first, then an Anne Arundel County patrol car. The security guard and two county police officers looked doubtful when I said a cobra was inside the storeroom with a dead man. One officer, short, his face scarred by acne, raised his eyebrows.

The taller cop, who had a severe buzz-cut, tried hard to suppress a dismissive smile as he pulled his night stick from his utility belt. Putting a hand on the doorknob, he turned it and eased the door open a crack.

Carmen and I exchanged an anxious glance and moved back.

Buzz-Cut creaked the door out farther and peered inside.

"Damn!" He jumped back, banging the door shut. "There's a big snake in there!"

The acne-scarred cop rushed to the cruiser's radio and Buzz-Cut called after him, "Get someone from county animal control. Someone who can handle snakes!"

The man had a talent for the obvious.

The twirling blue-and-red cruiser lights attracted a meager crowd. The words "snake" and "Tapply" drifted past me as the number of curious onlookers increased. Carol Merkel and Richardson pushed toward the front. Carol clutched my arm. "Is it true? Tapply's dead?"

"They've verified this?" Richardson asked.

"I don't know. The groom said he was dead. That snake is still in there with him." I shuddered.

"Bad way to go," Richardson said.

Ahead, a fast-moving van labeled "Anne Arundel County Animal Control" braked to a stop. I walked closer as a man and a woman hurried from the vehicle toward Buzz-Cut. The officers wore tan uniforms, and one carried a metal container resembling a trash can. The other grasped a long pole.

"Look, he's got a snake catcher!" a man in the crowd yelled. Like a school of curious fish, the crowd drifted closer to Tapply's storeroom.

The scar-faced cop stepped toward the crowd. "You people will have to stay back!"

One of the animal control officers pulled on a helmet with a wire face guard and picked up the pole. "Here goes," he said.

After opening the door a crack and peering into the storeroom, he slipped inside. Buzz-Cut closed the door firmly behind him. The hairs rose on the back of my neck as I waited. A snapping sound, thumps, and thrashing noises erupted from inside the storeroom.

"Got him!" The door muffled the man's words but not his excitement. "He's a big sucker! Darlene, get that can in here."

Darlene rushed inside. A moment later, her colleague emerged with the can, its lid fastened tight with metal clasps. The crowd broke into a cheer, but I didn't feel like celebrating. Was Tapply in there? I moved closer.

Darlene stumbled out of the storeroom. "My God, he's dead!"

r   r   r

Tapply had been found sprawled in a back corner of the storeroom.

I learned this shortly after the homicide detectives' plain, dark car eased up to the barn. A white van for the county medical examiner and more squad cars had rolled in behind it. Two male detectives hustled into the storeroom with the medical examiner on their heels and Buzz-Cut right behind.

Buzz-Cut came out shortly, and he and his partner rounded everyone up, saying the detectives wanted to interview us. With no backstretch bar, I knew it would be a long afternoon.

About an hour later, a detective in a drab, gray suit emerged and approached me. "Mrs. Simpson?" he asked, in a surprisingly rich baritone.

I nodded.

"You called it in, right?"

"Yes."

He pulled a badge. "Detective Trent Curtis, Anne Arundel homicide. I need to ask you some questions."

With a sudden pang, I realized how much I still missed my husband, Ed, who'd died two years earlier. He'd been so good at handling difficult situations.

After several throat clearings, I explained how annoyed Tapply had been when he discovered the door to his storeroom wasn't locked, how he'd gone inside, how I'd heard the muffled cry.

"Then around 10:30, I found Tapply's groom, Carmen, mesmerized by that dreadful snake." I nodded toward Carmen, who was waiting nearby.

"You see anyone else in the area, Mrs. Simpson?"

"No one other than the foreman and Carmen. But there is something you should know." I plowed ahead, telling him about Love the Money's death, the people involved with the horse, and how angry some of them had been.

Curtis stopped scribbling, then appeared to suppress a yawn.

"I appreciate your observations, but you should let us do our job. So far you're just speculating."

Well I'd just speculate some more. "Revenge is a motive."

"Could be." He nodded, but his eyes were lit with amusement. Or was it derision?

What did he know? Weren't these things always about passion . . . or money?

⌐　⌐　⌐

The next morning Kate and I sat on empire side chairs in the little den where I keep my laptop on an antique desk. My Park Place condo in Annapolis was small and pricey but wonderfully convenient after the rambling house I'd shared with Ed.

Kate folded back a page in the Metro section of the *Washington Post*. A pair of pearl pink reading glasses sat perched on her nose.

"It says here the autopsy could be in as early as tomorrow." She frowned. "Do they need one? Wasn't it obvious the snake killed him?"

I dipped my spoon into my cappuccino, scraping up the last of the hazelnut foam. "They never found fang marks, remember?"

"They probably will during the autopsy."

I glanced out the window at the historic cemetery lying across Taylor Avenue and suppressed a shiver, dimly aware of Kate rustling in her handbag.

Psst, psst. The eye-watering chemical smell of Kate's perfume drifted through the den, assailing my nose and eyes. No wonder they called it Predator.

"That stuff stings my eyes, Kate." I stood and crossed the hall in search of a tissue.

"Oh, pooh. I think it's sexy. You never know when you might want to catch a nice widower, Janet."

Not with that stuff. I grabbed a tissue in the powder room, dabbed under my eyes, and blew my nose before returning cautiously to the den. "I still can't figure out what a cobra was doing in that storeroom. How'd it get there?"

"Let's see." Kate moved to my desk and fired up my laptop. In moments she Googled the keywords Tapply, horse, and cobra together. I stared at her. A sharp mind hid behind that ditzy, pink routine. She found a few articles about Tapply's murder, but nothing with an explanation for the cobra.

"Try horse and cobra without Tapply," I suggested.

Kate ran the search, scanned the results, and pulled up an article. She whistled. "Says here there was a recent scandal in Kentucky involving a trainer using cobra venom. The venom blocks the nerves so the horse won't feel pain and will run when it shouldn't."

"That's disgusting." How could anyone be so cruel? "Do you think that might've been going on here with Love the Money?"

"I hope not."

"Look up Doc Dorset," I said.

Kate frowned. "Why?"

"Dorset's always around when things happen."

Kate's fingers tap-danced over the computer keys. "Oh my . . ."

"What?" I had trouble reading over Kate's shoulder.

"In 1996 Dr. Dorset's license was suspended at Philadelphia Park pending an investigation. He was never charged," Kate said.

"What did he do?"

"He was the state vet there, too. Someone accused him of allowing sore and injured horses to run. There were several fatal breakdowns."

Like Love the Money. I sighed and stared out my window. Behind the cemetery's wrought-iron fence the marble tombstones lined up like soldiers.

"Authorities suspected him of taking bribes from trainers. Nothing was ever proved. You don't suppose he was taking money from Tapply, do you?"

"I don't know," I said. "But nobody can ask Tapply now."

Our eyes met, and Kate lapsed into silence.

I thought a minute. "Carol Merkel was pretty angry at Tapply. See what you can find on her."

Kate searched but found nothing useful.

"Still," I said, "she was upset with Tapply when Love the Money broke down."

"Very upset," Kate said as my phone started ringing.

I grabbed it. "Hello."

"Mrs. Simpson?"

"Yes." I tried to place the man's voice.

"Detective Curtis, Anne Arundel homicide. I think we need to talk."

r r r

I headed right over to Tapply's barn to meet Curtis. The yellow police tape had been removed from the storeroom area. Curtis stood waiting by his cruiser.

"Thanks for coming," Curtis said as I walked up. "The reason I wanted to see you is some things have come to light. But first I want you to try and remember yesterday morning clearly." We walked to the storeroom door. I took a long look and focused. "You said Tapply was carrying a box."

"Yes."

"Did you see any writing or content identification?"

"No. It was plain cardboard."

"How did Tapply appear?"

"You mean his demeanor?"

Curtis gave the ghost of a smile. "Sure, his demeanor."

"His usual self. Looking like he owned the world."

"So he wasn't trembling or pale? Didn't appear to have difficulty breathing?"

"Hardly. He was hounding that pretty groom, Carmen, totally unconcerned his attentions weren't wanted. Anyway, he hadn't entered that storeroom yet, hadn't been bitten by the snake."

"Roy Tapply wasn't bitten by a snake, Mrs. Simpson."

"What?" A cool breeze kicked up, ruffling my hair with cold fingers. "The autopsy—they didn't find fang marks?"

"No," Curtis said, watching my face carefully. "If, as you say, Tapply was normal before he went into that storeroom, then someone must have injected him with a hypodermic after he went inside. A hypo loaded with cobra venom."

"The article was right . . ."

"What?"

"I read an article online about how some sleazy horse trainers milk cobras for their venom. Then they give it to horses so they'll run through pain. No matter the consequences. I guess what'll dull the pain in a horse will kill a human."

Curtis shook his head as if now he'd heard it all. He handed me his card. "Anything else happens, call me."

"There is something," I said.

"What?" His voice held a note of impatience.

Oh, phooey. He'd just have to listen.

I told him about the circumstances surrounding Doc Dorset's trouble in Pennsylvania.

Curtis studied me. The amusement and mockery I'd seen at our first meeting had disappeared, leaving his eyes flat.

"You need to stay out of this, Mrs. Simpson. You've gotten yourself too involved. Stop before you get hurt."

r   r   r

When the detective's cruiser disappeared through the gate, I glanced nervously around the stables. It was one thing to snoop from the safety of my condo. But here the vast grounds left me feeling vulnerable.

I dropped Curtis's card inside my handbag. When I glanced up, Carmen was walking toward me. As she closed the distance, she gave me a wan smile. Was she out of a job? I felt sorry for the woman.

"Holá, Carmen," I said, using almost my entire Spanish repertoire. "How are you?"

"Okay." She stared at the ground, frowning. "Is very hard Señor Tapply die."

"Do you need work, Carmen?"

She nodded quickly. "*Sí.*"

"I don't know if Leonard Cushman has work, but he might know someone who does. Come on, I'll introduce you."

Her quick smile gave her brown eyes a warm glow. We went to find Leonard. Maybe he'd hire her, and she'd take care of Pearl.

When we got near Leonard's barn, Carmen paused and said, "I have—how you say—resoo-may?"

She unzipped her red waist pack and pulled out a small notebook stuffed with papers. Opening the notebook, she searched through the contents.

The breeze strengthened and whistled through the barns, snatching at the papers, launching them into the air. As she raced to catch them, the contents of her waist pack spilled to the ground. She muttered angrily in Spanish.

"Let me help you," I said, picking up some photos, a few of the papers, and a small bottle that had rolled behind Carmen. I glanced at the bottle, startled to see the skull and crossbones stamp indicating poison. I stared at the label. The words "Cobra Venom" were like a slap in the face.

Jesus. Could this sweet girl be involved in Tapply's murder? I slipped the bottle into my pocket. A hurried glance at Carmen found her chasing a yellow sheet blowing toward Tapply's barn.

Quickly I examined the papers and photos in my hand. The last two pictures sent a tingle down my spine. One showed a close-up of the venom bottle on a table with a filled syringe next to it. The second was of the interior of Tapply's storeroom, with Richardson's hand on the bottle of venom as if he were picking it up.

What was Carmen doing with these pictures and the bottle? Looking over, I saw her fingers were closing on the elusive yellow paper. I hurriedly stuffed the venom pictures into my pocket with the bottle.

Carmen returned, and I handed her the remaining photos and documents. She shoved them into her notebook and handed me her resume.

"Can we go see Mr. Cushman now?" she asked.

I nodded, and we began walking toward the barn, but Carmen stopped abruptly, staring ahead. Pausing, I squinted and saw Leonard speaking with Richardson just outside the stable office.

I bet Richardson wanted to steal *my* trainer now that Tapply was gone. Tapply. Had Carmen tried to blackmail Tapply? Or Richardson? Or both? Had these men used cobra venom on Love the Money?

I needed some answers. Palming the bottle tight, I turned to Carmen and held it up.

"What do you know about this venom?"

Her eyes widened.

"Were Tapply and Richardson using it on the horses?"

Carmen looked like a wild animal deciding whether to fight or flee. She took a long breath. "I no sure. But they don' wan' anyone to see."

I bet they didn't. I marched over to Leonard. "Look at this." I thrust the bottle into his hand. "And these." I handed over the pictures.

Richardson stepped closer. As he stared, recognition flared in his eyes, and he glared at me. "Where did you get those?"

My gaze slid to Carmen who'd frozen in place.

Richardson's strange gold-brown eyes locked onto her. "This little bitch must have been blackmailing Tapply."

Carmen puffed up like an angry cat. "Is no true! You say you tell immigration if I no give you key to room." She paused a moment, and her eyes widened. *"You* let snake out!"

"You're crazy." A deep anger flushed Richardson's face. "Give me those things." He crowded Leonard.

"Just a minute!" Leonard said. "You and Tapply were using venom?"

I pointed to the bottle and tried to keep a tremble from my voice. "I bet they used it on Love the Money. And other horses too, didn't you?" Suddenly it all became clear. "And I bet Carmen hadn't blackmailed anyone. Tapply was blackmailing *you*. She merely found the evidence."

Richardson paled, but the hatred in his eyes grew stronger. Only I was too angry to be frightened.

"You were walking toward Tapply's storeroom early yesterday morning," I said, remembering. "You attacked him and slipped out before being noticed. You killed him!"

He blinked, and I knew I had him.

Richardson grabbed at the photos and the bottle in Leonard's hands. Leonard tried to jerk away. Richardson shoved him, knocking him into the stable wall.

I dug into my purse, searching frantically for Detective Curtis's card. Where was it?

Leonard was struggling with Richardson. Leonard was a tough old bird, but Richardson was younger, bigger, his face dark with menace. He punched Leonard in the nose. Blood spurted. Someone screamed.

I snatched the paper from Leonard's hand a second before Richardson could. Those pale eyes turned on me, and I backed away, digging in my purse for a metal nail file. Anything!

My fingers closed on something hard. I yanked the bottle of Predator from my purse and squirted perfume into Richardson's face.

He screamed, staggered back, hands clawing at his eyes. He stumbled against a post and held onto it for support.

Blood still gushed from Leonard's nose, but he shoved Richardson hard and knocked the larger man down, then grabbed a length of bailing twine hanging on a hook.

"Help me tie up this son of a bitch."

I did, and when we'd finished, I called security, then Curtis. The detective answered on the first ring.

"This is Janet Simpson. Are you still in the area?"

"What is it now? Are you in trouble?"

"Not anymore," I said, trying not to gasp. "I just found your murderer."

———

Sasscer Hill's "Pretty Fraudulent," the first story in the Janet Simpson series, appeared in Chesapeake Crimes 3. *Sasscer's short mystery "Game," featuring young female jockey Nicky Latrelle, appeared in an issue of* The Advocate. *Currently she is working on a novel-length Latrelle mystery series. Her novels* Full Mortality *and* Racing from Death *are under agent contract and in negotiation for publication. Another Latrelle book,* The Sea Horse Trade, *is in progress. Sasscer Hill lives on a Maryland farm and has been involved in breeding and selling racehorses for over twenty years. A number of her articles have appeared in the* Mid-Atlantic Thoroughbred.

DOUBLE DEAL

by Mary Ellen Hughes

I bit my tongue on purpose, for maybe the twentieth time that day. It's a wonder my tongue wasn't one huge callous, what with all the grief I was giving it lately. But clamping it between my teeth kept me from saying what was going through my mind, which kept me from losing this job. And I needed this job! Times were tough, at least for people like me, people whose old jobs had been eliminated through downsizing. The so-called "little" people who lived from paycheck to paycheck and, in my case, also needed a little bit extra to help support a daughter who was going through some tough times herself, what with two babies to feed. We had to scramble.

And believe me, I scrambled. Once I had cleaned out my desk at Human Resources, I was out pounding the pavement, as well as phoning and e-mailing, with no luck. Too many unemployeds were competing for too few jobs, and those with no gray hairs had all the advantage. So, with my bills piling up, I grabbed the first decent thing I could find—decent-*paying*, that is. I took a job as housekeeper for Cal Perkins. Honest work, and work I didn't, as a whole, mind doing—cooking, cleaning, and keeping his household running. Not exactly what I'd taken five years of night classes for, but it had its own satisfaction. What I minded was doing it all for Perkins. Or Perk the Jerk, as I came to call him.

Privately of course.

I started thinking of him as The Jerk when he stopped using *my* name and started simply barking out orders or, worse, snapping his fingers and pointing, generally when he was on the phone doing his wheeling and dealing. At least ten or fifteen years my junior, he'd already been divorced twice and had a steady parade of girlfriends marching through his bedroom, each of whom thought she was his one and only. I lost count of the times I'd overheard him placating one or the other with phony excuses about why he couldn't see her that night. Non-existent sudden business trips or fake illnesses (he could cough and wheeze impressively on cue)—all the time cradling the phone to his ear as he slipped on his diamond-studded cufflinks, dressing for a night on the town with the next gullible one.

I felt sorry for the young women, of course, and could only hope, since they were young, that they'd be able to bounce back and maybe learn a thing or two from the whole wretched experience. But some of the shady dealings I overheard him working out in his home office as I brought him his coffee or cleaned up his messes were another thing. Deals that sounded pretty close to the edge of illegal and definitely unethical. One morning in particular, my ears perked up as his voice took on an unnaturally (for him) genial tone.

"My dear Mrs. Morris," he was saying, and I caught a fake *I only want what's best for you* look on his face that matched the voice. I wouldn't have been surprised to see his right hand held piously over his heart. "Of course I'd be happy to stop by to discuss things. I understand completely how difficult it can be for a person in your circumstances to get around. My own dear mother suffered terribly from arthritis, and the poor woman—well, that's neither here nor there. Shall I come this afternoon around one? Or is that too early?"

Something big must have been in it for him. The Jerk didn't normally go out of his way for prospective clients. And his "dear mother," I happened to know, was currently drinking and smoking her way through Atlantic City, deftly flipping cards with those "arthritic" fingers at the blackjack tables, and hitting him up for a few more bucks to gamble away. Lots of luck, Mom. Exactly what was putting the smirk on his face that Mrs. Morris couldn't see, I didn't know. Until later.

"I can get the place for a song," I heard him say into his ever-present cell phone that evening as I set his baked potato and steak down before him at the dining table. He took one look at it, then snapped his fingers and pointed to the bottle of A1 sauce, set where he might have needed to lean an inch or two to reach it. I picked the bottle up and handed it to him as he continued talking.

"The old bag doesn't have a clue about the zoning change in the works that'll give Gridley the go-ahead to build their shopping mall. All she knows is she'll be needing cash soon to move to that assisted-living place. She thinks I'm a saint for overlooking the peeling wallpaper and old furnace. Yeah, I'll have the papers drawn up tomorrow. As soon as she signs we can kick her out and tear the dump down. Gridley will be begging us to sell to them within six months. We'll be naming our price."

As I turned to go back to the kitchen I heard him begin another call. "Hey, baby. I'm at the airport now. How about you meet me in an hour or so at my place? Great! Love ya, doll!"

The guy never missed a beat. I clamped down on my tongue again and wondered how he managed to face himself in the mirror each day. But then, I reminded myself, I was the one polishing that mirror and gratefully taking his money for doing it. So what did that make me?

Desperate, that's what. I still needed that roof over my head when I went home at night, leaky or not, plus my two little-angel grandchildren still needed what little I could send to help with their care. But it was definitely starting to get to me.

The next day, The Jerk actually hummed to himself as he gathered up the papers that'd been sent over for Mrs. Morris's property sale. "Tea?" I'd heard him say into the telephone. "Why that would be absolutely delightful, Mrs. Morris. In fact I'd love to bring along a beautiful home-made baklava that one of my clients gifted me with the other day. Just her sweet way of thanking me. But she was much too generous, and I'd feel so much better sharing it. May I do that? Wonderful."

As he hung up, The Jerk barked an order for me to rustle up some baklava quick. With no time for that kind of "rustling," I dashed to Anastasia's, a Greek restaurant a few blocks away, then re-wrapped the store-bought pastry in plastic wrap and foil to give it a homemade look. As I held the door for The Jerk to leave for Mrs. Morris's, I felt wretched, knowing that the poor woman was shortly to be fleeced out of a decent price for her home, and all for a gift of a pastry brought by a slippery, smooth-talking con man.

I worried about Mrs. Morris all morning as I dusted and vacuumed. While I washed and folded laundry later on, images of a sweet but gullible woman signing away her future floated miserably through my head. By dinnertime I'd just about tied myself in knots when The Jerk came in from the garage, flipped his car keys onto the hall table and, scowling darkly, demanded I fetch him a beer. I expected him to be jubilant and gloating. But instead he was oddly quiet. I couldn't figure it out until I heard him on the phone, explaining to his associate.

"Turns out she's one of those who'll take more time. She's skittish, you know? Likes to have everything explained to her a million times until she thinks she gets it. You push too hard, she's likely to shut down. But don't worry. I know how to handle her. She's coming around. Yeah, I'm going over there again tomorrow. Old bat doesn't see a soul all day. She's probably dragging this out just to get some company. I'll get her to sign, though. Might take a few days, but I'll do it. By the end of the week, she'll be thinking of me as her new best friend who's just dying to keep stopping in for tea for the rest of her life." His loud snort told me what he thought of that, as if I couldn't have guessed.

That last part got to me the most. It was bad enough The Jerk was planning to wheedle the poor woman out of her home. Even worse, he was also playing on her loneliness, turning himself into some sort of a thoughtful nephew in need of a kindly aunt. The thought of how she might suffer once she realized the truth was more than I could take. I decided I had to try to do something about it. I didn't know if it would make a difference, but at least it might keep me from wincing when I looked into those mirrors I'd been cleaning so thoroughly.

My problem, though, was finding out how to reach Mrs. Morris. The Jerk kept his papers close by that night, where I couldn't get to them. I tried the phone book, but the number of Morrises listed was staggering, with none, of course, matched up with "Mrs." Not having a first name, or even an initial to narrow the list down, I gave up in frustration and tossed and turned for several restless hours that night.

The next evening, The Jerk came home even more subdued. My hopes rose that he still hadn't gotten Mrs. Morris to sign. I wondered, briefly, if she somehow got to him, perhaps touching a soft spot that tweaked his conscience. But an overheard, snarly phone call instantly banished that thought, as he described his latest meeting to his associate, using words to describe poor Mrs. Morris that turned my ears pink. No, he had no conscience to tweak. But I could see he was growing frustrated. Enough so that he could barely finish the tasty beef bourguignon I'd prepared that night. And totally ignored the strawberry cheesecake I set out for dessert, usually a favorite.

Mrs. Morris apparently had turned into a tougher nut to crack than he'd expected and was becoming a challenge. He even blew off girlfriend number three that night without bothering to come up with a decent reason and spent most of the evening brooding in his chair. When he went in to take a shower and left his briefcase in the living room, I saw my chance and dug out Mrs. Morris's address. The next day was my day off, and I had plans for it.

I headed her way before noon, knowing I'd arrive well before tea time. I knocked on the door of a modest house that I judged to be at least fifty years old. Mrs. Morris and her husband might have moved into it as newlyweds. I hoped it looked a lot better then, because it was in sad shape now. The porch sagged, paint flaked, and the yard had long gone over to tangled weeds. A little money and enough elbow grease, though, might have spruced it up reasonably well.

As I waited, however, a glance at the surrounding neighborhood told me this was an area begging to be razed. Several other houses had an abandoned look to them, and the few blocks I'd passed through on my way here had clearly gone through recent transition to office and retail space. I wasn't surprised that the zoning board was ready to add this block to the fold.

A tiny, bent-over woman answered my knock and, on my brief explanation of who I was, readily welcomed me in. The inside of her home, I saw, was only slightly better off than the outside, though it was clean and tidy and warmed by a scattering of photos. Mrs. Morris noticed me looking at them and proudly identified several as children, grandchildren, and other family members.

"Do any of them live nearby?" I asked hopefully, and she shook her head.

"No. I'm the only one of my generation still alive, and as for the younger ones, their jobs have taken them all over the place. But they visit when they can."

She reached out one crooked hand for a particular photo, a snapshot of a pretty, blonde woman smiling into the camera beside a shiny, new-looking Saturn. "This," she said, "is my niece, Leila. Until recently, she lived close by. The day I took that picture she had just bought that car. She was so proud of it. Leila used to take me wherever I needed to go. 'Just call, Aunt May,' she'd say, 'and I'll be over.' A lovely girl."

Mrs. Morris set the photo back where it'd been, looking somewhat sad. She obviously was alone and lonely, which was why The Jerk was able to ingratiate himself so easily.

"Mrs. Morris," I said, "I came because I'm concerned. From what you said, you don't have anyone around to advise you, so I hope you'll listen to me and take my warning to heart."

"Warning? About what, dear?"

"About Cal Perkins. I hope you won't mention my being here because I could lose my job for what I'm about to say, and I really can't afford that. But I couldn't let things go any further. Cal Perkins means to take advantage of you, Mrs. Morris. The offer he's making to buy your house is way below market value because of the zoning changes that are sure to come through. He plans to turn it around when that happens and sell the property at a huge profit. He's trying to swindle you."

Mrs. Morris was quiet for several moments as she took in what I'd said. I expected shock, tears, maybe disbelieving protest. But her response surprised me.

"Please don't worry about me, my dear."

"But—" I began and was stopped by her gently raised hand.

"People tend to think because I'm a woman and because I'm old that I'm also helpless or feeble-minded."

"No, I—"

"That's all right, dear, it's natural. And you'll probably find, when your time comes, that's usually the case. Sometimes," she laughed merrily, "it can be rather fun!

"I appreciate your concern, though," she said, patting my hand. "You have a kind heart, and I hope you're rewarded for that someday."

"Thank you," I said, "But I wish—"

"Never you mind about all that, dear. I'll be just fine. There's not much, at my age, that I really need. Just a little company, now and then. Which is one reason I'm happy to see dear Cal. It's such a pleasure to have a reason to fix a nice pot of tea in the afternoon. And the lovely little treats he brings! Oh, my." She wagged her head saucily and laughed. A glance at the little clock on her end table, however, turned her more serious.

"I've enjoyed your visit, too, my dear, and I hope you'll come see me again so I can offer you a little tea as well. But not today, I'm afraid. Cal is coming a little earlier than usual. Since you asked me not to mention your visit, I assume you probably don't want to run into him."

I definitely didn't want that so I reluctantly got to my feet. "I wish you'd think over what I've told you, Mrs. Morris."

"Yes, of course, dear," she promised, as she pulled herself up and hobbled alongside me to the door.

"Button up!" she admonished me as she handed me my coat. "The wind is picking up out there, you know. Wrap that scarf nice and snug." She watched with grandmotherly sweetness as I did so, while I was feeling nothing but frustration at my visit having done no good whatsoever. Obviously Mrs. Morris preferred believing the best of people and had been too hoodwinked by The Jerk to take anything I'd had to say seriously. All that was left was to wish her the best, which I did, before cautiously checking in both directions and scuttling on my way.

The Jerk continued to work on her, although his phone conversations grew briefer and much less animated. When he cancelled out on his weekly golf date and put off a night of dancing with the girlfriend du jour, I asked him what was wrong. "A touch of the flu," he growled, waving away the beef medallions in wine I had just made for him.

Then the girlfriend showed up at the door carrying a container of chicken soup. "You look like shit, Cal," she said, pushing her way past him into the entrance hall.

I expected him to blow up at that and send her off. But instead he just shook his head tiredly and asked her to check what was on TV. That sent up a red flag. Perk the Jerk was many things but never a couch potato.

Though I had to force myself to do it, I suggested to The Jerk that he should check with a doctor. Despicable though he was, I couldn't really just let it go. I might have been able to ignore a sick alligator or a snake, but The Jerk, after all, was a human being. Or pretty close to one, anyway.

"Yeah, I probably should see a doctor," he'd said, dragging out the words with some effort. But it took him another day to get around to it, and even then, I had to look up the number for him and place the call. As he left for his appointment that day, I had mixed feelings. On the one hand, he was a lot more pleasant to be around in this new subdued state. On the other hand—well, I don't remember getting much further than that.

He took off, and I got busy cleaning the bedroom, which he hadn't let me do for far too long, what with all the napping he'd been doing lately. I stripped the bed, dusted, polished, and vacuumed the room, then worked on straightening up his closet. I had moved on to other chores and was setting up a second load of laundry when the phone rang. I almost let it go to the answering machine. But something made me go over and pick it up.

A male voice asked, "Is this the residence of Calvin Perkins?"

I confirmed that it was, expecting a telemarketing pitch of some sort to follow.

"To whom am I speaking?" the caller then asked, and I told him I was Mr. Perkins's housekeeper.

"Is there a next of kin there I can speak with?" The phrase *next of kin* chilled me, and I shakily found a chair and sat down in it.

Cal Perkins never made it to his doctor's appointment. Witnesses reported seeing his car weaving erratically on the freeway before crossing the median strip into oncoming traffic. There it was slammed by a cement truck being driven by an experienced driver who nonetheless had been unable to avoid Perkins's car, spinning it into a guardrail where it was swiped in rapid succession by several more cars before bursting into flames.

Little was left of Perkins to identify beyond the license plate on his car, which led police to call his home. Numbly I found contact numbers for Cal's mother and his close business associates and passed them along.

There was an autopsy, of course, but since his body had been burned to a crisp, they couldn't determine much. I was asked questions about his condition at the time of the accident. I explained about the doctor he'd been on his way to see and how he'd been clearly ill, and no, not under the influence of any drugs, as far as I knew. They searched his belongings, of course, but didn't turn up anything stronger than aspirin.

In the end they put it all down to an unfortunate accident caused by driver error.

After the funeral, Perkins's mother took over the house and asked me to stay on the job, but I'd had enough of that family by then. Besides, five minutes spent with Mom told me exactly where her son had learned his ways. So I politely declined and left.

But I found I couldn't put it all behind me. Perkins's death and what had gone on before it nagged at me, too many unanswered questions keeping me awake too many nights.

I went back to Mrs. Morris's house, hoping for some answers, but she was no longer there. A knock on a few doors eventually turned up a neighbor who told me that an ambulance had taken her away and never brought her back. I started calling nursing homes and tracked her down at Sunset Years, a combination assisted-living/nursing home in the area.

I went to visit, and the first sight of her was jarring. Though old to begin with, Mrs. Morris had aged visibly by several years. Hooked up to oxygen, her thin arms dotted by needle-induced black-and-blue marks and lying limply over the sheet, she nevertheless brightened when I walked in. "Do you remember me, Mrs. Morris?" I asked.

"Yes, I remember. You made it out just in time that day," she said with a hint of her old twinkle. "Cal showed up within minutes. But," she touched a finger to her lips, "I never breathed a word to him about your being there."

"He's dead. Did you know?"

She was silent for a while, but then she drew in a watery breath, and a smile formed on her dry, wrinkled lips.

"Yes, I know," she said. She was quiet again for several moments, and the Mrs. Morris I had first met—the hand-patting, doting grand-mother—seemed to recede, replaced by someone more somber and complex. "You're probably wondering," she said, "if I had something to do with it."

I couldn't deny it. She was watching me with clear, steady eyes that expected the truth. What I said, though, was, "It was ruled an accident."

She nodded, then said, "But you have doubts, I can see. You're bright. And you were good to come and try to warn me that day."

She drew once more on her oxygen, then began slowly. "There are many ways," she said, "to kill someone, you know. But the most direct—such as shooting or stabbing—leave behind a terrible mess, don't they? I mean, for the ones left behind. The perpetrator—no, I don't like that word—the *activator* may be perfectly justified in killing and willing to suffer the consequences, but there are always the killer's loved ones to consider. They'd have to deal with the negative publicity, the whispers and pointed fingers. It would be very hard on them."

It was a long speech, and she paused to get her breath. I waited, uneasy, but determined to get the full story.

"So," she continued, "to avoid causing unnecessary distress to others, the better way, to my mind, is to kill someone in a way that appears to be a natural course of events. After all, the end result is the same—a person who has been getting away with terrible things gets his due—but no unpleasant fallout settles on the innocent."

"That would seem the better way, certainly," I agreed, "if you had to choose. But killing someone seems a drastic step to take, if, say, the person were simply a swindling con man."

"Oh, yes, absolutely." She paused, gathering her thoughts as well as her energy. "But think, my dear, of a grizzly bear out in the wild. He sometimes behaves in ways we don't like, violent ways against other animals. It's part of life, so we let it go. But if that bear starts raiding our property, or worse, attacks and kills humans . . ."

"Kills humans?" Growing tired of metaphors, I asked bluntly, "Was Cal Perkins a murderer?"

Mrs. Morris sighed. "Not in a way that would put him in jail, but, yes, he was definitely a murderer."

"Who did he kill?"

Another deep sigh, and then I saw a tear work its way out of the corner of Mrs. Morris's eye and leave a track on her dry cheek. "Do you remember the photo of my niece that I showed you? She was standing next to her new car?"

I remembered. "She was quite beautiful."

Mrs. Morris nodded. "Cal Perkins thought so, too. At least for a while. She thought he was in love with her. He could pretend to be quite the perfect man, you know, for as long as it suited him. And when it didn't suit him . . ." Two more long draws on her oxygen.

"I told you," she went on, "that Leila wasn't around anymore. You probably assumed I meant she'd moved away. That wasn't the case. When Cal dumped her, Leila was heartbroken." Mrs. Morris's mouth tightened. "She killed herself."

I sucked in my breath.

"He didn't even notice her picture. I left it out, just to see, but he'd already forgotten her. She meant that little to him. That dear, gentle, vulnerable girl. She was just one of a string of others. Others who might be just as vulnerable. That's what drove me to go through with it."

"What did you do to him?"

She smiled tiredly. "Cal Perkins died accidentally. Isn't that what the police decided?"

"Yes, but—"

"I think that's quite the best way, don't you? A nice, tidy decision with no unnecessary complications. No fallout."

Someone tapped on the door, startling me, and a nurse entered briskly. "Sorry to interrupt, but it's time for your injection."

"It's all right," Mrs. Morris said. "We'd about finished, hadn't we, dear?"

I stood up dumbly, still absorbing what she'd said. The woman had just admitted to murder. Or had she? I could turn her in to the police, but what would they do? What was the evidence? The veiled words of a sick woman? A *dying* woman?

I looked at Mrs. Morris, and she smiled.

"I'm glad you came, dear. I feel better after our little talk."

I nodded and stepped out of the way of the nurse.

"I'm afraid," she added, as she glanced at the nurse preparing her hypodermic, "I never did get around to offering you any refreshments that day you came to the house. But time was short, you see, and Cal was on his way."

"Yes."

"He would have expected his usual tea. His special tea. With all he'd done for me, I certainly couldn't let him down."

I looked at her, and she returned my gaze steadily. "No, of course not," I said. I turned and left the room. As I walked slowly down the hall, I thought about what I'd just heard. Would I ever feel the same again about aged, helpless-seeming women? I doubted it.

A brisk wind chilled my face as I stepped through Sunset Years's outer doors, bringing on a shiver. Besides the cold, the visit had taken its toll. I badly needed something bracing before heading home. I paused to glance at the surrounding shops.

The battered sign on one dingy place a couple of doors down offered coffee, whereas across the street sat a picturesque, cozy-looking tea shop.

I turned and headed for the coffee.

Mary Ellen Hughes is the author of five mystery novels, including the Craft Corner mystery series: Wreath of Deception, String of Lies, *and* Paper-Thin Alibi. *She is delighted to have a short mystery included in* Chesapeake Crimes: They Had It Comin', *having participated as well in the first and the third volumes of the series, and she has had other stories published in various mystery magazines. Mary Ellen lives in Maryland, where nearly all her stories are set and where she often shares tea with her very trusting and supportive husband. Her website is www.maryellenhughes.com.*

COSMIC JUSTICE

by Smita H. Jain

Wealthy Businessman's Son Accused in Slaying of Servant Girl

Mumbai police arrested Ashok Patil yesterday on murder charges in connection with the death of Hema Daksha, the 15-year-old servant of his friend Vikas Singhvi. On the night the young girl was killed, Patil, Singhvi, and friend Rajiv Gupta were out toasting his recent engagement to Mumbai architect Prema Agarwal at Ambrosia, a local bar in the Colaba region of South Mumbai. The three friends left the bar to continue their celebration at Singhvi's house.

Prema put down the newspaper and sat on the bed. *They're just trying to sell more papers. Ashok could no more kill anyone than I could.* She repeated the words like a mantra; closed her eyes; took several deep breaths. Nothing worked. She reached into her nightstand drawer and pulled out a small plastic bag with a brown and gray clump in it. She pinched off a marble-sized piece, popped it into her mouth, and held her breath while she chewed it, swallowing hard to get the bitter morsel down.

At first it was just to help her sleep, something she had done little of since the police began investigating Ashok. Now she ate the opium like a common field laborer. She hadn't told anyone; they would think her weak, a degenerate. "What will people say?" she could hear her mother's voice. Even Ashok would be disappointed. He allowed her to drink alcohol, even though women in their families never did; but drugs were for the lower classes. It was just a little, she told herself, and it calmed her nerves, even when her nerves were the only thing fueling her through the day.

She stayed on the bed with her eyes closed, waiting for the opium to take effect. After several minutes, her breathing slowed to normal, and she opened her eyes. There on the bed next to her were the *kundlis*. Not the natal charts of old—handwritten cross-hatches of lines marking planetary positions, birth dates, and time zones. These were computer-generated printouts that separated data into eleven key areas and analyzed it to give families a simple "yes" or "no." She had had them cast before she and Ashok were engaged. Everyone had teased her. "You children are both from good families. Why do you need astrology to tell you what you already know." Because natal charts were never wrong. They were as deeply rooted in Hindu society as the separation between the classes. If they said she would be happy in marriage, she would be.

She stood up and crossed the room to take a final look at herself in the standing mirror—etched peacocks strutted around its walnut and sandalwood frame—adjusted the pleats of her *paloo*, and attached its tail end to her blouse with a simple safety pin. This was not the day for ostentation. She wore an organza *sari* in a pale saffron color, with only light beading on it. The matching short-sleeved blouse was longer than normal, covering more midriff than Prema's usual garments. She would save the bright colors and halter-topped blouses for after the trial.

⌐ ⌐ ⌐

From the backseat of her Toyota Innova, Prema directed the driver to go to the Sessions Court in the Kala Ghoda region of South Mumbai. Located in the premiere art district of the city, the Sessions Court was surrounded by Prema's favorite museums, restaurants, and regional art galleries. She and Ashok had plans to go there in February, during the annual Kala Ghoda Festival, a two-week celebration of the best in culture the area had to offer.

Prema wanted to stay in the cocoon of the drive from one of the city's most exclusive residential areas on Malabar Hill into its most culturally vibrant. She tried to lose herself in the vista flanking the car to the east, but not even the beauty of the Arabian Sea could distract her from what was coming.

She stepped out of the car in front of the historic Esplanade Mansion, India's oldest existing cast-iron building, which was situated adjacent to the more austere Sessions Court building. She didn't have even a moment to soak in the majesty of the architectural wonder—the type of structure she had always dreamed of creating—before the screaming and flashes started.

"Do you believe Ashok Patil raped and killed that orphan servant girl?"

"Will you still marry him if he's found innocent?"

"What do you know, Prema?"

She bristled at the familiarity from people who only wanted to use her to put her fiancé in prison. She pulled the *paloo* of her *sari* around her head and covered her face with the crisp fabric. The cameras and questions followed her to the entryway, and then, mercifully, the door closed, and the world outside faded.

Once inside, she dropped her *paloo* and let her head fall backward against the wall. She took a few breaths to steady herself, wishing she had taken a second pinch from the plastic bag.

By the time she entered the courtroom, the bail hearing was underway. She slid into one of the benches behind Ashok's father and uncle, while the lawyers for both sides pleaded their cases.

"This man will not flee, Judge; he has much family in Mumbai," Vinod Shetty, Ashok's lawyer, said.

"Sir, Mr. Patil has refused to be present at a test identification parade. There is a chance he will leave the city before witnesses can identify him at trial," the prosecutor countered. Prema did not know him except from news stories. A middle-class professional, he was not someone who would be in her circle. Cricket players, Bollywood stars, other privileged twenty-somethings like her—these were the people she knew.

"Judge, it was dark when Hema Daksha died. The witnesses would not be able to identify my client or anyone else. There is no need for a test identification parade."

The prosecutor opened his mouth, no doubt to present a counter argument, but was pre-empted by the judge. "Has the medical examination of the accused been completed?"

Both lawyers stood silent. Overhead, fans creaked rhythmically, circulating warm, stale air around the room.

"Mr. Patil has only now, after five days, turned himself in. There has been no time to complete a medical exam," the prosecutor said.

As soon as the accusations against Ashok became public, his father had advised him to go to Chandigarh while he hired investigators and lawyers to build his son's defense. Only then had he allowed Ashok to return to Mumbai. This was the first Prema had heard about a test identification parade, though. She understood the futility of having witnesses who had seen someone from across a dark street try to identify him. All the more reason for Ashok to let them try and fail. She would make that suggestion as soon as his father posted his bail.

"That medical examination must be completed before bail can be determined," she heard the judge order.

"What?!" The word came out of her mouth before she realized. Mr. Shetty and the judge turned to stare at her. She cast her eyes downward and shifted behind a large man taking notes—a reporter, she assumed.

She didn't see what happened next, but in moments, Ashok was in handcuffs, being removed from the courtroom by a uniformed officer.

He caught her eye just before passing through the doorway, winked, and made a loud kissing noise in her direction. His father and uncle turned to her and grinned.

␣␣␣␣␣␣␣␣␣␣␣␣␣**r   r   r**

Things Look Up for Ashok Patil, as Witnesses Recant

The prosecution in the Ashok Patil murder case cried foul yesterday, as witness after witness said they could not identify the accused son of millionaire businessman Ramchand Patil as the man they saw entering the home where slain servant Hema Daksha lived and worked.

Prema had thought it would be over by now, but the story had been picked up by the *Times of India*. It was too scandalous to pass up: rich kid accused of killing orphaned servant girl. People were hungry for more—details about what the judge thought, what he would do. The determination of guilt or innocence was his alone, since the option of a jury trial did not exist.

Prema had been at Ashok's proceedings. She put down the newspaper and drew from her own memory.

"You are Jitender Malhotra," the prosecutor had said to the first witness, "the Singhvis' neighbor."

Malhotra turned to the judge. "Sir is telling right. I am living next to the Singhvi family for nine years now." He turned again to face the prosecutor.

"Please tell us what you saw on the night Hema Daksha was killed."

"I went to Bangalore on business on January 10 and did not return to my house until the afternoon of January 11. I could not have seen anything." With that he folded his hands in his lap, dropped his head, and stared at the floor.

The next witness, another neighbor, claimed he did not even look out of his window that night because things were quiet.

"Did you not say that you saw Ashok Patil's Mercedes in the driveway, parked at an angle, as if he was drunk?" the prosecutor demanded.

"It would not be anything I would notice. Patil*ji*"—he added the honorific "*ji*" showing his loyalty to the accused—"comes often to Singhvi*ji*'s house. They are having a lot of parties there. It is not so unusual for his car to be there."

"You said Ashok Patil's car was parked crooked and the driver's door left open."

The witness gave a shy but encouraging smile to Ashok and said, "They are young men, and young men will drink. That is not a crime."

Prema recalled the last time she and Ashok had been at Vikas's house, for one of the many dinner parties Vikas enjoyed hosting. Hema had served them. Ashok's face lit up whenever she walked in, balancing a tray of drinks or food, her young breasts pushed against her threadbare *kameez*. At one point, Hema's *dupatta*, meant to provide additional cover, had slid off her shoulders. Ashok jumped up to replace it, Prema remembered. His hands had rested on her shoulder longer than necessary; his smile had dazzled, equally unnecessary to waste on a servant.

Prema tried not to think about that night, or the others like it; she focused, instead, on the *kundlis*. Everything would be different once she was married.

She shook away the memory and returned in her mind to the trial. Rajiv Gupta, who had been with Ashok that night, was being questioned by the prosecutor.

"At what time did you and Vikas Singhvi return to his house?"

Rajiv slumped in the witness chair, looking at neither the judge nor the prosecutor. Mostly he looked bored. He wore a dress shirt with metallic stripes, which reflected the ceiling lights every time he changed positions. The coconut oil slicking back his hair provided almost the same amount of reflection.

"Almost three in the morning, I think," Rajiv said, shifting on the chair.

"And what time did Ashok Patil arrive?"

"I don't remember, but it was after Vikas and me."

The prosecutor looked disappointed. It would have been so much easier for him if Ashok had already been there, waiting for his friends, hunched over the servant girl's corpse.

"After?" he said. "You said earlier that all three of you left Ambrosia around midnight. Where was Mr. Patil for three hours, while you were driving your, uh, *friends* home?"

Not surprisingly, Rajiv and Vikas had met two women at the bar and offered to drive them home, which explained Ashok's late-night visit to Prema.

"He said he was going to see his fiancée."

The prosecutor turned to look at her. It was true. Ashok had come by her flat, looking for a "proper goodbye" before his weekend trip to Dona Paula Beach in Goa with Vikas and Rajiv. She was very tired and would have trouble staying up much longer. So she told him she had to finish her designs for the new Mumbai Museum of Art. It was one in the morning when he arrived. He had left just a few minutes later.

The prosecutor called Shankar Kumar, the first investigating officer on the scene, next.

"Inspector Kumar, can you tell us what you found in your investigation of the Daksha murder site, on the night between January 10 and 11?"

The inspector pushed himself back in his seat and cleared his throat. Amidst side-to-side head motions, indicating both understanding and affirmation, he said, "When I get there, I find that the servant is dead and that all the windows and doors in her room and in the house are locked. Whoever kill her, she let in."

The prosecutor then asked the inspector about the change in so many of the witnesses' stories, from what he had included in his First Information Report.

"That is not what they tell me for my FIR. They tell me . . ." and he re-read his original interviews with the witnesses. Ashok's lawyer objected to each recounted statement, and it became a case of the inspector's word against all of the witnesses'. The prosecutor returned to his seat, mumbling under his breath.

When Prema had left the courtroom, she had heard the prosecutor talking to reporters outside the Sessions Court building. "The witnesses' testimony was a waste of time. No justice was served in that courtroom today."

▬ ▬ ▬

Public Outcry: "The Rich Get Away with Murder!"

In a shocking verdict yesterday, the judge in the Ashok Patil murder case found him not guilty of murdering orphaned servant girl Hema Daksha, saying there was not enough evidence to sentence a man to hang. "With no eyewitnesses, little evidence of the chain of events, and a poorly conducted police investigation, there can be no other verdict," Judge Saxena told reporters at a post-trial news conference.

Ashok laughed when he heard the verdict. He worked his way through the crowd of his family and their servants that filled the courtroom, grabbed Prema's hand, and led her out of the courthouse. The angry mob gathered outside shouted in protest when they saw him.

"This is nothing more than social bonding: the rich taking care of the rich!"

"Murderer!"

"You should be hanged!"

Their words only fueled Ashok's bravado. He swaggered to his Mercedes, Prema in tow. He knew they would be celebrating after the trial, he told her, so he'd had his driver bring the car to the courthouse. Only an innocent man would have such certainty, Prema hoped.

"Where are we going?" she asked when they pulled out of the parking lot.

"Madras Palace. Vikas and Rajiv are throwing me a victory party." He grinned and kissed her squarely on the mouth. When he turned back to the wheel, her hand floated up and wiped at the spot.

As they drove along Marine Drive, she watched the apartment and office buildings blur past on the left. On the right, nothing but a short embankment kept cars from hurtling into the Arabian Sea. Ashok whistled a song from the latest Abhishek Bachchan movie. They drove like that for several minutes, before Prema brought it up.

"What happened, Ashok?"

He studied a group of young girls in school uniforms crossing the street in front of his car and did not answer. She placed her hand on his arm and waited for him to look at her. The two of them stared at each other until, almost a minute later, he broke the silence.

"I was drunk, Prema. Still, nothing happened. That little girl wanted to, of course, but . . ." He waggled his eyebrows. "I have you. And soon, we will be married."

Before Prema could absorb the full impact of his words, they pulled up to the entrance of Madras Palace. A valet opened her door and waited for her to step out.

Ashok let himself out and strode toward the restaurant. He turned to Prema. "Come on. You will make us late."

In the private party room of the popular hot spot, Prema found their usual group of friends and a few hangers-on that Vikas and Rajiv must have picked up while waiting for Ashok to arrive. Neither man was especially attractive—dark skin, short stature, vulgar behavior. None of that mattered, though, with their family connections. Both of them would marry sought-after girls from prominent homes, and the girls would consider themselves lucky, just as she had.

She waited until Vikas was alone on the couch before approaching him. After a few minutes of small talk, she got to the point.

"Who found the body, Vikas?"

There was no harm in his talking about it now. Ashok was free.

He waited several seconds before responding. "Ashok."

A frown formed on her face. She stared at him without saying a word, thinking how easy it would be not to ask her next question. To go back to the celebration and accept the judge's decision. The stars had already revealed her future. She did not need to know anything else. Until she remembered they were talking about murder.

"What happened that night, exactly?" Her voice was soft, her eyes receptive.

Vikas sat up straighter and finished the contents of his glass. He stared at Prema, as if trying to decide whether to answer her. She didn't know if she should smile, look disinterested, or present some other façade. Before she could make up her mind, Vikas started talking.

"Ashok came only a minute after Rajiv and me and went straight to the bathroom. A few minutes later, we heard him screaming, something about Hema. We went to see what had happened, and that's when we saw that she was dead."

"A few minutes? How many minutes?" she asked. She didn't realize she had been holding her breath until she heard her words tumble out without pause.

"It was only one or two," Vikas said.

Not enough time to kill her, she thought, feeling less relieved than angry.

▐ ▐ ▐

Second Chance for Justice:
Police Move the High Court

Mumbai Commissioner of Police Dr. J.S. Mehta moved the High Court yesterday to re-open the murder case against textile heir Ashok Patil. Patil was found innocent of capital murder charges last month in connection with the slaying of 15-year-old Hema Daksha.

"This is such shit, *yaar*!" Ashok tore the newspaper into several pieces, leaving a wake when he stormed out of the room.

Prema picked up the piece with the rest of the article on it. The police commissioner cited the change in the witnesses' testimonies, possible coercion or conspiracy by someone involved in the case, and a judge who should have asked for further investigation of the discrepancies as the reasons for his decision. He denied accusations by Ashok's family that he was bowing to public pressure to convict Ashok Patil.

Prema kept reading.

When asked about the accused's chances for appealing this decision based on double jeopardy, the commissioner had this to say: "In Indian law, double jeopardy prevents a person from being tried for the same offense in separate cases. This investigation will look to see if there was witness tampering or even bribery by Ashok Patil. What is important here is that criminals do not cock a snook at our legal system, just because they have money."

                   r   r   r

Six weeks later, Prema stood outside the Bombay High Court. The building's Gothic revival façade was majestic in the early-morning April sunlight. The statues of Justice and Mercy stared down at Prema from the building's roof. Prema shifted her eyes away from them, suddenly uneasy. She scanned the crowd, gathered outside, who were craning their necks to catch a glimpse of the key players in the most anticipated drama to take place in the august structure in four decades.

Inside the courtroom, Prema listened for days as the prosecution brought up point after point about "false" witnesses brought forward by the defense to say Ashok Patil returned to the bar Ambrosia an hour after midnight and stayed there until close to three in the morning; about incomplete investigations conducted by the police; about the ease with which Ashok Patil could have killed Hema Daksha and gotten away with it. He grew bored waiting for his friends, the prosecutor suggested; Hema resisted, screamed. He stifled her, realized what he had done, and climbed out of her window, only to return after seeing his friends arrive, close the window, and "discover" the body. The defense attorney screamed, "Circumstantial; it's all circumstantial! Where is the evidence?" The judge nodded, the same look on his face as the first trial judge had had. And through it all, Ashok sat relaxed, confident, as he had been in the bail hearing, the first trial, and all the encounters with angry protestors.

As the evidence pointing to another acquittal kept mounting, Prema finally understood the message of her *kundli*. She left the courtroom early to prepare things for Ashok's arrival home, smiling for the first time in months.

                   r   r   r

Prominent Mumbai Architect Prema Agarwal Weds

Socialite Prema Agarwal, who gained some notoriety as the once-fiancée of twice-acquitted murder suspect Ashok Patil, was married yesterday to millionaire cricket player Sandeep Pandya. Her first fiancé died six months ago in a drunk-driving accident. The coroner had reported finding over 100 milligrams of opium and several ounces of alcohol in his system. Friends say he was driving back after an acquittal victory party at Madras Palace, arranged by Agarwal, and drove head on into an embankment. Miss Agarwal, the architect credited with creating an architectural wonder with her design for the Mumbai Museum of Art, disappeared from the public eye in the days following the accident. She surfaced on the arm of playboy cricket player Pandya only last month, sporting a five-carat diamond on her ring finger. The couple is said to be honeymooning in Goa. "It was in the stars," Prema said when asked how she met her husband. "I couldn't be happier!"

———

Smita H. Jain was born in Amravati, India, and raised in Mumbai; attended Wellesley College and Columbia University; and now lives in Fredericksburg, Virginia. A lifelong fan of the mystery, she finally decided to try her hand at it, in between working full time, homeschooling two daughters, and not getting enough sleep. "Cosmic Justice" is her first published work in mystery fiction.

IT'S ALL IN THE NUMBERS

by B. V. Lawson

She hated begging. The boss had turned down her three previous requests for a raise, but even so, she stayed up until 4 a.m. rehearsing her latest spiel until she thought it sounded professional and not pathetic. She'd proudly typed up a cost-benefit analysis, printing it out in triplicate and signing her name—Andy Playne—on each copy.

Andy. She hated that name. Her father had wanted a boy and that was how she came to be saddled with it. Not Andi or Andie or Andee, just regular old Andy. At least her father, cold and distant, hadn't beaten her as a child. He'd just shut her in the closet whenever she got a C, usually in English or social studies but never math. She'd always made straight A's in math.

Struggling on just two hours of sleep, Andy tried not to take it as a bad omen when the first glitch of the day came, a broken-down subway car making her twenty minutes late for work. Hoping her boss was also late—as usual—she ducked into Starbucks and ordered his usual venti caramel macchiato and, for herself, the only thing she could afford as office manager at the end of a pay period, a plain coffee.

The clerk pulled out a pocket calculator. "Our register's down. This should just take a minute." Glitch number two, but it was only a minor inconvenience, right? She tried to wait patiently while he punched the buttons, but he hit a wrong key, and an error message showed up on the display.

The clerk looked at her apologetically. "I don't use these much."

Andy wondered if they even taught math in school anymore. After all, it had been two decades since she'd won the state Math Bowl, much to her father's surprise since "girls weren't good with numbers." Before the clerk had finished fumbling with the calculator, Andy held out her hand with the bills and coins she'd counted, saying, "The macchiato and coffee plus 7.5 percent sales tax comes to $7.54 exactly."

He hesitated, "I don't know . . ." but when he saw the line forming behind her, he grabbed the money.

Avoiding the balky elevator, Andy ran up the stairs to the top floor dedicated solely to the offices of Artemis Brown, LLC, relieved to see her boss's office empty and the gossipy junior partner's door closed. So far, so good. She'd barely had time to plonk the macchiato down on Artemis Brown's desk when he breezed in, whistling and wearing one of his Gieves & Hawkes suits, which cost more than Andy earned in a month. Not that the extravagant suit was anything unusual. Brown's haircut at Salon Louie last week had set him back at least $250 and she was pretty sure he'd had Botox injections a couple of months ago—at $520 a shot. Too bad they didn't have injections to fix high-pitched nasal voices.

"Good morning, Andy. How's the office party animal today? I hope you had as fantastic an evening as I did. Orchestra tickets for *Les Mis* at the Imperial with dinner at Masa."

Andy did a quick calculation. Those theater tickets usually went for several hundred each and Masa was three to five hundred *prix fixe*. If he could afford that, maybe her small raise request would seem a trifle. Right in the middle of that happy thought, Brown continued, "Oh and I need you to draft a memo for me. We're establishing a moratorium on staff pay raises through at least the end of the year. The firm's had a lot of investment losses recently, and it's just not a good time."

Unbelievable.

After a quick trip to the bathroom to get the impending tears under control and dab more concealer on the dark circles under her eyes, Andy managed to type out the memo and make progress on her inbox, operating on autopilot, not really conscious of what she was doing. She also barely noticed when Brown left at 11:30, as always, for a two-hour lunch. Vaguely wondering if Brown had even touched the macchiato, she entered his office to retrieve the cup and glanced at his monitor.

That was odd. She'd been the one to set up the office computer filing system, but Brown had been working on something in a directory where employees didn't store files. He'd even made it password-protected, but when he left in a hurry, he'd forgotten to log out. The title didn't make sense, either, *Bats-Score*. Brown wasn't particularly computer-savvy— he didn't have to be, with his minions doing everything for him—but apparently had managed to learn the basics of Excel spreadsheets.

Andy was a team player, always had been. Good ole reliable Andy Playne. Still, smarting from the pay raise news, she couldn't help herself and peeked at the *Bats-Score* file. There were a lot of names and figures, but she couldn't tell at a glance what to make of it. Worried she'd be caught, she did something else very un-Andy-like and forwarded an unprotected version of the file to herself.

Since it would be at least two hours before Brown returned and she had nothing pressing in her inbox, Andy opened the mysterious file on her computer. Even though she hadn't been able to afford college to get that accounting degree, she soon realized the numbers in the file weren't on the official books. She pored over them painstakingly, entry by entry, checking the numbers several times, but it didn't change the painful truth—Artemis Brown was bilking millions from elderly, court-appointed clients, all women with senility or Alzheimer's—the "bats" in *Bats-Score*.

Dear God in heaven, what should she do? She needed this job desperately, a job she'd held for ten years, the only real job she'd ever had. It was hard enough to pay the bills after her ex drained their bank account and ran off with his secretary. She didn't dare turn Brown in. Everyone knew what happened to whistleblowers—usually sacked in disgrace. She'd never have a chance of getting work anywhere else. For every office manager job, there were usually fifty applicants, all younger, prettier, and able to work for less. But she couldn't stand by and let Brown continue to exploit all those women, could she?

Andy pulled off the acting job of her life, behaving normally for the rest of the day, saying all the right things, doing what was expected. But as she rode home on the train that night, she kept thinking about the file and those accounts. She stewed about them all evening. She tried to sleep, but sleep wouldn't come. Short of divine inspiration, she didn't think she could do anything for those elderly women.

The next day the trains were on time and the Starbucks register was working. She'd ordered Brown's macchiato extra hot so it would still be warm when he arrived. Life would go on as usual, as it always did.

Brown rolled in thirty minutes late and approached Andy's desk. "I'm sorry about the pay-raise situation, Andy, but I got one of these for everyone. Here you go." He handed her a box of chocolates, the budget kind you get at the local CVS, the ones that taste like plastic. Some consolation prize! He could have splurged on Godiva, at least.

Then he said, "I have an important press release to go out later this morning. You'll be here to type it up for me when it's ready, won't you, Andy?"

"Certainly, Mr. Brown. Any special prep work I need to do?"

"It's about the award I received from the Bar Association. I want it to go out to all the major news media in the state. We'll need that database with newspaper, radio, and TV addresses."

"Very well, Mr. Brown. I'll have everything ready."

"Terrific, Andy. I want to send it before I leave for lunch. I knew I could count on you."

Oh, he was counting on her, all right—to get his coffee every morning, to work at the same rate of pay six years in a row, to work long days while he took two-hour lunches, even coming in on Christmas last year to meet an important deadline while he was sunning on a beach in Aruba.

Andy seethed in her chair with its broken back and jammed wheels. Then, like Seuss's Grinch, she had a perfectly wonderful, awful idea. Before she had a chance to change her mind, she called Brown on the intercom. "I know you're rewriting the official announcement the Bar sent you, but I think it would be a nice idea to attach the original document along with your press release, don't you? Give it extra impact."

Brown sounded distracted. "What? Oh, yes, yes that would be fine. Let's do that."

So far, so good. If neither of them had any interruptions, her idea might actually work. Andy was nervous, though, certain everyone could read on her face what she was planning as each second of the clock ticked by. When Brown's wife showed up unexpectedly at the office at 10:50, Andy almost had a heart attack.

She actually liked Brown's wife, who had one of those pretty names Andy had always loved—Rosaleen. Today Rosaleen had even brought Andy some peach-colored roses, Andy's favorite.

"I hope you don't mind, Andy, but this office is so dull. Almost like a hospital. I thought it could use a touch of color."

Long ago Brown had vetoed Andy's suggestion to add plants to the décor, calling it an unnecessary expense. But Rosaleen was right—the office, with its gray paint, metal furniture, and windowless walls, had all the charm of a police interrogation room.

Andy arranged the roses on the side of her desk. "Thanks very much, Mrs. Brown. How did you know these were my favorite?"

Rosaleen laughed. "I guess I have a head for tidbits like that. Personal details aren't my husband's strong suit, so it falls on me to remember."

No doubt that's why Mr. Brown made sure Andy's office calendar included his wife's birthday and their anniversary so Andy could use Brown's credit card to buy cards and presents to send in his name. Andy had a sneaking suspicion Rosaleen knew this. Which could explain the peach roses.

Rosaleen, by all accounts a self-assured and vivacious woman before her marriage, now stood in front of Andy's desk, looking down at her feet and twisting her hands together absent-mindedly. "I shouldn't be barging in like this. I know Artemis's been extra busy lately and just got back from that business trip to Reno. But since I was in the neighborhood, I thought I'd stop by, in case he might be free."

Andy cast a surreptitious glance at the clock and calculated how many minutes Rosaleen could spend with her husband without interrupting Andy's plan. Twenty minutes, tops. Andy hesitated before asking, "Would you like me to interrupt him?"

Rosaleen studied the closed door to her husband's office, then shook her head. "No, it's not urgent. I just—I missed him, that's all." She gave one last longing glance at the closed door, and with a sad smile and a wave, left Andy alone. Andy felt relieved, but at the same time, part of her wanted to run after Rosaleen, give her a hug, and tell her to get as far away from her husband as quickly as possible.

Andy wondered if Rosaleen suspected what Andy had discovered from Brown's credit card records—Artemis Brown had a mistress. He'd taken the mistress around the world on trips to exotic locales and expensive resorts. Resorts with perks like a $5,000 bath in Evian water sprinkled with rose petals and a $1,000 massage using oil with flecks of gold.

Meanwhile all those disabled and senile women in *Bats-Score* were probably eating cat food and shivering in unheated houses. Andy could see herself like that in thirty or forty years, and her obituary would read just the same as theirs: "Elderly woman's frozen corpse found decomposing after newspapers piled up outside her door. No one noticed her missing."

She glanced at the clock: 11:02. Brown said he wanted the press release to go out before he left for lunch at 11:30. She remembered when he first told her about this award. "You'll never guess what happened, Andy. The state Bar association is giving me their public service medal. This should help bring in higher-caliber clients. Ka-ching!"

Brown could have simply sent out the Bar's official announcement, but he didn't feel it was glowing enough and decided to rework it. By the time Brown exited his office at 11:10 and asked her to type up his release from his hand-printed notes, the memo was definitely glowing, all right—glowing so brightly with words of self-praise, Andy half expected the paper to catch fire.

A quick typist, she finished the task in minutes and e-mailed it to Brown to check over. He okayed it so quickly, he'd obviously only skimmed it. She knew he trusted her work and, for a moment, had a slight pang that she was getting ready to abuse that trust, but the names of the victims in those secret records gave her strength.

She entered his office and asked, with as normal and encouraging a voice as she could, "Since you've worked hard for this award, would you like to do the honors in e-mailing the press release to the media?"

He grimaced. "You know I'm not comfortable with computers. I'm sure I would just make a mess of things and send out a porno web site or something instead."

"Oh, it's not hard at all, Mr. Brown. Here, I'll show you. I've got it set up so that all you have to do is click twice and it will be transmitted automatically."

"Just two clicks?" He looked doubtful.

"Just the two. It's foolproof."

He laughed. "Well, since this is such an important moment that could change the course of my career, how could I refuse?"

She called up his press release and showed him how to click on the Bar's official announcement to attach it. Then with a flourish, Brown clicked on send and e-mailed the press release via instant binary gratification to hundreds of television, radio, and newspaper organizations across the state—complete with the attached and newly renamed embezzlement file that Andy had substituted in place of the official Bar document.

Andy returned to her desk, humming Led Zeppelin's "Your Time is Gonna Come." She didn't know how long it would take for the proverbial excrement to hit the fan, but she could wait. She'd read about another attorney involved in a similar crime who'd gotten nine years plus restitution, which turned out to be $1.2 million for each of those nine years. Andy worried a little about Rosaleen but figured she'd do just fine on her own. After all, she was a pretty woman with a pretty name, good breeding, and a wealthy family to boot.

As she watched Artemis Brown leave for his luncheon, blissfully unaware, Andy began to wonder if she could find an equally clever way to put his charge card records into Rosaleen's hands. And how hard would it be to dig into her ex-husband's finances? She recalled some questionable business practices at his car dealership. It should be quite easy. Because if there was one thing Andy was good at, it was numbers.

———

B.V. Lawson's short story honors include a Center Press Masters Literary Award, first place in the Armchair Interviews "Summertime Blues" contest, and honorable mentions for Deadly Ink (published in the 2007 edition of that anthology), Mysterical-E, Crime and Suspense, the Press 53 Open Awards, and the Derringers. *Other publication credits include* Mysterical-E, Great Mystery and Suspense, Cantaraville, ESC! Magazine, Mouth Full of Bullets, Northern Haunts: 100 Terrifying New England Tales, Static Movement, Powder Burn Flash, and PMS: Poison, Murder, Satisfaction. *In addition, she has written for* Mystery Readers Journal, *the* Washington Times, *and special-interest magazines. Her website is www.bvlawson.com.*

PASSING THROUGH

by Audrey Liebross

It was a warm morning in September 1894 and I, a grandmother of three, was content with my life. Although I had lost my beloved husband two years before, my mood had greatly improved in recent months. I lived with my only child, Thomas, in Hagerstown, Maryland, and thought of my daughter-in-law as the daughter I never had.

When I finished my morning ablutions in the modern bathtub complete with hot and cold running water, I buttoned my fashionable white blouse with its leg-of-mutton sleeves and piled my graying hair on top of my head. After a quick check in the mirror, I descended to the sitting room to read to the three children.

A young man, straw hat in hand, rose from the davenport to greet me. My daughter-in-law introduced him as Mr. John Drummond, of Philadelphia, but the name meant nothing to me. Katherine told me, "Mr. Drummond is here to deliver a letter from his late mother, whom you apparently knew during the war."

I took in Mr. Drummond's milky white skin, wavy, blond hair, and pale-gray eyes, and more than thirty years melted away. I knew in an instant whose son he was. His mother had figured prominently in the events of another September day, when the Confederates had passed through town during Robert E. Lee's first invasion of the North.

Mr. Drummond, as if reading my mind, told me that his mother, before her death three months prior, had insisted he deliver this letter to reveal the truth about all that had transpired. I sat in my favorite chair, heart thumping. I had always had my suspicions that there was more to the story regarding what happened that day, and now I was finally about to know.

In August of 1862, I was a young girl of eighteen with three unwed brothers in the Union army. I lived alone—with no chaperone—in our large house in Hagerstown, my father having died in July. In war time, people were more apt to forgive what would ordinarily be a severe breach of etiquette.

One sweltering day, a young woman who introduced herself only as Daisy Smith (not as "Mrs. George Smith," or whatever her husband's Christian name might have been), knocked on my door. She was obviously in a delicate condition and carried two worn carpetbags. I invited her inside and offered her lemonade and cold chicken, both of which she readily accepted. She told me that her husband was a Union soldier and that she had left Kentucky to come north, wanting her child born in federal territory. She planned to make her way to Pennsylvania, but said that traveling was too difficult now because of the movement of both armies. Mrs. Smith was seeking employment for the next month or two, until she was able to move on again.

Young and naïve, I did not think to question her story or her lack of a wedding band. Instead I found myself staring at her milky white complexion and her pale-gray eyes, with their sorrowful aspect. Despite the grime of the road, her golden tresses, with just a hint of curl, remained neatly pulled back into a bun at the nape of her neck, as was the fashion of the day. With my darker skin and hair, I envied her appearance. I took pity on her unfortunate circumstances and reasoned I could use some help in running the house. I offered to hire Mrs. Smith to assist me—and serve as my chaperone—until she was ready to move on.

As it happened, the Confederates shortly invaded the North. For days, Hagerstown buzzed with rumors of their coming. I had visions of Stonewall Jackson's soldiers stealing every drop of food that they could find and burning what they could not carry. My fears were especially acute because I knew our own beloved soldiers had not always treated Virginia's residents with civility.

Fortunately Longstreet's men proved polite in their invasion and offered to pay for what they took, albeit in Confederate currency. Nothing had prepared me, however, for their wretched condition. On that fateful day in September, a ragged Confederate soldier came to my back door and knocked. I opened it and fell back three paces, not out of fear, but from the stench of his unwashed body.

"Please, ma'am," the appallingly thin creature said, "I've been marching for days and ain't had nothing to eat but green apples and green corn. Can you spare something?" As he spoke, he was joined by about twenty companions. They referred to themselves as North Carolina "boys."

These men were the enemy, but they were God's creatures. I took pity on them, and showed them the well in the backyard, where they could wash. I called Daisy, who was cleaning upstairs, and told her that we needed to prepare breakfast for at least a score of hungry North Carolina Confederate soldiers.

Daisy descended the steps, looking wan and frightened. Silently she boiled oatmeal in a large pot, while I fried eggs and bacon. The Confederates needed shoes as desperately as food, and I gave them my father's three pair, wondering if that's why the Lord had bade me keep them after his death. I could only hope that my generosity did not result indirectly in the deaths of Union soldiers, but I could not let human beings march hundreds of miles in such a sorry state.

As the company prepared to resume their journey, the lieutenant asked if anyone had seen Private Howell. After a brief search, the officer decided to leave without him. He asked me to tell the missing man, if we saw him, that his companions had resumed their march along the Hagerstown Pike. I thought no more of it, assuming that the soldier in question had departed before his comrades did, and that they would catch up with him. I commenced cleaning up, hoping these were the only Rebels who would pay us a visit. As it was, they had consumed much of our food store.

I heated water with which to wash the pots and called to Daisy for help but received no answer. Wondering at her absence, I rolled up my sleeves and started to scrub, whereupon Daisy quietly entered the kitchen. "Are they gone?" she whispered, her face the color of ashes.

"Yes, and thanks to your disappearing, I had to feed them mostly by myself. Where were you?"

She did not answer at once. I was not usually so waspish, but the Confederates' visit had taken as much out of me as it seemed to have taken out of Daisy.

Daisy looked as if she would cry. "Miss Henrietta," she said, "there's something I need to tell you. I I knew one of those soldiers."

"Not now," I snapped, in no mood to engage in polite conservation. As we worked without speaking, each of us clattering pots in fits of pique, I wondered how a loyal Kentucky woman was acquainted with North Carolina Confederate soldiers.

When we finally finished cleaning the kitchen and I got a look at her red-rimmed eyes and her pasty face, I suggested, more kindly, "Take a rest. That is what I plan to do, and let us pray that there are no more visitors from General Longstreet's army."

I took her hand and began helping her up the steps.

"Miss Henrietta, please don't go in there," she begged as we approached her bedroom, located down the hall from mine on the second level.

"Why in heaven's name not?" I demanded, at the end of my rope. "Not that I would intrude upon your privacy," I added, when I saw the expression on her face.

Daisy convulsed into sobs. "The missing soldier is in there. He's dead. He . . . he must have hit his head on something. I went upstairs and saw him lying by the fireplace."

I dropped onto the steps to avoid swooning and struggled to unhook my corset through my dress. When I felt able, I insisted she show me the young man's body.

The soldier lay on his back, not breathing, his eyes staring straight up at the ceiling. There was not a mark upon the front of him, but blood pooled underneath his neck. Daisy helped me roll him over. What I saw made me rush for the wash basin in the corner of her room.

After I finished vomiting, I looked wildly about, trying to focus on something normal. However my eyes kept returning as if of their own accord to the area around the fireplace. One of the pokers had a small puddle of water underneath it. Dear Lord, Daisy must have killed the soldier with the implement and then washed the blood off the weapon to cover her deed.

Was a woman in a delicate condition capable of cold-blooded murder? Was I in any danger from this mother-to-be whom I had taken into my home? Despite my shock, I managed to think rationally. The soldier had no proper business in a lady's boudoir, especially a lady married to another man and expecting his child. It was clear Private Howell had been up to no good.

Daisy could barely meet my eye. "He was waiting for me up here. He offered me money to do unspeakable things. He grabbed me and tore at my clothing. I picked up the fireplace poker and hit him." I noticed for the first time that Daisy wore a different bodice from that morning—one that did not match her skirt. She must have changed her clothes in a hurry. Indeed the old bodice lay on the floor, partially hidden underneath the bed. I picked it up. Several hooks and eyes were torn off, and the white collar had separated from the neck. Clearly a struggle had taken place.

"I believe you," I told her. "The problem is what to do with him." I nodded toward the body.

After a hasty discussion, we decided to pretend we had been nursing Private Howell when he expired, if we later had to answer any unwelcome questions. We lifted the soldier onto the bed and cleaned and bandaged the wound. This operation necessitated two more trips to the basin for me, but Daisy was surprisingly calm, especially for a woman in a family way.

The next hours brought second thoughts about our plan, which now seemed naïve and dangerous. We could not leave the body where it was for long, lying on the bed in Daisy's room where the odor would soon become intolerable. Yet we did not dare remove the corpse from the house with the streets still swarming with Confederate soldiers.

Daisy and I devised a different plan. We struggled to carry the late Private Howell's remains down to the coolest part of the cellar and wrapped them in a rubber mat, which we placed in one of my father's old crates. I sent Daisy out to buy as much ice as she could and we packed it in next to the body. The good Lord must have been with us, because we received no further Confederate visitors, although several units marched by.

"Get some hot water from the stove. We are both going to wash," I said now that our grisly deed was done. I did not yet know of Dr. Lister's germ theory, but I instinctively wanted to cleanse myself of the miasma of death.

A half hour later, when we were both clean, I burned our blood-stained dresses in the kitchen fireplace. "Dear Jesus, please forgive us for what we have to do," I prayed. "And let us dispose of the body without being caught."

The Confederates left Hagerstown after only one more day, but it seemed an eternity. Fighting broke out nearby at South Mountain and Crampton's Gap. That night we lugged the body, wrapped in burlap, to the wagon and drove out of town, praying that we would meet no patrols or snipers from either army.

The moon was only half-full. We found a suitably deserted spot where corpses lined the road, extinguished the lamp, unwrapped the burlap, and rolled Private Howell's body out. Anyone who found our erstwhile visitor would assume he had wandered back dazed and wounded from battle and fallen by the side of the road, never to rise again.

At home, I threw the burlap and the rope that had secured it into the fireplace and gratefully watched as they were consumed in the flames. Would that the images of the past two days could be as easily obliterated.

Daisy went into labor on the morning of September 17, 1862. All day she suffered, assisted by a local midwife, a freed slave. Even the terrible sounds of battle at Antietam Creek couldn't mask her screams of pain. We did not know it then, but that day turned out to be the bloodiest of the war. Yet in the midst of the carnage, a new life came into the world, John Herbert Smith, Jr., named for Daisy's soldier husband.

Thankfully my brothers came through the battle without a scratch, but many other soldiers weren't as fortunate. For six weeks, the house was filled with wounded Union soldiers, and Daisy and I spent our days nursing them.

Finally the last soldier was well enough to be moved to a hospital in the District of Columbia. Daisy volunteered to accompany him. From there she and the baby would continue on to Philadelphia.

"And thank you for everything, Miss Henrietta," she said, hugging me for at least the fifth time.

"Why do you call me 'Miss' after all we've been through together?" I asked, although I should have given up by then. Perhaps I was just trying to avoid concentrating on our parting. I would miss Daisy and the infant. Yet, in some ways, I was hurt that she hadn't chosen to stay with me.

"I have to get to the North," she said firmly. "This area is too close to the fighting."

"I'll pray for you," I said.

A few weeks later, I received a crudely written letter from Daisy bearing terrible news—her husband had been killed in a battle out West. Yet she seemed curiously detached from the matter. The rest of the letter was cheerful; she had found a position with a widowed doctor. Within six months, another missive, her last, arrived informing me they had wed.

My brothers returned home after Appomattox with a desire to open a store together. My brother Michael's new wife, Alicia, had a twenty-four-year-old brother, Hanford Scott, to whom she introduced me. Mr. Scott and I were soon married. Thomas, our pride and joy, came a year later. But, alas, there were to be no more children.

Over the years, I often thought about Daisy Smith and what had become of her. I hoped she was happy in Philadelphia, but I could not understand why she had broken contact so abruptly. Had I offended her in some manner? Try as I might, I could not think how.

Perhaps now, after thirty years, I would learn the truth.

My daughter-in-law offered Mr. Drummond coffee and cake. While we sipped and ate and engaged in small talk, I opened the envelope.

"Dear Henrietta," the letter read. As I glanced down, I saw that Daisy's handwriting, grammar, and syntax had improved dramatically over the years. "Before I die, I must tell you the truth of who I am and what happened that day in 1862.

"I am an octoroon. I never married till dear Joseph Drummond took me to be his wife. He knew the whole story, as do our beloved children. All are passing for white.

"Shortly before I met you, I escaped from my life as a slave on the Dunstan Larrimore plantation in North Carolina, where Private Howell was a frequent visitor, a friend of my master's son. My pregnancy resulted from my master's animal desires. A man almost sixty years old, he liked me best because he could pretend he had seduced a young, white woman, instead of forcing himself upon an unwilling Negro slave. When I conceived, my aunt (another slave) took me aside and told me the horrible truth: Dunstan Larrimore was my father as well as the father of his own grandchild.

"I managed to leave the plantation and located the Union army, where I worked as a laundress. Because of my fair skin and hair, I passed easily as white, and I safely made my way into Maryland, where I happened to approach your house. I have never forgotten your kindness, but I could not risk my family's future by telling you my secret or by remaining in Maryland, a slave state.

"Now that I am near death, however, I must unburden my conscience. Private Howell, of course, knew that I was a fugitive slave. He threatened to report me to his commanding officer. Aware that the Confederate army rounded up runaway slaves and returned them to bondage, I believed him. He told me that first he was going to have a little fun, and he started tearing at my clothes. I hit him with the poker because I felt I had no other choice. I hope you can forgive me for not telling you the full truth."

Without looking up, I folded the letter and slipped it into my pocket. I excused myself to use the newly installed water closet, but mainly I needed to compose myself; I felt as if someone had kicked me in the innards. Poor Daisy! The whole time she had been cleaning my house and weeding my garden, she had been burdened with her shattering secret. How could she love the beautiful infant who came to her in such a vile way? Yet there was no question that she did love her son.

I went to my room and hid the letter under my pillow. The tears poured down my face, and I struggled to regain control before I returned downstairs to face my daughter-in-law and our guest.

Mr. Drummond was ready to take his leave. "If you are ever in Philadelphia, I would be honored to have you visit, Mrs. Scott. Both Mrs. Scotts."

"And we would be honored to visit," I replied.

After John Drummond departed, my daughter-in-law eyed me critically. "Mother, what was in that letter? You look as if you've seen a ghost."

I had to unburden myself to someone, and I trusted Katherine as much as I trusted my beloved Thomas.

When I had finished telling the story, her eyes flashed. "That is terrible," she said.

"To think what that poor creature went through," I replied.

"No, to think that a Negro ate from my dishes. I will instruct Moira to wash them twice."

I barely spoke to my daughter-in-law for three days. And I burned Daisy's letter in the stove. Let the past be forgotten and the dead rest in peace.

———

Audrey Liebross, a contributor to Chesapeake Crimes I *with "Sisters and Brothers," has written a series of columns for* Independent Agent *magazine, which humorously presents technical insurance material. Audrey's short stories have also appeared in* Penny-A-Liner *and* Woman's World *magazines. Audrey is currently marketing her two unpublished novels,* Chicken Soup Justice *and its sequel,* Oy the Bloody Bridegroom, *both featuring Cindy Katzmann, a newly ordained Reform rabbi in a small, southern town. Audrey is an attorney who works for the federal government. She is married with three sons.*

ANCHORS AWAY

by C. Ellett Logan

Gina paused in her kitchen doorway to listen to the message on the answering machine.

"Axel Boyette? Swinson Concrete here, confirming your 10 a.m. appointment for Saturday the seventeenth. We want to remind you to complete the required site prep: clear all brush and debris—then rake smooth. If you need to reschedule for any reason, you must do so at least forty-eight hours prior to your reserved time by calling 703-3 . . ."

Gina tuned out the rest of the message, furious that her husband had followed the instructions to the letter, destroying her roses in the process. She stepped from the kitchen onto the dirt and stones of their side yard—a no-man's land bathed in the perpetual shadow of the house, where even weeds would not grow. From her shady post, she observed that the noonday sun rendered everything else a washed-out white, especially her husband's bass boat. Around twenty feet in length, including outboard motor and trailer, the thing was covered with a canvas tarp that somehow made it look like a whale in a silly cap, waiting to go for a ride.

Skirting the boat, she knelt beside a pitiful pile of plant remains, suffering as if it were her own body parts dumped in a heap on the hardscrabble ground.

"Oh, my sweet babies," she said, carefully picking up the severed limbs that had once been her Knock Out roses. Aromatic blossoms stubbornly clung to the stems, heads bowed and petals limp.

"I'm so sorry." Gina swallowed hard, wiping the wetness from her cheeks on the back of her thick gardening gloves. She carted the bushes close to her body like injured children until she filled the compost pile around back, the pricking of their thorny teeth barely registering through her sorrow.

"He said he had to take out some flowers for the carport, but I never dreamed he meant my roses," she exclaimed to the wilted foliage, cooing gently as she had when their shoots had been tender.

Gina had only half listened when Axel explained about contractors coming to install a cement parking deck for his boat. Even though they had a two-acre lot full of possible sites for his project, she should have realized that he would want the damn boat where he could admire it from the dining room window. The same window she used to look through to enjoy her flower beds.

"Why didn't I pay more attention?" She stepped back into the shade for a moment's rest. "Maybe I could've stopped him."

To be fair, much of their property was covered in pine trees, more difficult to clear than her garden. Gina had been grateful when Axel gave up his womanizing for fishing, relieved to know his destination when he drove off every Saturday morning pulling his boat and trailer. But the fact that he was capable of destroying the one hobby that gave her pleasure, just to accommodate his, was cold even for him.

Gina, who was in the best shape of her life because of gardening, worked the small pitchfork with ease. She thoroughly mixed the lifeless branches into the rotted manure and leaf litter of the compost pile then put the yard tools away. She had the urge to call the concrete company to cancel the pour. But it was only Wednesday, and the job still ten days away—her husband might discover what she had done. She didn't have the nerve to risk it.

 ▗ ▗ ▗

The next afternoon, Gina climbed up and down on a footstool taking apart light fixtures for a good soaking, disgusted by the dried insect parts that rained down. From her perch in the hall, she heard the slam of a car door, followed by Axel's gruff voice calling goodbye to his ride home, a fellow traveling salesman. She continued her chore until she got the etched-glass cover washed and dried and back in place. Her husband usually parked his suitcase on the small front porch, then went around to the side yard to examine the flex-fit cover on the boat for tightness, or the trailer tires for air pressure; anything to spend time and attention on his boat. And money—2009 had been an expensive year. First he traded in their paid-for car for a used truck with a trailer hitch and a monthly payment. And now they owed good money on a concrete pad and steel cover.

So it was a good thing her husband had a stable job selling office products. On Mondays he checked in at the local office to talk to his manager about the coming week's goals and turn in his travel expenses. On Tuesdays he set up appointments. Wednesdays through Fridays he drove the company van from town to town in the surrounding counties, servicing his outside-sales route, delivering toner cartridges, and taking new orders. He performed his "adore the boat" ritual every Friday after he was dropped off, before he saw fit to gather up his bag and join her.

Finally he came through the front door. "I'm home."

No kidding. "How was the trip?" Same question she always asked.

"Business is really down. But gas prices have come down, too, so things are about even."

Next we'll talk about the weather, she predicted.

"Yard looks like we didn't get a drop of rain," he said as he hauled his garment bag into the laundry room. He would secure it on a hook behind the door and fish his toiletry kit and shoes out of the bag's corners.

Oh, really? she thought. My dead roses didn't notice.

Instead she replied, "Supper's almost ready. By the way, they called to confirm that you're on the schedule next Saturday to get your carport poured."

 r r r

After fifteen years, Gina was used to Axel's weekly travel, but it always took until Sunday afternoon to get used to having him underfoot again. That's when she emptied the dirty laundry from his hanging suitcase. Underwear and socks went straight into the wash. Suit jackets and dress shirts ended up on the pile for the dry cleaners. His mealtime spills never made it past his big belly to his pants, so a couple pairs of slacks usually lasted another trip. She knew which pairs because he re-hung his quasi-clean pants. In his hotel room, Axel would open whatever magazine he had with him when he packed, slide it over a wire hanger, and drape his pants over the magazine. The rigid support prevented a crease at the fold.

As she sorted the laundry, Gina partially registered the magazine titles: *Bass Assassin* and *Extreme Boating*. She was brought up short when she noticed the magazine cover under the lightweight wool slacks she had in her hand. *Cosmopolitan*? She squinted at the address label, and the laundry room seemed to sway.

"Tricia Peller? Red-Mazda-sports-car-driving-husband-stealing Tricia Peller?"

She slammed the dryer door, knocked hangers off the rod, and cussed.

"I'm not putting up with this." The nasty names she called Axel were drowned out by the squeal of the high-pressure nozzle outside the window as he hosed off the boat and trailer, a ritual he did every Sunday afternoon. But she did not cry. The last time he swore off that bimbo, three years before, she had vowed not to waste another tear if he ever went back to his cheating ways.

Gina went to the window and glared at her husband. "How dare you do this to me again?"

She yelled and bawled him out through the glass until he disappeared around back. How naïve she'd been. All this time, she had foolishly believed the rumors about Tricia and the pastor of the Brethren of the Desert church, thinking that the tramp had moved on to her next conquest. She took a deep breath and looked over his boat. His precious boat, which he treated better than their home. Better than her. The slob made one mess after another, and Gina dutifully cleaned them up, sneaking his old magazines, newspapers, and mail out to the trash one piece at a time, so he wouldn't notice and make her life even more miserable. Well, not anymore.

"You better watch your back, Mr. Boyette."

r r r

Gina waited patiently till Wednesday, when Axel left on his weekly business trip. She took a late afternoon nap, even though falling asleep had been difficult at first. When the only light outside was the soft luster at the horizon and a few stars, she went on a reconnaissance mission, starting in the storage shed leaning against the side of the house. She removed the lock that always hung from the hasp in a simulated locked position, since Axel could never remember the combination, slipped into the shed, and closed the door. Feeling for the flashlight hanging from a hook to her left, she lit the cramped space.

"Come to me, my darlings," she said to her worn and familiar gardening tools. She set down the upended flashlight and gathered a shovel, spade, and the bucket in which she carted plant detritus from her garden to the compost pile. She turned off the light and eased the door open. Quietly she laid the tools on the stony ground. Their lot was large, and heavy tree cover hid the house from nosy neighbors, but she wanted to be on the safe side. She reached in again and felt for the protective netting she used to keep the squirrels from getting at her bulbs around front, remembered the rake, and placed these items outside with the other implements. Quickly she slipped back into the house to wait for deeper darkness to fall.

After an hour or so she returned to the boat in the faint moonlight and climbed up on one of the fenders of its trailer. She loosened the cover's drawstring and pushed the canvas over to the other side of the boat. Inside she could just make out oars, a gas can, and two anchors made from gallon milk jugs filled with something, maybe sand. Otherwise the boat was clear of clutter (his fishing poles stood lined up in the corner of the den; the cooler, bleached clean, waited on the back porch). Axel was way more particular about his floating obsession than the other areas of his life.

Gina carried the anchors one at a time, hoisting them by twisted nylon ropes over to a spot close to the shed. She lined the bottom of the boat's hull with an old tarp. Soon the boat's contents were tucked inside the shed. All the garden tools were hidden in the boat. She tidied up, pulled the cover closed, and went inside to wait some more.

There was a certain time of the night when Gina thought she could best carry out her plan and not be detected. Once, when she was a girl, she had gone with her father and uncle into the woods to hunt, well after midnight. The world outside their truck on the way to the blind had been so still. No breezes blew. No cars passed. Every self-respecting dog lay dreaming, legs jerking, behind the dark windows of the houses they passed.

She wasn't sure what the actual time had been that night on the way to the hunt, but it felt late enough now. She was right—in the yard, she didn't hear activity of any kind. At the center of what used to be her rose garden, she started digging a hole about two feet out in each direction: scooped a shovel full, stepped up on the fender, and tossed the load of dirt into the bottom of the boat. Then back to the hole again. After a time, she began to dig down and not just out, getting into a rhythm. Several times, overcome by exhaustion, she almost stopped, but memories of her lovely Peace Roses floating in a bowl of water on her table in spring, or of drinking in the fragrance of her Iceberg roses in late summer, kept her working. Eventually she had to lean a small metal ladder from the boat up against the side of the hole. She added another three beats to her rhythm.

When she heard the rumble of a trash truck several blocks away accompanied by barking dogs, she put all the tools on top of the substantial pile of dirt in the boat and replaced the tarp. She quickly anchored the protective netting from the shed over the hole in the ground by pinning it with pieces of stem she had saved from her decimated rose bushes. Scattering stones in a random pattern along the edges, she completed the camouflage by covering the entire surface with pine straw from her yard.

It was almost dawn by the time she finished, so after her shower, she stayed up and went through her usual routines. By two in the afternoon, she had to lie down, falling quickly into a deep sleep. When she awoke, she was able to run a few errands before meeting her aunt for dinner, as though it were just a normal day in the life of a woman whose husband traveled.

Thursday night Gina only needed to dig for three hours to get the hole to the perfect depth. It was a good thing she was finished because the boat was full of dirt, stem to stern, and she had trouble crawling out of the hole, even with the ladder. She retrieved the gas can from the shed and set it inside the kitchen. She raked the pine straw back onto the net-covered hole, mixing in some of the small stones that plagued their yard. She sprinkled the entire area with pine cones in what she hoped looked like nature's way. She showered and scrubbed under her fingernails with a brush.

In spite of the shortened work night, by the next afternoon Gina had worn herself out pacing from the truck to the front porch and back again. She was waiting to distract her husband as soon as he was dropped off at the foot of the driveway, desperate to keep him from his usual Friday afternoon love-fest with his boat.

She could see the self-satisfied mien of his mouth turn into a frown as the car pulled up to the curb. He leaned over and said something to his co-worker, who then nodded and wiggled a quick wave in her direction as Axel climbed out of the passenger side.

Gina started in about how the truck wouldn't start as soon as the car pulled away, describing the *pop, pop, pop* sound it had made, trying not to make eye contact.

Axel walked over and laid his garment bag on the front stoop like always, then reached for the keys swinging from her fist.

"What the hell'd you do?" he asked and got into the driver's seat. "Leave the lights on?" The engine caught immediately and roared loudly as he stomped down on the gas pedal.

"Well it works now." He rolled his eyes at her. "I don't know what the problem was."

Her husband's grousing was ramping up when the shrill racket of a smoke alarm inside the house stopped him mid-sentence.

"What's that?" Axel jumped out of the truck and ran down the sidewalk and up the stairs quick as a flash. Gina closed the truck door he had left open and retrieved his bag.

The upper portion of the foyer and hall were clouded with smoke. A crackle and hiss issued from the kitchen. Gina knew the fuel was only the few rashers of bacon she'd left frying on the stove as a back-up plan to keep him away from the side yard.

Axel grabbed the handle of the skillet with a pot holder and shoved the pan of flames off the burner. "What's the idea of going outside when you've got food on the stove? What's the matter with you?"

He threw open the kitchen windows. "Why are you cooking bacon anyway?"

"I'm making black-eyed peas," she said.

He left the kitchen mess for her to clean up. "Well, make sure you don't walk away from the next batch."

Even though her ploy to redirect her husband had worked, Gina didn't stop shaking until she heard the earsplitting sounds of a car chase on the television in the den. Axel would stay glued to his recliner unless there *was* another fire.

r r r

A couple hours later, Gina was strung tight as a drum as she finished preparing Axel's favorites for dinner, hoping to lure him to the table. She stopped to make sure the colorful array of sliced red tomatoes, rice, black-eyed peas, pink ham, and yellow cornbread would do the trick before setting down his plate.

"Supper's ready," she called as she dipped up her own meal at the stove.

"I thought I'd eat on a tray in here," came the answer from the den.

Gina knew there would be hell to pay if she insisted he join her. But if she just didn't answer, or take him his plate, the smell of the special dinner might entice him into the kitchen. She wanted his full attention when she confronted him. And sure enough, after a few minutes, he dropped his bulky body into his chair at the table.

Gina picked at her food while Axel downed most of his first helping. His vigorous chewing was the only conversation, but it still seemed as if he was taking forever to finish. She fidgeted as she held the magazine and its inflammatory address label in her lap.

"Where were you Thursday night?" The words popped out before she could stop them.

"Same place I always am." His fork never broke stride.

"I called the hotel in Eversville, and they said you already checked out."

"After I saw my last customer, I run up to see my brother," he answered and brought another forkful of peas to his mouth.

"Nobody in your family talks to you, Axel. You're lucky they let you go to your own momma's funeral." Gina slammed the *Cosmo* down and slid it across the table. The peas on her husband's fork bobbled off.

He crisscrossed his knife and fork at the top edge of his plate and blotted his lips with his napkin. "What the hell do you want from me, woman?"

"I want an explanation for this." She shoved the magazine closer to him, jabbed the label with her fork, and leaned in to get a good look at his lying face.

He shoved it back. "It's a woman's magazine."

"Would you mind telling me what the address label says?"

Instead of answering, he laced his fingers and perched his elbows on the table. He didn't say anything. Gina didn't say anything. The *Jeopardy* contestant on the television in the next room said, "Viscous Liquids for a thousand, Alex."

A bundle of nerves, Gina got up and went to the fridge to put away the iced tea pitcher, waiting for the battle to commence.

Axel stood. "I'm gonna finish my dinner in the other room and watch *Jeopardy. Best Gol' Durn Videos* comes on next," he said over his shoulder.

Disappointed that he hadn't defended himself so she could shoot down his lies one by one, she inwardly raged as she wiped the stove and counters and chased down peas under the table. "He doesn't even have the gumption to challenge me, to deny it," she muttered.

For the rest of the evening, every annoying sound he made—the swooshing of water in the bathroom, the bang, bang, banging to dry his toothbrush on the side of the sink—strengthened her resolve.

Later Axel stuck his head into the den where she sat stiffly on the couch. "If you think I'm going to get into another argument on this subject," he said, "think again. You sleep in the guest room."

Gina got up and squeezed past him.

He shrank back against the frame of the door, contorting into a question mark as though he couldn't stand for her to even brush against him. "Now what?" he asked.

She returned quickly with a crocheted coverlet. "Might get chilly in the guest room. There's only a sheet on the bed."

"Yeah, whatever."

She watched him walk down the hall and clenched her fists. She knew he thought this was like all the times before when she had watched him drive away in the little red sports car with the Jezebel. Pitch a fit for a few days, pout a few more, and then forgive him everything. She whispered, "Just keep thinking that way."

＊　＊　＊

Fully clothed, Gina sat in the den until that perfect-shield time of night. She had put the gas can full of water just outside the kitchen door. She carried the long, slender, fireplace Bic in her hand. Before she called out to her husband, she paused by his bed and listened to him snore. She had to yell his name four times before he sat up, sputtering. "Is there another fire?"

"Will be. I'm going to burn your boat," she said and turned on her heel.

She grabbed the can and navigated cautiously so she didn't disturb the target area, even though the moon spilled its light through the ragged cloud cover and she could see a little. After she got into position, it seemed like an eternity before he flew out the side door. She had taken the bulb out of the porch light, but she could still make out the angry contortion of her husband's face.

"Gina. You know I'm not letting you get away with this," he said, but, agonizingly, took only two steps closer to the trap.

"You got this comin', Axel." She turned and splashed water on the boat.

He charged, moving faster than she had ever seen him go. And then he snapped from view.

She listened to the night, suddenly worried someone might have heard them. At first all was quiet. Then she heard a moan and saw the top of Axel's head pop out of the hole.

Adrenalin surged as she jumped up on the trailer fender and grabbed the shovel, then flew down and bashed him on the head. The impact wasn't really a loud sound, but the meaty thud made her stomach lurch. Worried about the loss of cover with the moon out, she moved quickly and mechanically. Up, get a shovel full of dirt, down, throw it over him. She was horrified that the gravelly dirt made so much noise as it hit his body. She intensified her efforts: step down to the edge of hole, let the dirt slide down the walls, back up on the fender, and scoop. Finally she gathered up the soiled tarp from the bottom of the boat and pushed it in on top of him. Thank goodness she had toiled in the garden season after season, building up her stamina, because it took until dawn threatened to top off the hole. Only minutes though, to rake the area smooth in preparation for the cement job.

"Guess you wish that I *had* canceled tomorrow's pour now," she said and inspected her work.

⌐ ⌐ ⌐

As she wiped the garden tools across the grass to give them a preliminary cleaning, she thought about the rose bushes in their burlap coats that she had tucked away in the shadows behind the house. They stood ready to be planted around the edges of the new carport when it cured.

Axel planted in his hole meant that all the dirt wouldn't fit back in, so she had gone ahead and piled the extra soil in a mound (such handy planting material) beside the roses.

Gina was sure it would be a long time before anyone noticed he was gone, what with his travel all week and his fishing on weekends. His boss sure wasn't going to call her, or anyone else for that matter, to ask about his missing salesman. The guy had covered too many times in the past when Axel was off with that woman. If anyone ever did come looking, they'd find the boat parked right where he left it on the concrete deck that Axel himself had ordered.

She went into the shed to retrieve the hidden *Cosmo* to plant in the boat's storage compartment. The address label would make a nice piece of incriminating evidence to tie the witch to her husband. Tricia Peller: a person of interest.

Gina had hidden the magazine on the top of the tool cabinet, and she stretched to fetch it down. Once in her hands, she couldn't help encircling the address label within the flashlight's beam for one more look.

"Tricia Peller," Gina sneered. And then some bold type at the edge of the illuminated halo caught her eye.

Gina read, "Christmas Edition: December 2006."

―――――

Logan spent her formative years in the Deep South, an experience that informs her settings and troubles her characters, Southern-Gothic-style. She moved with her family to Northern Virginia in 1985. Logan's found the perfect home in the crime-fiction community, coveted spots for her short stories "Backseat" and "Anchors Away" in the Chesapeake Crimes *anthology series, and a position on the board of Sisters in Crime, Chessie Chapter. Her novel in progress is* Miasma.

A WOMAN WHO THINKS

by Debbi Mack

"I'm . . . so upset, Dr. Fein," Lila said, alternately rubbing and clasping her long-fingered hands as she stared out the window. Her mouth crumpled and tears flowed down her cheeks. "I don't know where to start." Her last words came out as a sob.

Dr. Morris Fein thought about how to respond to this, keeping his expression bland, as he did with all patients no matter what crazy things they might say. Thinking is what Dr. Fein did best. Thinking about the nutty things distraught patients said and formulating a well-reasoned response.

It had taken most of their hour to get to the heart of Lila's problem. She'd danced around the issue, talked about her frustrations at work, her lousy love life, her financial problems. After this extensive prelude, it seemed like she'd finally come to the reason for her visit.

"Why don't you start with whatever you're most comfortable telling me," Dr. Fein said. Lila needed to be handled with care, like a carton of fine china.

Continuing to avoid his gaze, Lila raised a fist to her mouth and bit it. Finally she said, "I . . . can't. I've done something very stupid. And I think I'm in trouble."

Dr. Fein cocked his head to one side, as if examining a specimen from a different angle. He kept his expression impassive but spoke in a warm tone. "I'm here to help. Perhaps you could tell me more about this thing you've done."

"I've been—" She broke off the thought in mid-sentence and, bowing her head slightly, looked up at Dr. Fein with wary, deep-blue eyes. "Everything I say is confidential, right?" she said in a husky voice.

Dr. Fein pursed his lips. "For the most part, yes."

"When you say that . . . does that mean if I'm involved in something criminal, you have to report it?"

Dr. Fein felt unease stirring within him. He hated questions like that.

"That depends." He leaned forward, clasping his hands between his knees. "If we're talking about something that's already happened, no. Or something involving, say, minor property crimes like shoplifting. But something more serious like murder or child abuse . . ." His voice faltered, despite his best efforts to the contrary. He needed to sound sure so patients would have confidence in him, trust him. "If a patient told me she intended to hurt someone, I'd be legally required to report it. You can understand why . . ." Again his voice trailed off, but he searched out eye contact with her as he asked, "Are you involved in such a crime?"

She shook her head with such force, he thought he saw tears fly from her cheeks. "No, no," she said. "Nothing like that. I just . . . got involved with the wrong people. And now I'm afraid they're coming after me."

"Please," he said, his unease quelled but not eradicated. "Why don't you start from the beginning?"

"They wanted me to deliver something," she said, staring before her as if a spider too tiny to see were hanging a few inches from her face. "It was strange because they told me not to tell anyone. But they were willing to pay me a lot of money to do it, plus the costs of the trip and everything. I was supposed to take a locked suitcase to this place near the Canadian border." Her eyes finally turned his way, refocused on Dr. Fein. "I think it may have been drugs. Maybe something worse. They . . . they wouldn't tell me."

"Who is 'they'?"

"Two men. They never mentioned their names." Lila shook her head and shrugged. "They said they got my name from Mickey. That should have tipped me off the whole thing was bad news."

Her ex-boyfriend. Dr. Fein had jotted the name in his notes. He sighed, thinking about how often people were in denial and didn't see the obvious error of their ways until it was too late.

"And you agreed to do this?"

Lila buried her face, pink from crying, in her hands. Her dark hair fell over her cheeks, brushing her shoulders. When she looked up, her desperate expression had transformed to self-derision. "Stupid, wasn't it? I never thought I'd be dumb enough to get involved in something like this. But when they told me how much they'd pay me . . . I guess I just didn't think. I needed the money so much."

Dr. Fein nodded and glanced surreptitiously at the wall clock hanging behind Lila. Ten more minutes. He knew this wouldn't be solved in the time they had left but wanted to bring things to enough closure to satisfy Lila until the following week.

"Anyway," Lila said, giving her runny nose a backhanded sweep. "I did what they asked. I put the suitcase in this locker at a bus station and mailed the key to a PO box. But I'm scared now. I think these people are watching me."

"Why?"

"How the hell should I know?" Lila's eyes reminded him of a wild animal stuck in a trap. "Maybe they think I'm going to tell someone!"

"No," Dr. Fein said, keeping his voice low and even. "I meant, what evidence do you have that someone's watching you?"

"Evidence?" Lila sounded as if she'd never heard the word before. "I've been followed. The last three days. They've followed me home from work." She paused and sniffled before adding, "Then they wait outside my house for hours. Like they're watching me. I'm afraid to go anywhere when I see them out there."

Dr. Fein nodded. "Are you sure?"

"Am I sure?" Lila's lips curled and he received the kind of look she'd have given a reeking pile of dog doo. "You don't believe me, do you? You think I'm crazy. Well, I'm not crazy, Dr. Fein. I'm not!"

She picked up her purse and pulled out her cell phone. "You want evidence, fine," she muttered. "Here!" Hitting a few buttons, she held up the phone to show him a photo. Dr. Fein scooted forward in his chair and reached out to draw the phone closer. He saw a black Escalade with a sparkling chrome grill parked along a leafy, residential curb.

"This is right outside my house," Lila said. The photo noted the date and time. Three days ago at 5:47 p.m. Lila clicked a button on the side to show him yet another photo of the vehicle, dated the following day, around the same time. She hit the button again—same Escalade, the next day, from a different angle. This one provided a rear view. There appeared to be a bright red decal on the back window, setting it apart from the no-doubt many black Escalades roaming the state of Maryland. The windows were darkly tinted. The license plate was a standard black-on-white type—not a "Save the Bay" or colorful "Farm Preservation" plate. He tried, without success, to read the tag number. The characters were too blurred to make out, but they didn't appear to be vanity plates.

"And you know for a fact this vehicle is connected to the people you . . . did business with?" Dr. Fein said.

Lila looked at the floor and shook her head. "I've never seen it before."

"Well," Dr. Fein said. "There could be other explanations."

"I do something that's probably illegal. Then this car turns up the next week—follows me home and sits outside my house for three days in a row. And you think there's no connection?" Lila looked incredulous. "I think they're watching me. Making sure I don't tell anybody, I guess."

The whole thing sounded absurd to Dr. Fein. Who had done this to Lila? Why would they do it? Why would they assume she'd tell anyone else? Surely it would only hurt her to do so. He wanted to ask all these questions, but time was running out.

"Are you sure this vehicle was following *you*? Maybe someone in the building where you work happens to know one of your neighbors."

She shook her head. "No. I just know it's them. I think . . . I think my life may be in danger."

Dr. Fein shifted slightly in his seat, tensed and ready to rise and show Lila to the door. His next client would be waiting. "If you feel that way, maybe you should contact the police?"

"After what I've done?" Lila gave him a look that expressed a low opinion of Dr. Fein's IQ. He could feel himself flush, realizing his gaffe. "They've paid me way too much to make what I've done legal. Now I'm supposed to go to the cops for protection? And say what? That a bunch of criminals I did a job for are watching me? I mean, isn't that why they're watching me? Because they think maybe I'll tell the cops?!"

Dr. Fein had no idea why the people who'd paid Lila would want to watch her and found her reasoning about the matter to be confused and twisted. Even so, as her voice rose with each derisive comment, he could feel his embarrassment and discomfort rise with it. He felt as if she was scolding him, the way his ex-wife did toward the end of their marriage.

"I can see your dilemma," he said. "I confess, I'm not sure what to suggest. You live alone, don't you?"

"Yes." The word came out as a sob. "Now I do."

Dr. Fein nodded. Mickey had left Lila several months ago. She hadn't dwelled on the topic, but he could tell it still tugged at her consciousness.

"Perhaps you should consider staying with a friend or relative if you feel scared," he said, trying hard to stay seated. The minute hand had inched past the appointment's ending time.

"I have no relatives. There's no place I can stay." Lila raked her hair back, and it fell like a dark curtain framing her perfect oval face.

"I'm afraid our time is up." Dr. Fein rose—giving Lila her cue to stand, also—and he placed a reassuring hand on her arm as he escorted her to the door. Lila paused and gave him a damp-eyed, beseeching look. Her eyes were an incredibly dark blue—indigo, really. Dr. Fein resisted the urge to touch Lila's cheek.

"Try not to worry," he said. "I'm sure you'll be all right."

▗ ▗ ▗

After twenty years as a therapist, Dr. Fein had observed that female patients often jumped to conclusions, read too much into situations, and were swayed more by wayward and unpredictable emotions than by reason. Dr. Fein had learned to tolerate these traits in female patients, as he'd learned to tolerate them in his wife. That is to say, his ex-wife.

Despite the somewhat bizarre, even ludicrous, nature of Lila's tale, Dr. Fein couldn't help but worry. Whether Lila had bungled her way into becoming a runner for a drug cartel or was simply nuts, she believed herself to be in danger. That was a fact. And if she felt scared, she might do any number of crazy things.

Dr. Fein knew this all too well. He had ignored similar warning signs in another female patient, Jenny Mahoney. One who, in retrospect, he realized he should have monitored more closely.

He had tried with Jenny. Tried to explain that she needed to curb her irrational impulses and focus on how to make the best of a bad situation with her parents. Tried to explain that homosexuality was a difficult concept for them to accept. In point of fact, it was a difficult concept for Dr. Fein to accept, too. Jenny was a beautiful, young woman, with wavy blonde locks that flowed gracefully down her back. She had light-green eyes and a peaches-and-cream complexion. Dr. Fein knew that the field of psychiatry no longer considered homosexuality an aberration, but he found it (secretly, for he would never say so outright) a shame that such loveliness was being wasted in another woman's arms.

Jenny was dead now, exactly three months ago to the day. Suicide by pills and carbon monoxide poisoning. Dr. Fein didn't like to dwell on his mistakes—it made no sense to dwell on things you couldn't change—but that mistake . . . well, it insisted on dwelling with him. The memories crept into his consciousness, like roaches creeping through a tenement wall. Each time Dr. Fein tried to squash one thought, more thoughts would appear to take its place.

The following week, Lila failed to appear for her scheduled appointment. Dr. Fein had warned her she would be charged for not showing up, but this was not the first thing to cross his mind when he didn't see her in the waiting area at the appointed hour.

His first thought was, what if she had been right?

Dr. Fein tried to reach Lila at her daytime phone, only to get voice mail. He tried her home number, too. The phone just rang. Dr. Fein listened to it ring on and on. He'd counted twenty-five rings when he hung up.

Not good, he thought.

That evening, after the last patients had unloaded their sorrows or shared their latest breakthroughs, Dr. Fein locked up his office and climbed into his silver Lexus.

The car was his pride and joy, and one of the few possessions he'd been able to salvage after the divorce. Sarah had done a thorough job of laying claim to most of their assets and gaining custody of the children, forcing him to pay the mortgage on what was now her house, along with three years of alimony, child support until the kids turned eighteen, and all the rest.

Dr. Fein fumed over the fact that this outcome had been driven by Sarah's quitting her job as an office manager for a law firm to "spend more time with the kids" and "be a real mother to them." So she'd said. Dr. Fein believed now that her ten-plus years outside the workforce had been part of a larger strategy. An exit strategy, in which she would end up with the house and kids and he would end up footing the bill.

Dr. Fein scowled as these thoughts revisited him, once again making him feel impotent and used. Why were men always paying for women's petty schemes? Sarah could go and throw away a job, extra income, benefits—all for the kids. Everyone would "ooh" and "ahh" over her and admire her motherly instincts. But if he did that—well, people would think he was insane. What kind of a man quits his job to be a house-husband? No real man. Not even by today's loose standards.

As he pulled into the lot of his favorite Chinese restaurant, Dr. Fein found himself mentally comparing Sarah to Lila. Now Lila (for all her irrational fears and impulses) was a woman he could respect to an extent. She wasn't looking for a meal ticket; she was earning her own keep. Her desperation for money may have driven her to make a foolish decision, but it was her own decision and, he had to admit, required pluck and nerve on her part.

Sarah would never have done such a thing. Sarah was too conventional—in every possible way—to get mixed up in such business. No, Sarah chose a time-honored and conventional way to get her money— by extracting it from her ex-husband.

Dr. Fein seated himself and ordered his usual chicken lo mein. He dined at this restaurant about once a week since moving into his apartment. He'd never been there with Sarah—he avoided all restaurants they'd frequented, hoping not to see her or deal with her unless it was absolutely essential. Yet despite these evasive maneuvers, he could often feel her invisible presence—like a ghost—across the table from him. He could even hear her voice. Her endless chatter, which had seemed to get more and more inconsequential the longer she'd been out of the workforce.

Even now Dr. Fein could feel Sarah's presence in the empty chair opposite him, hear that voice—that voice!—and he concentrated hard on tuning it out. Concentrated on exorcising the ghost. Replacing her, perhaps, with Lila. He thought of Lila and wondered what it would be like to have her in that seat, instead.

r   r   r

When he finished his dinner, Dr. Fein decided to call Lila once more. He pulled out the patient list he kept in his briefcase in case of emergencies and dialed her number.

The phone rang endlessly. Maybe he should run by her house, he thought. Just to make sure she was okay. He noted the address, then made his way to Route 29 and took it north toward Columbia.

Lila lived in an older section of Columbia, a well-manicured planned community. Her small house had a cramped rectangle of yard, but tall, leafy trees lined the road. Dr. Fein parked across the street, several feet up from the house—a spot with a good view of the front, flanked by trees. He sat for a moment, watching the place.

Evening had fallen, and the house was still—the entire neighborhood was still, as if no one lived there—as if he were on a vacant set for a television series about life in the suburbs.

As Dr. Fein pondered this, a light snapped on in Lila's house, emanating from the front window like a beacon. Lila marched into view talking on a cell phone. She appeared upset—waving her free hand about, her expression drawn, her brow furrowed. She wore a robe, loosely tied at the waist. As she walked, Dr. Fein could see flashes of black pubic hair or dark underwear—he wasn't sure which. One shoulder of the robe slipped off to reveal a black bra strap. Dr. Fein was still staring as Lila walked to the side of the window and drew the curtains shut.

Through the light-colored curtains, Dr. Fein could just make out Lila's silhouette as she paced about the living room. The light went out.

A few minutes later, a black Escalade pulled up in front. Two men climbed out, walked to the door, and knocked. The living room light came back on. Lila answered, and a conversation ensued. One of the men—the taller, thinner one—seemed to be edging his way inside. Dr. Fein couldn't read Lila's expression from where he sat. Eventually she appeared to relent and let them in.

The living room light went out.

Several seconds later, light came from another window facing the street—possibly a bedroom. Dr. Fein slipped out of the car and approached the house. He thought of calling again but decided against it. If the men were threatening Lila, she wouldn't be able to talk freely.

As he walked by the SUV, he checked the back window and saw a red decal with writing on it that he couldn't make out. He didn't stop to read it.

Dr. Fein crept toward the window where light filtered out from behind a blind. Suddenly the blind snapped up and one of the men stood in its place, looking out at the darkened yard. Dr. Fein pitched face-forward to the ground. His middle-aged body landed with a dull thud. He ventured a peek at the window, where the man, framed by shutters and light from the room, didn't seem to notice him. Dr. Fein realized the man was squinting, not looking his way at all. The light indoors was probably obscuring his view. In fact the man might simply have been looking at his own reflection.

Finally the man walked away from the window, leaving the blind up. Dr. Fein grunted as he rolled over and brushed off his grass-stained khakis. Creeping on hands and knees, he made his way to the window and crouched near it. Then he rose slowly, hugging the brick façade. Cautiously he craned his neck to peek inside the room.

The three of them were in her bedroom. The tall man, who had his back to the window, must have been doing all the talking because Lila just stood, nodding, her lips parted and her chin quivering. The shorter, stouter man leaned against the wall by the door, a smile plastered on his face and one of those silly-looking phones clipped to his ear—the kind that make you look like a robot. The tall man gestured broadly as Lila kept nodding, her indigo-eyed gaze riveted to the man's face.

The robe had slipped further off Lila's shoulder, revealing one cup of a lacy, black bra. When Lila finally tried to speak, the tall man grabbed the robe and ripped it off her, flinging it aside. Lila stood, shaking, in her bra and matching bikini panties. The man with the ear phone laughed and applauded, as if his friend had performed a magic trick.

Dr. Fein's mouth hung agape, allowing a gnat to fly in. He coughed and spit it out, then looked inside to see if anyone had noticed. Apparently no one had. Relief washed over him, but tension took its place as he thought that if anything more happened, he should call the police. Give an anonymous tip. But then they'd have his cell number. And how would he explain his lurking around outside a patient's house? A female patient, no less. What a field day Sarah would have with that. It was already hard enough to enforce his visitation with the kids. He could picture her painting him as a Peeping Tom. Then there was the licensing board to think about. Jesus. Dr. Fein cursed Lila's stupidity for getting involved with these men, even as he fretted over what they might do to her.

Fortunately the tall man merely said a few more things to Lila and abruptly turned and left, followed by his companion. Dr. Fein scuttled around the corner of the house until the two men appeared outside, crossed the yard, and sped away in the Escalade.

Dr. Fein ventured once again to the window. Lila, who'd apparently forgotten the blind was open, lay on the bed, face down, banging her fist against the mattress. Eventually she rolled onto her side and stretched out, facing the window. Her face was red and eyes puffy. She stared without apparent comprehension.

Dr. Fein was torn between wanting to comfort her, wanting to help, and wanting to steer clear of the whole business, for his own good. He stood arrested by the sight of her slim, young form in her underwear. Body so firm, skin so creamy. He couldn't tear his eyes away, and he drank in the image, impressing it in his memory.

He remembered then that he could take photos on his cell phone—a function he rarely used. He cursed himself for not remembering this before the men had left.

Lila's expression changed suddenly, and she scrambled off the bed. Dr. Fein dropped to a squat as she walked to the window, cupped a hand against the glass, and looked out at the street where the Escalade had been. Apparently she didn't notice Dr. Fein cowering nearby. Then she pulled the blind shut. But not before Dr. Fein had snapped several photos of her.

As he drove home, the memory of Lila's body made Dr. Fein's head reel. He was breathing so hard the windows were fogging as he pulled onto a quiet side street to park and get his bearings. Glancing around and seeing no one, he opened his phone and viewed the series of shots—not great on detail but good enough—of Lila's lithe, barely clad body. Before he knew it, his pants were unzipped, and he was fondling himself. As he clicked through the photos, fogging the windows all the more, he couldn't help thinking of Sarah's voice—reprimanding, reproachful, whining—but helpless to stop him. The satisfaction of this knowledge brought him to a climax that left him astonished and gasping.

▗ ▗ ▗

"They say it wasn't there! And they want all the money back."

Dr. Fein had called Lila the next day. After assuring her it wasn't about payment for the missed appointment (though he normally would have insisted she pay in full), he asked whether she was all right.

What followed was a lengthy, tearful account. Parts of it he already knew, parts he could guess, but some details came as a complete surprise, including the fact that the suitcase had somehow gotten into the wrong hands and the people who'd hired Lila to make the delivery now wanted back the money they'd paid her.

"Then pay them." Dr. Fein tried, without complete success, to keep a note of irritation out of his voice.

She gulped loudly enough to be audible through the line. "It's not that simple. Most of the money . . . well, it's gone."

"How much money is that?"

"Twenty thousand dollars."

"How could you possibly—?" Dr. Fein cut himself off. The note of irritation threatened to flare into anger, disgust and disbelief.

"There were old debts. Plus . . ."

The line went quiet. Dr. Fein counted slowly to ten, then kept going, instead of screaming "What!?" as he might have done otherwise.

A deep, shuddering breath came from the other end. Wait for it, he thought.

"I gambled a lot of it," she said. "A whole lot of it . . ."

Dr. Fein fell back in his chair, and his eyes rolled skyward as Lila told him about her visits to the Laurel racetrack, where she couldn't resist playing the ponies. She'd win a small, safe bet and gain the courage to try something bigger, riskier—only to see her money slip away. She kept going back, tried several times to recoup her losses by placing more bets. Of course she lost more than she won. In the end, the money that didn't go toward her debts was frittered away at the track.

Dr. Fein despised gambling. Lila might as well have flushed her money down the toilet.

"I'm scared, Dr. Fein." Lila's voice quavered over the line. "If I don't pay them back, they'll . . . they'll kill me. Or worse." Her voice broke upon uttering the last two words.

Dr. Fein could feel pain run like a thread being pulled between his temples. He massaged his forehead and tried to think.

"What am I going to do, Dr. Fein? I don't know what to do." Lila moaned. "I don't have their twenty thousand dollars. I have nothing of that value to sell. No one will lend me the money. I rent my house, I have no collateral, and these people . . . well, they don't exactly take credit cards, do they? I just don't know—"

"Lila," Dr. Fein interrupted, in a soft, but firm voice. He continued to knead his forehead. "Hold on for a moment while I think."

"But I'm scared. What am I supposed to do?" Lila's voice took on a whiny edge. Then she started babbling. "I could run away, but I don't know where to go that they won't find me. I have to do something. Maybe I should buy a gun. I can't afford a bodyguard, and I have to protect myself. But I . . . I just don't know. Could I really shoot someone if I had to? Maybe, maybe not. I'm just—oh, God! I just could *kick* myself for letting this happen. I just could—"

"Lila!" Dr. Fein barked as a surge in the pain seared through his forehead. His imperative tone had the desired effect this time. "Lila," he continued, more quietly. "Please just let me think for a moment."

After half a minute of silence, Lila said in a halting voice, "Dr. Fein? Are you still there?"

"I'm still here, Lila." Dr. Fein could feel the pain subside. "Can I call you back in ten minutes?"

"Oh—okay." Lila sounded hurt, like she didn't believe him.

He started to put the receiver down but heard her faint, childlike voice—like a toddler's whimper—calling his name before it hit the cradle. Bringing it up to his ear again, he said, "Yes, Lila?"

"Just ten minutes, right?"

 ⌐ ⌐ ⌐

Dr. Fein started his ten minutes thinking of Lila's body, recalling the powerful urges he'd had the night before in his car. Her voice—like her body, so helpless, so fragile—only deepened the intensity of his desire for her. He had promised to call her in ten minutes. Dr. Fein wanted to think about how he could help Lila—but it was impossible with images of her, half-naked, giggling, pleading, sighing with pleasure, images that appeared one after another, rolling around in his head like a kaleidoscope. He finally gave in and, with a nervous glance at the clock, he locked his office door, grabbed a box of tissues, and indulged himself in the fastest self-gratification session he could recall having since puberty.

When finished, he sat spent for a moment, feeling himself growing limp on his sticky palm. He absently fingered himself as he considered his proposal. Yes, he could get the money—after making the proper arrangements. He could have her sign something for his files—to cover his ass, because Lord knows, her mind and story could shift like the wind. He'd refer her to another therapist. And after that he'd be free to help her in any way possible. He would be free even to see her—if she wanted that. And if she were grateful enough, it was quite conceivable that she would agree to see him. Perhaps even welcome the chance to do so.

After all, twenty grand could buy a whole lot of gratitude.

 ⌐ ⌐ ⌐

Dr. Fein proposed his solution. Lila was wary of taking his money but ultimately agreed. He e-mailed her the termination letter, which she signed and returned to him.

They arranged to meet at a small park, about a forty-minute drive from his office. He would bring the cash in an old briefcase. Dr. Fein had it wired to him from an account he kept in Paraguay—an account he'd managed to keep secret from Sarah and her grasping lawyer.

Dr. Fein picked up the cash at a Western Union office. He carried the briefcase to his Lexus and set it on the passenger's seat. He smiled and started the car. With the money he gave her, she'd be free again. Or, to be more precise, in debt to him, not those ruthless thugs. Her debt to him would be one of gratitude. And he would never hold that over her, use it to hurt her.

He wondered if she would be free for dinner that night. Maybe Saturday.

*   *   *

As he drove to the park, Dr. Fein listened to an oldies station on the radio. He loved oldies. Sarah always called him "an old fart" and couldn't understand why he refused to listen to more contemporary music. But the old music reminded Dr. Fein of better times. A time when the world seemed nicer. The rules about everything were clearer, better defined then. Today the rules had been thrown out, and no one knew how to act, what to do. He knew that from listening to his patients.

Sarah's taunting words came back to him as he hummed along to the Lovin' Spoonful. *How can you listen to this all the time? Could we please change the station just this once?* He could almost picture her beside him, whining and pouting—except that the briefcase was there, which made him think of Lila. Lila, smiling, perhaps even hugging him with joy after he gave it to her.

The thought of her breasts pressed against his body made Dr. Fein grin from ear to ear.

Dr. Fein parked the silver Lexus, grabbed the briefcase, and walked over a grassy knoll toward a bench near a stand of trees by a lake. It was early afternoon, and the park looked deserted. Dr. Fein hiked down the gentle slope. The day wasn't overly warm, but he could feel sweat collect under his arms, dampening his shirt. Dr. Fein wasn't in bad shape for a man in his early fifties, but his breath came hard and fast, as if he'd been running a sprint instead of strolling down a hill. He was surprised at how winded he felt by the time he'd reached the bench. He'd seen only one car in the lot—an old Toyota that he assumed was Lila's. But Lila wasn't waiting for him.

The bench was empty. Dr. Fein wiped his brow and took a seat, placing the briefcase on his lap.

Glancing around him, Dr. Fein wondered if anyone he knew would see him. Not likely, he thought, but not impossible, either. He hoped Lila would get there soon.

Dr. Fein watched a pair of ducks paddling across the lake. He'd heard mallards mated for life. He couldn't imagine such a thing. Spending the rest of his life with Sarah would have been unbearable.

Lila, on the other hand . . . Dr. Fein drifted into a reverie, imagining Lila cuddling naked beside him in bed. Her head on his shoulder as he stroked her hair and whispered, "It's okay. I'm here now."

The ducks had just reached the shore when the back of his skull exploded with pain and everything went black.

▗ ▗ ▗

The first thing Dr. Fein noticed when he opened his eyes were trees. He was seated on a bare patch of dirt surrounded by trees, with his legs slightly parted and extended before him. Pain radiated in waves from the back of his head. Blinking, he tried to get his bearings.

The terrain was hilly. He was on a slope facing uphill. His hands were tied behind him, digging into his back. And something propped him up from behind. As he twisted to glance over his shoulder, his hands scraped against a hard surface—a boulder, as it turned out. A boulder the size of a VW bug. Dr. Fein didn't think he was in the park anymore.

He froze at the sound of footsteps.

Someone trudged up the slope behind him. More than one person. Dr. Fein's heart raced. In vain he tried to free his hands from whatever was restraining them. His head pounded as he persisted in his fruitless efforts. He finally stopped, gasping for breath.

A man chuckled.

Dr. Fein looked toward the sound and, several feet to his right, saw the two men who'd been to see Lila. Both of them were smiling, but neither looked friendly.

Dr. Fein tried to ignore the pain screaming through his skull. He licked his dry lips, cleared his throat, and said, "What's going on here?" with all the authority he could muster.

He realized as he said it how preposterous the question must sound. A demand for an explanation of what was happening would sound ludicrous, he thought, coming from a man sitting in the dirt with his hands bound behind his back. Apparently the two men agreed, for their smiles broadened, and they started laughing. And their laughter was no friendlier than their smiles.

Dr. Fein felt an icy ball of fear congeal in his stomach. Had the men followed Lila to the park? "Where's Lila?" he demanded. "What have you done to her?"

His questions only made the men laugh harder. One of them wiped tears from his eyes, he was laughing so hard.

Dr. Fein fought pain and confusion to make sense of the insane situation. They must have followed Lila. How else would they have found him?

"You have your money," Dr. Fein said. "What more do you want? And where's Lila?"

The men stopped laughing and merely looked at him. The short, stout one frowned. In fact, he started to look angry. The taller man just stared at him with faint disgust, as one might at a maggot.

No one spoke. Dr. Fein's chest heaved with the effort of breathing. He tried to scramble to his feet, but it was difficult facing uphill and with his hands tied. Dr. Fein braced himself against the boulder and tried to inch his way up, only to have the tall man saunter over and, with a sideways kick, sweep his feet out from under him, letting him land on his ass with a jarring thump.

Dr. Fein could feel his face redden with rage and frustration. His breathing was labored now, his head felt ready to explode. He sat gasping in the dirt, the tall man towering over him. Looking up, Dr. Fein wailed in anguish, "What is it? What the hell do you want?"

A moment of nothing but Dr. Fein's breathing followed. Then the shorter man said, "It's not what *we* want."

More footsteps. Dr. Fein's guts twisted with anxiety. The briefcase hit the ground a few feet from him. He turned to see who had thrown it and couldn't believe his eyes.

It was Jenny Mahoney.

Dr. Fein shook his head, as if to clear his vision. He was hallucinating. That crack on the head must have done it. Or maybe the men had drugged him. But he looked again, and there was no denying it. She looked a little thinner, but the wavy, blonde hair, the green eyes, even a peasant blouse he recognized. Jenny Mahoney was standing right there, her arms crossed, her lips curved in a slight, triumphant smile.

"Jenny?" Dr. Fein croaked. "I thought you were dead."

In response she walked up and kicked him squarely in the groin.

The pain was so intense, it took Dr. Fein's breath away. He doubled over choking, then threw up the remains of his lunch.

As he tried to recover his wind, Jenny crouched beside him, placing her lips to his ear so they brushed against it as she whispered, "You goddamned bastard. You killed me. You made me feel worthless. You *killed* me."

Dr. Fein spat bile from his mouth. "What are you talking about?" He stared at Jenny. "Where's Lila?"

Jenny rose and looked down at him with scorn. "Don't worry. We've taken care of her."

"What do you mean? Where is she? What do you want?"

"An apology," she said.

"Huh?"

"I want to hear you apologize for killing me."

This is insane, he thought. "How can I apologize for killing you when you're clearly not dead?"

"Would you believe that I've come back from the dead to haunt you?" Jenny threw her head back and laughed.

"How stupid can you be, old man?" The tall fellow spoke. "Obviously she's not Jenny."

"Ohhhhh." Jenny—or the woman who claimed to be Jenny—shot him a look to match her protracted moan. "And I was having so much fun, fucking with his head." She put a hand on her hip and looked at Dr. Fein. "No, I'm not Jenny. I'm her sister. And I was in the SUV that night you were peeping into your own patient's bedroom."

"We followed *you* there that night," the shorter man said. "We'd been following you for a while. And our girl here was in the SUV, telling us what you were up to, lurking outside the window like a perv. Naughty, naughty, doctor."

My God, Dr. Fein thought. Jenny had mentioned a sister, close to her age. He could see now that, though similar in appearance, the girl was definitely thinner, her features slightly different. The eyebrows a bit darker—she must have highlighted her hair to match Jenny's. In any case, he finally had a rational explanation. And an enraged relative to placate.

"Is this blackmail?" he said, thinking of how photos of his escapades outside Lila's house could ruin him. "You have my money. What more do you want?"

"I told you, doctor." The woman fixed a cool gaze on him. "I want an apology for what you did to my sister."

"Okay, I'm sorry," he blurted. "I'm really, really sorry. I should have paid more attention to Jenny. I should have been more responsive to her needs."

"What you should've done," Jenny's sister held up a didactic finger, "is not make her feel like a freak because she was a lesbian."

"I never . . . I didn't . . ." he sputtered.

"Now, now, *Doc*-tor Fein," she said with exaggerated formality. "You did. You made it pretty clear that you didn't approve of her sexual orientation. From what she told me, you didn't take her very seriously as a person at all. Like you don't take women seriously at all."

"No, no!" Dr. Fein's protests grew louder, and he could feel his face redden. "That's not true."

"Oh, but it is. In fact," she continued, her voice getting louder as she spoke. "You went so far as to suggest her lesbianism might be the cause of her depression and other problems."

"I just . . . thought it was a shame." He hung his head. "She was so beautiful. Like you."

The woman frowned, and a deep line formed between her eyebrows. "Nice try, doc, but no dice. No one here is buying. Especially her lover."

"C'mon over, sis," the shorter man said with a wicked grin to someone Dr. Fein couldn't see. "Say hello."

"Her lover . . ." Dr. Fein's voice was faint.

He heard the click of the gun being cocked before he felt the barrel against his right temple. "That's right, Dr. Fein. I was Jenny's lover."

The voice was unusually cool and steely, but he knew it all too well. Dr. Fein glanced toward the woman who had quietly taken her place beside him. "You can't be serious," he rasped, feeling ready to vomit again.

"I'd say it's only fair. An eye for an eye. A life for a life. You understand."

"Please . . ." he whispered. "Don't."

"Plus a little monetary compensation from you—like an informal wrongful death settlement."

"I . . . don't believe it," he mumbled.

"I know you don't, Dr. Fein," she said in a mocking tone. "You simply couldn't imagine it, could you? That you might be dealing with a woman who thinks. But you're a believer now, aren't you, Dr. Fein? Aren't you?"

Lila gave him a cold smile before she pulled the trigger. And in the moment before the bullet hit his brain, Dr. Morris Fein's head was filled with the sound of Sarah's voice, berating him once again.

Debbi Mack has worked as an attorney, a news wire reporter, and a reference librarian with the Federal Trade Commission. She has published one novel, Identity Crisis, *a hard-boiled mystery featuring female lawyer Sam McRae in a complex case of murder and identity theft. Her short story "Deadly Detour" appeared in the first Chesapeake Crimes mystery anthology. Debbi currently works as a freelance writer/researcher, writes crime fiction, and raises money for research to cure dystonia (a rare movement disorder). A native of Queens, New York, Debbi, her husband, and their family of three cats live in Columbia, Maryland.*

BOOKWORM

by G.M. Malliet

If the book hadn't been facing the wrong way out, he might never have noticed it, or the photo. The title was familiar because of all the publicity the book had received. He was an avid reader, as his mother had been, and devoured every *Washington Post* book review.

The name he'd never have recognized. He'd never known her name, it hadn't mattered. But the face . . . hard to forget that face. Before. Or after.

He smiled, picking up the thick hardback for a closer look. It struck him so funny he laughed aloud, causing other browsers to glance up and smile at him, tentatively. It was just days before Christmas, and the downtown Borders was crowded. Then he saw their smiles falter. He was used to that, or should have been. Even working his solitary job as a night watchman, he couldn't avoid people entirely.

A voice from behind him asked, "Something funny?"

He turned and saw a middle-aged woman with blonde hair dyed the color of shredded wheat and of about the same texture. She wore a blue store clerk's apron.

"Oh," she said, noticing the book he was holding. There were rows and rows of it, jacketed in heavy, shiny, black paper. The four letters of the title—*ACID*—and the author's name screamed against the black in a thick, embossed font, dripping scarlet red. More copies were stacked on a nearby table where an overhead sign said, "Best Sellers."

"Jeanne Robinson's latest," the clerk told him. "Just got it in yesterday. From what I hear, it's nothing to laugh about, though." She picked up a copy and read aloud from the starred reviews set beneath the author photo. "'A complete departure for the Queen of Romance.' 'A dark, bleak, terrifying foray into the mind of a serial killer and his victim.' 'Read this one with the lights on.'"

The clerk looked at him expectantly. Even if Cliff had felt like talking with this old bag with the fried hair, how to explain he was laughing because he knew the photo was at least ten years out of date? A *recent* photo of this Jeanne Robinson would have shown her the way he'd left her.

He shrugged, mumbled what might have been, "Thank you," and shouldered away abruptly. He carried the book to the checkout counter, paying with his credit card.

Once outside the store, he called in sick to his supervisor. He started reading *Acid* as he waited for the Metro that would carry him toward the Maryland line and the old brick row house he'd inherited from his mother.

He spent all that afternoon and night reading, barely stopping for a sandwich dinner, becoming more enraged with each chapter.

He'd warned her, this—who was it?—this *Jeanne* person: If she ever told anyone, he'd find her and make her even sorrier. So what does she do? She writes a book and tells the world. Not just that, but she fills the book with insults and lies. "Pathetic," she wrote. "Psychotic," she called him. "Deformed." Worst of all, "Impotent." *Impotent?*

He should have killed her. She'd managed to pull off his mask, but he'd spared her anyway, the ungrateful—He should have killed them all. But part of their punishment was that they should live, so scarred and damaged no one would ever want them.

The ones who'd died had been accidents.

Accidents. So he'd gotten a little overenthusiastic. So what? She'd gotten it all wrong, the stupid—

There was one consolation. A blind woman couldn't see him *now*, could she?

Closing the book, Cliff rose from the couch and went to his computer on the partners desk by the window, the desk he'd once shared with his mother. He used to do his homework while she read a book or the book reviews. He was glad she was gone so he could have the desk to himself.

He was glad she was gone for a lot of reasons.

The dust jacket copy only said this Jeanne Robinson lived "in the Chesapeake Bay region." Guess she thought she was so important she had to be vague about her whereabouts, otherwise hysterical autograph seekers might beat down her door. But his search engine turned up a phone interview she'd done six months ago for her hometown newspaper. The "reclusive Jeanne Robinson, our most famous resident" lived in some place in Maryland called Braemer's Point.

It was ridiculously easy. He pinpointed Braemer's Point on an online map, finding an isolated dot on the Eastern Shore. He searched awhile longer and learned it had a population of 927, give or take a few.

927, soon to be 926.

It shouldn't be too hard to find a woman like that in a town that size. He'd just ask someone where the freak lived, the one with no face.

The thought cheered him so much he could finally sleep. The next day, he'd pack what he called his hunting tools, drive east from D.C., and complete her punishment. This time, she'd learn.

⌐ ⌐ ⌐

"You really think this will work?"

Detective Denton hadn't a clue.

"I do," he said.

She turned in the direction of his voice, the small, slender woman with the unbearable scars. The detective guessed it was as well she couldn't see him, except as a moving collage of blurs and shadows—it was impossible for him not to avert his eyes, harder still to hide the involuntary jolt of revulsion. No matter how often he'd seen her over the years, working the case that wouldn't let him go, it was still a shock. What the bastard hadn't accomplished with a knife, he'd finished with the acid. Her features were distorted, the muscles atrophied into a grimace, despite repeated operations.

Many of her fellow victims had died from shock, exposure, blood loss. Or pure fright. What steel-spined strength of mind and body had allowed Jeanne to survive, Denton couldn't begin to guess. But he liked to think he'd created a little hope in her mind now. Not *too* much, in case this gamble didn't work.

Thank God the rest of the task force had agreed to the gamble. And let him lead this operation—despite that he now stood outside his jurisdiction, 100 miles away from the D.C. suburb where Jeanne used to live. Where she was attacked.

The whole world was reading this book of hers, and her photo—that old publicity head shot that had appeared on all her books for the past ten years—was in all the major papers, thanks to a major push from her publisher. If all this attention turned her book into a best seller—well, a pile of money was something she'd get out of it, at least.

Meanwhile, all they could do was wait here in her house. Hope this maniac found the book, read it, reacted to it. Denton knew it was a long shot. But the only clue they had after a dozen cases was a fresh, clean copy of a newspaper's book review section left behind at the scene of every crime. No fingerprints or DNA, of course. The guy was meticulous as a cat. Also incapable of sexual assault, according to the ones who'd survived.

Denton's private code name for this freak was Bookworm.

Books. Jeanne had made her start as a romance novelist, of all things. She'd been out for a walk, plotting her latest bodice ripper, when the guy had grabbed her. She was the only witness who'd seen his face, and he'd left her with only her verbal powers to describe him to the police sketch artist.

At the time of the attack she'd been little known. None of the freak's other victims had been authors or had anything else in common—Jeanne's had been a random attack like the rest. Denton was sure of it.

She was telling him now about how her blindness had forced her to talk her books into a tape recorder for transcription by someone in New York. It was a story he'd heard before, but she seemed to find strange comfort in the repeating, so he was glad to listen again.

"And it was then I really started to sell," she said, wrapping up. "It turned out it was easier for me to invent the spoken than the written word. I should be grateful to him, eh?" A sound, something like a cough of amusement. "Can't think why I'm not," she said.

"You never thought of writing about crime before? Judging by the way *Acid* has taken off . . ."

"Morbid curiosity. Rubberneckers, all of them, 'my reading public.' Can Jeanne Robinson pull it off?"

"I think you're wrong, you know."

She nodded, whether in agreement or irritation, he wasn't sure.

"Okay," she said at last. "Maybe I'm wrong about the morbid part. No one except the police and my two helpers know what happened to me. Not even my agent, my editor. They accept that I'm a recluse, a regular J.D. Salinger. I wasn't famous when—this—happened." She made a sweeping gesture, one hand fanning across her face. "No one makes the connection between Jeanne Robinson and some poor woman who was attacked."

"I can only guess how difficult this has been to write about, but—"

She sighed, and a silence drew out in the small, stone-walled room. He'd lit a fire against the cold rain that had chilled the day earlier; the flames now shimmered against the old-fashioned furniture, her collection of artwork. A cup of tea sat on the table by her chair. He guessed she was framing her thoughts, editing in advance of speech. It seemed to be a habit of hers.

"Romance was my means of escape. I never knew in those early days how much I would need escape one day. Until escape wasn't working any more. It was time to write about . . . what happened, even in fiction form. What Capote called a non-fiction novel, although no one knows that's what it is. Except *him*, we hope." She paused. "I guess I hoped it would be cathartic."

"Was it?" He wanted the answer to be yes. It was he, after all, who had talked her into it. She should have called the book *Gamble*.

Again she turned toward him, a middle-aged man, bald, unremarkable in every way except, perhaps, for his tenacity. When this case had started, he reflected wryly, he'd had hair. Now he was looking at retirement and there was no way he could leave with this failure gnawing at his mind. He'd called in every favor, from every direction, every chance acquaintance and long-term friend, to lead this operation and try to draw this guy out of his cave.

She said nothing for so long he thought she wouldn't answer.

"Nothing will ever make the memories go away. If anything, it reinforced them, made me dwell on every detail. Worse was letting him live inside my *brain* while I wrote the book—you understand what I mean? Still, if it catches him . . . If it means he's sentenced, condemned as I am . . ."

"We're ready for him," he said. "We'll get him."

She couldn't read expressions, either, thank God, or she'd see the doubt in his.

"Your tea is getting cold," he told her. "Can I get you some more?" Her helpers had been told to stay away until told otherwise. But someone had first made her some tea.

She shook her head.

"Write what you know," she said, her voice now a harsh whisper. "Isn't that the standard advice given to writers? So that's what I did in *Acid*. I described him to the last pore on his face, the stench of his sweat. He was a real Ted Bundy, you know. Until he smiled. Only then did you see the creature beneath. That deformity of the jaw, could it really turn him into something subhuman, completely lacking compassion?"

"It's what the profilers thought, of course," Denton said. "He needed to destroy beauty, particularly a woman's, because women had always rejected him. Starting with his mother. Et cetera. Blah-de-blah. They always say that. But I don't think anyone knows. There is no explaining these guys. His—"

The ring of his cell phone broke the quiet of the remote, tree-shrouded house—the refuge where Jeanne had retreated after her last surgery. He listened a long time to the voice on the other end. He turned to her, his voice jubilant.

"They think they've got him!"

Denton listened intently, then punched the air like a golfer after a hole in one, allowing himself a little two-step of pure pleasure. "We've got him!" he amended. He heard the squeak of her chair as she leaned forward, her body language radiating impatience. Denton was again moved to pity: She'd waited years to hear this.

"He wasted no time," he relayed. "My men nabbed him after he broke into the grounds. He was crawling toward the house, armed to the teeth—knives, ropes, acid, the whole . . ." He stopped as he saw her flinch from the memory. "I'm sorry. But you flushed him out, all right—he matches your description perfectly. It turns out he bought your book just yesterday—the receipt was still in his wallet. He must have driven up here like a demon."

And God knows, he must be a speed reader, too, Denton thought; *that book weighed in at four pounds.*

"We've got him," he repeated. "Motive. Intent. And hauling that nasty bag of equipment behind him."

And when I'm done with him, Denton thought, *we'll have a confession, too.*

"What do you want to bet there's some DNA on his . . . belongings . . . that he couldn't scrub away?" Denton went on. He knew he was grinning like an idiot, but he couldn't help it. "His name is Cliff Basie, according to his ID. That name mean anything to you?"

She shook her head. "No." There was a giddy lilt to her voice, a tone he'd never heard before. He imagined he was hearing for the first time the young woman who had been Jeanne.

"Let's hope," she said, "*Acid* turns out to be a real Cliffhanger."

He laughed.

"Let's hope," he said.

"You haven't forgotten?" she asked.

He hesitated only a moment, then spoke again into the phone.

"Bring him in. I know. I *know*. I don't need any lessons in procedure from you, sergeant, thanks anyway. I said bring him in."

It was the least he could do, and what was the harm? She'd waited so long. She wanted to "see" him face-to-face, she'd said. She'd made Denton promise: If they caught him, she could "have a few choice words," as she put it, before they hauled him off.

A knock at the door, and Sergeant Crew came in, a manacled Bookworm in tow. She'd been dead right in her description, which might have been taken from chapter one of an FBI manual on serial killers. Youngish, handsome, but with the closed-down look of a loner. He was older now, of course. But then—

"Tell the sergeant to step back." When Denton hesitated, she insisted. "Stop *worrying*. He can't hurt me now," she said.

Denton nodded; Crew stepped away.

Years later, Denton would still be asking himself if he knew, at least on some level, what Jeanne was up to. He was never sure.

Maybe he didn't care.

Mostly he just remembered the Bookworm's scream as she threw the cup of acid.

———

G.M. Malliet's Death of a Cozy Writer, *previously a Malice Domestic Grant winner, won the Agatha Award for Best First Novel of 2008. It has also been nominated for 2009 Anthony, David, and Macavity awards and a Left Coast Crime Award for best police procedural. It won an IPPY Silver Medal in the Mystery/Suspense/Thriller category.* Kirkus Reviews *named it one of the best books of 2008. The second book in the St. Just series is* Death and the Lit Chick *(April 2009) and the third is* Death at the Alma Mater *(January 2010). Malliet and her husband live in Virginia. Visit her at <www.gmmalliet.com>.*

PLEASE DISPOSE OF PROPERLY

by Ann McMillan

When my husband left me, he locked me out of my life. That was when I discovered I hadn't really been a resident but a visitor there, all along.

I came home from tennis at the club to find ten $100 bills in an envelope on the kitchen counter, with a note saying that the mortgage and utilities were paid, and I was to make that last for the month. Also in the envelope was a business card engraved *Joseph A. Lyle, Esq., Attorney-at-Law.*

A series of images flooded my mind: Eric caught with his hand in the till, literally—my handsome husband trying to free his fingers from an old-fashioned cash register; Eric on a plane, cash-stuffed briefcase clutched between his knees; Eric in some dusty south-of-the-border town with no cell phone service . . .

I grabbed the phone and punched in Eric's mobile number. After a few rings, it went to voice mail. I hesitated to call him at work—maybe they didn't know he was gone and my call would be the tip-off. But my mind worked slower than my fingers. Eric's secretary answered: "I'm sorry, Mrs. Donovan, he's out of the office." *Out of the office?* That could mean anything. I picked up the lawyer's business card and tried that number. It was answered on the second ring by Joseph A. Lyle himself.

"It's Elise Donovan—Eric Donovan's wife. I . . . Is Eric all right?"

"He's fine." Joseph A. Lyle sounded slightly surprised.

He probably didn't get that question often. He was a divorce attorney, he told me. Eric had instituted divorce proceedings. "Any questions, any messages you have for Eric should be relayed through us," he told me. *Us?* I pictured a room full of expensively suited men answering phones, scribbling on notepads. Apparently the bad-news business paid well.

I thanked him and set down the phone, then grabbed the edge of the counter and shut my eyes, waiting for the room to stop its crazy spinning. When I opened them, my gaze fell on the microwave's digital clock. It was after noon; I would have to hurry to pick up Danny at preschool. I rinsed my face and dried it with a dish towel, then ran out the door.

Danny didn't seem to notice Eric's absence that evening or my preoccupation. As soon as he was settled in bed, I searched the house. Eric's closet looked half-empty, but it was his business suits that were missing, not the beachwear I imagined him packing for an escape south.

Where had that notion, that Eric had been bilking his company, come from? My vision of Eric on the lam finally crumbled, giving way to the image of Eric living his successful-executive life as usual, only without me. Without everything that life entailed. Including our son.

Circling back to the kitchen, I upended the envelope and fanned out the bills. Was a thousand dollars enough for a month? I had no idea.

I plopped onto a barstool and sunk my head in my hands. Okay, "The mortgage and utilities are paid," his note had said, but what did that mean? I'd never paid a utility bill, never even looked at one, though Eric would sometimes wave them in the air to complain about the expense. I'd married Eric after my sophomore year in college. His parents paid for the condo we lived in up until five years ago, when we bought this house. Eric handled all the bills, the taxes . . .

I wiped away the tears that were stinging my eyes. Focus, Elise! *Utilities.* Electricity, gas, phone lines, stuff like that, right? What about the groundskeepers, the pool cleaners? They must send bills. Had Eric paid those guys ahead? If not, would they just not show up? Or would they show up and be mad because I couldn't pay them? The maid, Maria, I always left cash for, but Eric gave it to me. All those ten dollar bills would take a bite out of the thousand dollars. But what to do? Tell her not to come? It was always so hard to get in touch with her, even when she had a working phone. Tell her in person, and face those sad brown eyes?

What about the club? A country club membership didn't sound like a utility. Had he paid for that? If not, how would I find out? Would they turn me away at the gate? Escort me off the tennis courts with everyone staring, whispering?

What about Danny's preschool? Eric had signed Danny up for the McGregor School about a week after we found out I was pregnant. Danny had started there when he turned two-and-a-half, just two months ago. He'd barely made the deadline for potty training. He was still wearing pull-ups at night. He . . .

I began to sob.

r r r

Some time later, I raised my head. Eric kept receipts and checkbooks in the big antique desk in his study. I ran in and tried the drawers. The ones I could open held instruction manuals for electronics and appliances, stuff like that. The shallow drawer in the center and the deep one on the right side were locked. Eric kept them locked to keep Danny from getting into them. I tried to jimmy the locks with nail scissors—no luck.

I searched in vain for the laptop he'd bought a few weeks before. At the time I'd wondered why he wanted a personal laptop since he carried his work laptop with him everywhere. Now I knew: he'd been preparing for a quick exit.

I finally found the clunky, old desktop computer in the kitchen closet behind the bags of papers and cans awaiting recycling. I hoisted it onto the counter, plugged in various cords and cables, and turned it on. The screen came to life. Password-protected. Once again, I was locked out.

This time failure worked like an old-movie slap in the face. *Thanks; I needed that.* I jumped off the bar stool, determined to do something.

Out in the gardening shed, I searched for an appropriate tool for the job I had in mind. Chainsaw? I shuddered. Hammer? Too small. Ax? Perfect.

I carried the ax into Eric's study, lifted it over my head, and let the blade fall onto the polished executive desk. I'd never really liked tennis, but at least it had built up my shoulder muscles. After only a few repetitions, I could see into the two locked drawers. They were empty.

Sad. Eric had loved that desk. Oh well—as someone said, we all got problems.

⌐ ⌐ ⌐

For the next few days, I blundered about like someone robbed of her sense of touch. After an embarrassing encounter at Whole Foods proved to me that my Visa card no longer worked, I froze, unable to take any action that could not be handled with a small amount of cash. Still, I couldn't bring myself to call Joseph A. Lyle, Esq., with a list of questions for my husband. I would get my own lawyer, I told myself; have my people call his people. I even spent some time looking up attorneys in the Yellow Pages. But I didn't call any of them. I guess I believed, deep down, that if I didn't acknowledge what had happened, it wouldn't be real.

I kept Danny home from preschool—better that than have the coolly perfect headmistress call me in to her office to ask if there was a problem with the payment. Of course, she tracked me down. I answered the phone one morning to hear her upper-class purr: "Mrs. Donovan, this is Genevieve Carr from the McGregor School. How are you?"

Hearing her voice put me right back in her plushly carpeted office. Eric and I had met with her several times, the two of them aiming their charm at each other like guided missiles while I looked out the window at the children playing. She'd worn a different gray suit each time—pearl, slate, graphite—with heels and pantyhose that had an expensive sheen. Of course the school employed other people who actually touched the children.

Now she said she was concerned that Danny had missed several days of school. "We're just taking some time off," I told her, knowing how lame it sounded, and ended the call quickly. Thereafter, when she called, I let the phone go to voice mail. Danny didn't need to go back there, now that I was no longer playing tennis or lunching with the ladies whose husbands could help Eric get ahead.

╭ ╭ ╭

Despite my worries about money, it did feel like a vacation. Danny and I spent our days on the move, driving to distant parks where we wouldn't see anyone we knew, eating at fast-food restaurants with playgrounds. I hated being in the house, especially the kitchen. The brushed-steel appliances and granite countertops reflected my image in a flesh-colored blur, like an incomplete erasure. But it was there that I'd set up the computer, and there that I spent most of my time.

If only I could get into its workings, I thought, I could orient myself to this new world, find out what had and hadn't been paid and how far in advance, maybe get hold of a credit card number I could use. It killed me that I couldn't figure out the password. I'd seen on TV that security experts advise the use of meaningless numbers, but Eric surely was too confident of his own invulnerability to worry overmuch about such things. I tried Danny's birthday, the name of Eric's old dog. They didn't work. His mother's maiden name, the name of his prep school. No dice. His favorite golf resort, his brand of aftershave. Nothing. I would sit late into the night, coffee growing cold at my elbow, trying everything, trying nonsense, damning the "password invalid" message.

At last I admitted defeat. I couldn't bear to have that annoying machine in my presence another day. Through a series of phone calls to county offices, I discovered I could dispose of the computer for a small fee at the main county recycling center. It was all the way across the county, so I planned to make it an outing for Danny and me. I opened the back of the Escalade and heaved in the computer tower, the deep-backed monitor (so out-of-fashion, it was a wonder Eric had stood it so long), the keyboard and mouse, a printer, and a tangle of wires and cables. I packed water and juice and snacks and wipes and pull-ups and an extra set of clothes for Danny, as I always did when we would be away from the house for a while.

Just as we were heading out the door, the phone rang. It was Joseph A. Lyle, Esq. The McGregor School had reported some concerns about Danny, and Eric was preparing to claim custody.

It was a pretty drive past old Virginia farms and deep, tangled woods—what our exurban community's developers had mown down and covered over with tract mansions. Markers commemorating events from the Revolutionary and Civil wars appeared at regular intervals, whipping by too fast to be read. I called out to Danny to look at the cows. Soon this grew into a game in which he would ask me, "Is that a cow?" I would say yes, and he would say, "No, silly, that's a dog" or "lady" or "horse" or "mailbox." All the while I was thinking about Eric's wanting custody of Danny. Not rational, legalistic thoughts. Just: No. Not gonna happen.

I passed the entrance since the only sign I spotted said Cormier Regional Prison. The GPS reprimanded me. I turned around and, on the way back, noticed a smaller sign saying County Landfill. Visible from the road was a small, utilitarian building. Behind it stood dark green bins. No prison walls were in view. All right, I could drive up to that building, no problem. When I pulled up, a man stepped out. I told him I was bringing a computer to recycle. "In there?" I indicated the bins, with their triangular recycling logos. He shook his head and pointed further down the road.

I drove on slowly. A thick stand of pine trees stretched on either side of the road, hiding whatever lay beyond. I was nervous to be so near a prison and ashamed of being nervous. It wasn't maximum security, after all.

I asked Danny to help me spot a computer.

"Is that a computer?" he asked me, pointing to a tree.

"Yes!" I replied, picking up the game in its new version and thinking as I did so how much it would annoy Eric. After the first couple questions he would be telling Danny to stop, first good-humoredly, then not so much. Eric wanted custody? Why? So the McGregor School could take Danny and make him into another Eric?

Off to the right I saw heaps of dark brown mulch and a chipper. Beyond those, grass-covered hills rose unexpectedly from the flat ground. Metal cylinders, maybe a foot tall, stuck out from these hills at intervals. The landfill, I reasoned—those chimney-like cylinders would be venting gases. I passed a second sign for the prison pointing off to the left. Here coil-topped wire fencing, cloaked in places by the dense woods, rimmed the perimeter.

I drove straight on. Beyond the trees, encircled by them, was a big structure like a barn but without a front. Just past it, among scraggly pines, were more big green bins, trailers without their trucks, stacks of wooden pallets.

"Look, Mommy. Computers!"

Lined up in front of the three-sided building were at least a hundred computer monitors. Well, this must be the place.

I turned into the lot.

There were a half-dozen workmen in the building. Most wore orange jumpsuits. They turned and observed my approach. I rolled down the window and smiled at them. "Can you take my computer?" I asked.

One—the tallest—approached the car and smiled back. He had the worst teeth I had ever seen. "Sure," he said, nodding emphatically. "Open 'er up."

"Smiley" motioned a couple of the men to follow him around to the back of the Escalade. In the rearview mirror, I could see him gesturing and them nodding. I handed Danny a box of animal crackers to keep him distracted, or at least keep his mouth full, lest he comment on the bad teeth and dirty hair.

"It's $5, right?" I asked the friendly man, who had returned to stand near my window. "Oh, no, ma'am, no charge," he replied. "There used to be. Now we got somebody who can work on 'em, fix 'em up for resale, the good ones, anyway. Make some money for the county." He gestured toward the open-faced building and the men. I worried briefly about information that might still be on the computer—bank accounts, credit cards. Then I remembered I had no reason to care.

I had a vague sense of the car being weighed down as one of the men leaned in, bouncing up as he removed one heavy piece, tower or monitor, then the process repeating with the other piece, then some scrabbling as they scooped up the smaller items. Then the car sagged again, more than before, and a smell of unwashed body reached me. I realized—even as the tall man held my gaze—that one of the men had climbed into the back of the Escalade. I turned around. He was holding something concealed in his hand, very close to Danny's throat. If Danny had been frightened, had cried or called out, I would have lost it. But Danny was playing with his animal crackers, oblivious.

"Get out of the car. Don't try anything." The smiling man spoke those words, leaning close to the open window.

🐾 🐾 🐾

They didn't drug me or knock me out. I'm pretty sure I walked to take a seat on one of those wheely desk chairs, way in the back of the open-faced building, though I don't remember doing it. My daze cleared to the sound of voices. Both Danny and the Escalade were out of sight.

The men were talking, earnestly and without menace, except for the fact that they had Danny.

"Elise, we need you to do something for us." Smiley spoke slowly, the way Eric did when he explained something he thought I might not understand. "Danny's going to stay here with us until you come back with the money. No police."

I thought about this prohibition a moment. I felt strangely calm—or was it numb?

"Aren't you prisoners?" I asked.

"Trusties," another man piped up, glancing toward Smiley for his approval.

Smiley nodded. "And that feller there's a guard," he added, gesturing toward the farthest-away member of the group, whose back, I now noticed, was turned to the entire proceeding.

Then another question occurred to me. "How do you know our names?"

Smiley held up my purse. I'd left it on the car seat. So they had my cards: driver's license, health insurance, Social Security . . . Once again someone else held the keys to my life. But I kept cool. I wouldn't give them any excuse to hurt Danny.

Another man—better groomed than Smiley, with little, round-framed glasses—handed me a small piece of plastic. I looked, then stared. It was a Virginia driver's license, authentic-looking, with a blurry photo of a blond woman, Beverly Wirtz. Her address was an exclusive subdivision pretty much the clone of mine.

"You see?" Smiley asked eagerly. "We've been waiting for just the right person." Beverly Wirtz had more than a passing resemblance to me.

"Doc, here, made that driver's license and all the other stuff," Smiley told me. The bespectacled man nodded acknowledgment. "Look here. He took the mug shot from this picture that was on a computer someone dropped off." Smiley showed me a casual photo of a big family group at some outdoor event. The head of one of the women was cut out.

"It's quite amazing what people will leave on their computers," Doc said in a schoolteacher's voice. "I hope you cleaned out your hard drive." He was smiling, looking at me over his round-framed glasses. I suspected he'd already spotted me as the careless type.

"I couldn't. My husband locked me out." Why was I apologizing to these men?

Next Smiley gave me a list of bulleted instructions and a sheaf of printed documents. A half-dozen looked something like checks, only more institutional than the ones I was used to. He and Doc took me through each point with painstaking care. Then Smiley summed up: "All you got to do is show 'em these papers and withdraw the Wirtzes' cash."

At last they decided I was ready. Smiley gave a signal. A few moments later, the Escalade rolled into view. The man who'd taken Danny, whom I had smelled—Stinky, I'll call him—climbed out of the driver's seat, and the two of them walked me over to the car, not strong-arming me but ready to if necessary. The back seat was empty. They had kept Danny, his car seat, and the bag with the pull-ups, wipes, snacks, and toys.

"Please," I begged, "I'll do what you want. Just let me take Danny home. Please."

Smiley shook his head, serious now. "We ain't stupid."

I tried to convince him, but I knew he was right. If they let Danny leave with me, I would start driving and never stop, not until I crossed a major border. Canada. Mexico.

"Don't worry." Smiley was smiling again. "The kid will be fine. We reckon it'll take a few hours, is all. Just be sure you get back here before seven. They lock the gates at seven. And no cops."

I thought for a moment. "There's enough food and drink for him in the diaper bag. He's potty-trained, but . . ."

Smiley shot Stinky a glance. "I'll take care of it, boss," Stinky assured him, then turned back to me. "I got kids," he said.

They put me into the car, and I drove away, dry-eyed and determined to follow their instructions.

r r r

Later I wondered briefly why I had been so quick to fall in with the convicts' plans. But that wasn't really much of a mystery. I'd always lived according to other people's plans. I'd been raised and schooled to think that making a fuss and calling attention to oneself were simply not acceptable. Eric had picked up where my parents and teachers and other well-intentioned people had left off. He had come very close to making me a perfect wife, interchangeable with so many others. Interchangeable with Beverly Wirtz. But he'd walked away from the project. Had I failed, or had he just lost interest? If I had been a better wife, would Eric be here with me now? More importantly, would Danny?

I pulled into the parking lot of the first bank on the list, but I couldn't loosen my grip on the steering wheel. They would know I wasn't Beverly Wirtz. I would be caught, taken to jail . . . I wouldn't make it back in time. The police wouldn't believe me. Danny . . .

I forced myself to calm down. The bag with my tennis things was still in the seat behind me. I reached back and grabbed it, took out the visor and sunglasses, and put them on. As long as I got Danny back, I didn't care what happened next.

Cool as a seasoned crook, I strolled into the bank and took my place in line. I pretended to text on my cell phone so as to keep my head down. When I got to the window, I gave the fake driver's license and one of the check-like documents to the teller. I answered her questions as I'd been coached, and she handed me the cash. I couldn't believe it was so easy. The walk out was like stepping through a mine field. I had to force myself not to run, not to scream, not to look over my shoulder to see if security guards were after me. I drove away slowly, listening for sirens.

On to the next bank. It was easier. The third bank was easier still. And why not? My actions would have been legal if I had been Beverly Wirtz. And I almost was.

Then, pulling out of my parking space, I got careless and almost backed over a Mini Cooper. The driver honked her horn and mouthed something at me. I went hot, then cold, and began to shake.

The air conditioning in the fourth bank froze the sweat on my body. I knew I looked a wreck. I felt nauseated and couldn't keep my hands from shaking. To my surprise, this transaction went as smoothly as the others. My mood shot up to elation. Danny would be safe. I was so hyped up that the fact I was carrying almost $30,000 in cash that didn't belong to me fazed me not at all.

It was after five o'clock. I headed back to the landfill, cursing the rush-hour traffic that was clogging the highway.

Just before six, I turned off onto the country roads. Only ten more miles. I would make it. I forced myself to keep up an appearance of unconcern, waving and smiling at anyone who happened to turn my way. But as I passed a barricade of trees, my heart began to twist like a wrung-out washcloth. What would they do with Danny if I didn't get back before the landfill closed? What if they had already hurt him? They had an entire landfill in which to hide a body. What if they were lying in wait for me? It gave me an odd sort of courage to realize that, if they had killed Danny, I didn't care what they did to me. I drove on.

Finally I pulled the Escalade up to the frontless building. It looked to be the same bunch of men standing around. I picked out Smiley and Doc among them. Stinky walked up the road to see if I was being followed. I rolled down the window and sat, gripping the steering wheel and holding in my scream. What if this had all been a plot to prove what an unfit mother I was? I would never, never be able to explain why I had left Danny with these men . . . why I hadn't called the police . . . why after a lifetime of not being allowed to raise my voice I had been unable to scream for help . . .

They watched me for a full minute before approaching the car. I smiled, a reflex of subordination; if I'd been a dog, I'd have showed my belly. I handed Smiley the four bank envelopes. He took out the bills and fanned them, showed them to Doc and the others. One fellow pulled loose a bill and held it close to his face, turned it this way and that, rubbed his thumb over it, then examined the thumb.

Stinky must have doubled back. He came trotting up with Danny riding on his shoulders. I got out of the car and walked to them, suppressing my desire to run. He swung Danny down, and I gathered him into my arms.

"We wasn't really gonna hurt him, you know," Stinky said by way of apology.

I clutched Danny so hard he squeaked in protest. He seemed grubby but healthy and happy, pleased to see me but only that. He showed me a blobby plastic monster toy, a fast-food restaurant tie-in from a movie popular a couple years ago. Recycled. I looked at the men with tears in my eyes. "Thank you." I kissed Danny and fastened him in his car seat. Then I went back to the men. The money had vanished. We presented the same tableau as that morning, except that Danny and I were scruffier. More like them. I looked at them with fresh eyes. Smiley, Doc, the guy with the thumb—Thumby? Four others. Seven dwarves. Did that make me Snow White?

I thought about whom to ask my question. Doc, the brains, or Smiley, the executive? I chose Smiley. "Is that all?"

"All what?"

"All you needed me to do."

He glanced at the others, and they shared a chuckle. "Well, pretty much, I guess."

"Okay. Now I need you to do something for me."

Their chuckles froze, then shattered into laughter. I waited until the merriment died down, then got deadly serious. "It's about that computer I brought in earlier?"

r r r

The next afternoon, I left Danny to play at a neighbor's and returned to the landfill.

Doc greeted me with a question: "Who's Gene V. Eve?" I peered at the monitor over his shoulder. Eric's password was *Genevieve*. "I'm sorry to have to show you this, ma'am, but I think you ought to know." Doc clicked the mouse and brought up a series of photographs of Eric and the headmistress. I gasped. She wore *that* under those gray suits?

This was just the beginning of the bad news for Eric. I'd been right the first time: he'd been carving out the innards of the company he worked for and leaving a shell, like a jack-o'-lantern. They weren't on to him yet, was all.

🠞 🠞 🠞

With Doc's help, I now had the passwords to all Eric's files and accounts. I spent a few more long nights with his old computer back on the kitchen counter, hooked up to a new color printer this time.

I'd wanted to crack open his computer to get back my life. At most I'd hoped to find a credit card number I could use. But what I got was the keys to my husband's life, proof of things he had done that could get him sent to prison.

The trusties would get a cut of Eric's (soon to be my) money. I would use some to replenish Beverly Wirtz's bank account. That was only fair. Maybe the moving around of funds would pass for some sort of computer error. As for the rest of it—my vision of flying south with a briefcase full of cash now starred Danny and me. I would wire money ahead, too, just to be on the safe side.

The information I found got me Eric's complete attention for the first time in years—ever, probably. I told him what I wanted, when and where and how I wanted it, and he delivered.

"Oh, and one last thing," I told him, pointing to the old computer on the counter. "I want you to take that to the landfill. Yes, I'm quite serious. You can drive the Escalade."

————

Ann McMillan is the author of four Civil War mysteries set in Richmond, Virginia, published by Viking Penguin. Civil Blood was a Library Journal book of the year for 2001. Learn more at Ann's website: www. civilwarmystery.com.

CLIMACOPHOBIA

by Bonner Menking

"You're a dead man!" I stifled the urge to throttle my brother, nearly crushing the remote control. Good thing Steven James Ross was at least four states away. A murder trial would be the last straw.

"I could argue justifiable homicide," I muttered. And win. Unless they found out how much I talk to myself.

I flopped back on the bed and stared at the living room ceiling. Steve had been so sweet and helpful when his "poor big sister Lizzie" first came home from the hospital.

I should have been suspicious.

My dear, darling kid brother had come all the way down from Connecticut and brought a big box of movies specially picked out to entertain me while I recovered from popping a ligament off my right ankle in a stupid fall.

Specially picked to drive me nuts. *The Man Who Came to Dinner*, *Misery*, *Forrest Gump*, and of course *Rear Window*. Every single movie included a character with an injured leg or confined to a wheelchair. Can you search IMDB.com for movies with gimps? Even *Sense and Sensibility* had turned on me. I'd forgotten that Marianne met Willoughby when she sprained her ankle out on the downs or the moors or wherever, while taking a stroll in the rain. Marianne was up and walking the very next day of course. No such luck with me.

"No weight on that leg for six to eight weeks," my surgeon had announced after cheerfully detailing the surgery to install the screws that would keep my foot from falling off. Sure. No problem. Except I "failed" crutches by tipping over into the thorn bushes outside his office. (Who landscapes a doctor's office with thorn bushes?)

So now I spent most of my days and nights in a hospital bed smack in the middle of my living room on the first floor of my three-level townhouse. I could hop short distances with a walker, but mostly I was stuck circling one level in a wheelchair. Just enough room to roll past the bed for a full counterclockwise circuit. First the attached dining room—nice and open with the table pushed against the back windows. Then squeeze into the kitchen—I could spin like a top on the linoleum. Back on carpet for the tight turn to avoid all the furniture crammed against the windows in my little "front parlor." Past the heavy filing credenza to the right of the front door—I guess Steve *had* been useful; he moved all that stuff out of the way.

The patch of parquet I called my "foyer" offered a little spinning room by the front door and at the foot of the three steps going up to a wide landing. A careful turn on the carpet to safely pass the three steps going down on the right brought me to my powder room. Here I would abandon the wheelchair for the walker and do an ungainly hop-and-turn maneuver to access the door-less facilities. (Talk about a loss of dignity!) Finally I could hop back to the chair and roll into the living room to collapse in the bed and enjoy the view.

Not that there was much of one. I could only see the outside world when I propped the solid front door open and used my glass storm door as a window. All the shades on the actual windows were down for privacy, and with the furniture shoved against the outer walls, I couldn't get close enough to any of the windows to operate them. So I spent a lot of time looking out the front door. Just looking. A tantalizingly beautiful fall day might beckon outside, yet the six steps down to the sidewalk might as well be a cliff overlooking the ocean. Without two men and a van, the only way I could get out of the house was to fall out.

"Time to survey my kingdom," I muttered. Before I could even grab the bars on the sides of the bed to haul myself to the edge, Kato pounced on my shoulder meowing with satisfaction. How do cats know the least convenient time and place to plant themselves?

"Off! Damn cat. You're lucky I haven't thrown you over the fence to play with the MacAfees' Rottweiler." The adorable little ball of fluff I'd rescued from the animal shelter had turned out to be a big-game hunter. Her sneak attacks were so frequent, I'd changed her name to Kato, after the valet in the old Pink Panther movies who was always attacking Inspector Clouseau when he least expected it.

Kato was the reason I was trapped in this ludicrous situation. I had been halfway down the stairs carrying a fully loaded laundry basket when she leaped from the balcony railing, landing on my shoulder with all claws deployed. I'd screamed, dropped the basket, and lost my balance. Kato abandoned ship when I tripped and went down wrong. Very wrong.

Stairs. I sighed and gazed at my carpeted nemesis. Someday I'd use the stairs like an adult instead of having to bump myself up on my ass like a two-year-old. Talk about a pain. It had taken half an hour for my physical therapist to teach me to haul myself up one step at a time. Sadist! At least I could flop onto the first landing before working my way up the long flight along the common wall, doing a ninety-degree scoot around the second landing, up the last three steps, then onto a taped-together pile of phone books that gave me the height I needed to ease myself into the armchair Granny left me. He kindly let me sit at the top catching my breath for ten minutes. What a sweetheart.

Then he clapped his hands and grinned. "Now I'll show you how to go down the stairs. It's much easier. Even if you do it wrong, you end up at the bottom." What a comedian.

After he had left, I decided there was no way I'd be going up or down the stairs on my own. Not till I could put weight on the bad leg. Too much effort; and I sure didn't want to take *another* tumble when I was at home alone.

What a production that had been. After I fell, I had to drag myself to one of the phones sitting inconveniently in its cradle, find something long enough to knock it off to where I could reach it, call 911, then drag myself close enough to the front door to unlock it.

Where's Marianne's Willoughby when you need him?

At least now I never "wandered" without my cell phone.

"Enough whining." I was expecting my best friend, Shannon, soon. The pain was better after two weeks, but they don't give you pills to deal with the grumpiness. Best friends are the only cure for that.

I transferred over to the wheelchair—admiring my expert pivot and drop—and wheeled around to the kitchen to tidy up. Well, put a few things in the dishwasher and shift around the stuff I could reach on the counter.

The dying doorbell made a pathetic little *thunk*.

I wheeled into the front room to see, not Shannon, but a casually dressed man with mirrored sunglasses standing on my small porch. As I rolled up, he opened a wallet to show me a badge through the glass. He stepped back, and I pushed the door open. When he shifted toward me to hold the door, I saw a second man standing at the foot of the stairs and a patrol car parked in my neighbor's spot.

"Excuse me, ma'am, I'm Sergeant Peters and this is Officer Jeremiah from the Montgomery County Police. We're looking for your neighbor at 1778, a Mr. William Carlson." He pointed to my left. "Do you know when he normally gets home?"

Yes, I live at 1776 Liberty Lane—too cute for words. But that doesn't mean I know what's going on next door. "No," I told the officer. "All I know is that renters moved into 1778 a little before I did this." I indicated the bright orange cast practically glowing on my right leg. Tip: Never tell a med tech, "Oh, surprise me."

"I don't get out much these days," I continued. (To put it mildly.) "And I have no idea what their names are. We haven't actually met."

At least the MacAfees in 1774 were nice enough to ask if I needed anything. Not the new people. So much for neighborliness.

The officer on the walkway leaned forward and handed me a photo. "Do you recognize this man?"

I glanced at the smiling face of a pleasant-looking man in his mid-thirties. "Yes, I saw him when they were moving in, also a time or two before I fell." I handed the photo back, relieved that it wasn't a mug shot.

"But you don't know what time he normally gets home?" the sergeant persisted.

"Not a clue. Sorry. Why are you looking for him?" Parking tickets? Jay-walking? Driving thirty-eight in a thirty-five mile-per-hour zone? I'm a little bitter about the newbie cop who pulled me over a month ago for no apparent reason and gave me a five-minute lecture on safe driving and regular brake maintenance.

"We just need to ask him some questions, ma'am."

Big surprise there. Not gonna warn me that he's a mass murderer or anything useful? Where's the fun in that?

"If you do notice that he's at home, please call me at this number any time of the day or night." The sergeant scribbled on the back of a printed business card and handed it to me.

I tucked it into the pocket of my sweater. "Certainly, officer, but I'm not likely to notice much. This is my only window on the world." I waved at the glass storm door.

Officer Jeremiah frowned. "Do you often leave your door open like this?"

"When I'm expecting a guest or delivery." Or to keep Kato entertained.

The cops exchanged a glance. "Ma'am, you should always keep your door shut and locked for your own protection."

"I'm expecting a guest shortly."

"Well, we recommend that you lock your door until then." Sergeant Peters stared at me significantly, or at least his mirrored sunglasses did. Friendly type. Better not tell him about the key under the mat.

"Will do." I forced a polite smile, rolled back, and shut the solid front door. I had a sense they were waiting to hear me throw the deadbolt. Bossy busybodies. I should get a peephole installed at my new eye level, then I could check to be sure they were gone. I couldn't peek out the windows with all the shades drawn.

Five minutes after I was pretty sure I'd heard doors slam and their patrol car drive away, I re-opened the solid front door. (Odd that plain-clothes cops were driving a marked car.) I rocked the gnome statue—my joker brother's idea of a housewarming present—back into position as a door stop. Really got to get something less hideous, not to mention lighter. Never seemed like a chore till I had to work it around the wheelchair foot rests and a bum leg. Another task for the "when I'm back on my feet" list.

The physical therapist would like that.

* * *

"Where did you find real Philly cheesesteaks?" I took another heavenly bite.

"I'm not telling . . . yet." Shannon dodged the balled-up napkin I tossed at her head.

"Some best friend you are."

"I'm a terrific best friend. I brought you the biggest one on the menu exactly the way you like it." South Jersey girls like me are as picky about cheesesteaks as South Philly girls like Shannon.

Kato purred like a diesel truck, trying to con Shannon into sharing her sandwich. Darn cat knew better than to try that with me.

"Warning," I offered when I came up for air, "the cat wants your lunch, and she's eyeing your shoulder."

Shannon shifted her seat farther away from Kato's current perch. "She'd make a great attack cat. You should train her."

"She's already an attack cat. I'm becoming phobic."

"Would make you a scaredy cat or, what, felophobic?"

"Nope, ailurophobic. That's the fear of cats."

"You would know that! So Queen Elizabeth of Trivia, should I wrap up the rest of that for later?" She pointed at the remaining two pounds of sandwich nestled in its wax-paper-and-foil cocoon.

"Absolutely. Never toss ambrosia!" I rolled back from the table, balancing my plate in one hand.

"Put that down. I'm doing the clearing up. You can go all Superwoman later." She relieved me of the plate.

"Yes, ma'am."

"And don't you dare *ma'am* me. By the way, do you want to practice the stairs before I go?"

"Weighed down by Philly's best? I can barely lift myself empty."

"Sounds like an excuse to me. Maybe that phobia you're developing is of stairs." She gave me that look moms give kids claiming a fever on the morning of a math test.

"I'm not climacophic either."

"You made that up." She turned back to finish loading the dishwasher.

"Did not. Climacophobia is the fear of climbing up or falling down stairs. It's just as real as domatophobia, fear of being in a house; isolophobia, fear of being alone; traumatophobia, fear of injury; or barophobia, fear of gravity."

"Liar, liar, pants on fire. You're worse than my kids." She wiped down the counters and grabbed her purse.

"I looked up phobias online. There's even a word for fear of otters."

"What, otterphobia?"

"Nope, lutraphobia."

Shannon looked heavenward, no doubt invoking the saint of patience, whoever she was. "You have *got* to find something better to do with your time. Speaking of time, if you're not doing the stairs, I'd better go relieve the babysitter. I need her alive and willing to come back on Saturday."

I rolled her to the door.

"I can't thank you enough for coming out here, Shannon. You're a lifesaver."

She leaned over to hug me. "No big deal. Call me if you need *anything*. Don't just mope around feeling sorry for yourself."

I opened my mouth but stopped when she gave me another "mom" look.

"Don't try to deny it, Lizzie. I'm not buying this whole 'enjoying the rest' crap. I know perfectly well that being trapped here is killing you. You're not the dependent type."

"A nice way of calling me a control freak? Can't argue with that." I shrugged and grinned at her.

"Hang in there."

"Got no choice. Now leave before I throw you out!" I rolled menacingly toward her, aiming at her knee with my cast. She laughed and easily hopped out onto the porch, nearly tripping over the *Gazette*, rolled up in a blue, plastic bag.

"Show off! Hey, could you hand me the *Gazette* so I can recycle it?" How do you stop delivery on a free paper?

"Sure, but don't you want to know what's going on in your neighborhood?" Shannon eased the weekly tabloid out of its wrapper. "Speaking of which, I wonder if they have any news on that poor woman who disappeared."

"What woman?"

"You know, the day-care teacher who left work one afternoon last week and just disappeared. It was all over the local news."

"I was on Percocet all last week." Makes you nice and fuzzy, but I stopped taking it a few days ago. I'd rather endure a little pain and remember how to spell my name.

"Here it is. They found her car in the parking lot of the Giant over on Rosedale the next morning." She pushed the paper at me, open to the police-blotter page.

"*My* Giant? Thanks a lot, Shannon. I'll be sure to call *you* when I wake up with nightmares at two in the morning." I let the storm door close, smiling and waving as my last link to the outside world abandoned me. Alone again in the big bad 'burbs.

Sunset was approaching—my house's shadow had just reached the far end of my forlorn car. "Rats!" Forgot to ask Shannon to start it up and run it for a while to save the battery. Better write that down before I forgot again.

I wheeled back from the open door to scribble on the notepad on the front hall credenza. Predictably Kato jumped onto the credenza and planted her butt directly on the notepad, purring and turning her head almost upside down. Translation: "Aren't I adorable? Feed me!"

"Well, Miss Priss, it's a little early, but you can have dinner now." The ungrateful beast darted under the wheelchair and bolted into the kitchen. I'd shut the door later—the cops didn't have to deal with a hungry cat. I ditched the *Gazette* in the recycling trolley. Kato ran back, yelling at me to hurry.

"Like that speeds me up. Sheesh." As usual, I had to see-saw my way through the turns back into the kitchen. Why was it so easy to roll *out* of the kitchen but so hard to get the angle right to get back *in*?

"Here ya go. Damn!" I looked up from dumping kibbles in her dish and noticed that Shannon had left the dining room shade up. With the table and chairs pushed up against the window wall, I couldn't get within three feet of it. "Great. Hope Shannon hasn't gone too far."

When I pulled my cell out of my pocket, a slip of paper fluttered to the floor. I'd pick it up later. The floor is surprisingly hard to reach from a wheelchair, especially if you don't want to tip over.

I waited for the phone to turn on; I usually just kept it on all the time now. Nuts! Turned itself right back off. Battery was too low. Must have forgotten to charge it. And I'd been off Percocet for days.

At least I'd left the landline in its charger base in the living room. I rolled into the dining room, turning to the right, heading for the bed. Of course, the landline was all the way over on the far side of the bed. I'd have to climb into bed to reach it. I looked for my handy-dandy grabber tool. Also on the far side of the bed. Brilliant.

I looked out the dining room window. The sun slipped below the line of trees behind the townhouses. Sitting a full ten feet above my backyard, gazing out the wall-to-wall windows through the still-green leaves, felt like being in a tree house. Better than the view from my walk-out basement—just patio, fence, and tool shed.

What the hell, I'd just enjoy the view. The MacAfees haven't been out on their deck much lately, and even if they did look in, all they'd see is the foot of my bed. Nice to be reminded why I'd bought my now-prison—a spectacular view and excellent privacy. Leaving the shade up for a day or so wouldn't matter.

I backed into the kitchen, unwrapped a "specially imported from Philly" Tastykake Koffee Kake—hard to find in Maryland—and rolled into the dining room to enjoy my dessert and the sunset. I made a mental note to move "add a deck" higher on the remodeling list.

The waning sun reflected off the clouds in deepening shades of salmon pink. Something moving at the edge of the woods caught my eye. Probably just those kids who liked to cut across back there to get to the next development.

I shaded my eyes with my hand. Not kids. A man, dragging something. He put down his burden and crossed the open yard of the house next door. I smiled. I was twelve again, sitting in the dark, peeking out the window and spying on the cute high-school boy across the street. I loved being sneaky.

I leaned as far out of the wheelchair as I dared and watched him go in the back door of 1778.

Was this the guy the cops were looking for? Carl-something. Carlson! Too dark to be sure. But this guy was up to something.

I didn't feel twelve anymore.

"Stop scaring yourself. Even if it was him, he's just walking into his own house. Probably illegally dumping leaves."

After dark? With no lights on in the house? Maybe I should call the police.

I reached into my pocket for the sergeant's card. Empty.

"Doh, the paper that fell out." I rolled back into the kitchen. Where was it?

Earlier Kato'd been batting something around. I prayed it wasn't the cop's card. I reached for the light switch. No, don't turn on the light; don't want to draw attention to yourself.

Doesn't matter. Just call the police.

"Idiot!" Didn't plug in the cell to recharge. For that matter, where did I put the phone down?

I tried to quickly back out of the kitchen. Slammed into the door frame. Tried again. Scraped my left knuckles on the way out. I rolled the wheelchair around on the carpet and got to the bed. I hopped up but forgot to lock the brakes and nearly smashed my face on the footboard as I pitched forward onto the mattress.

"This is ridiculous." So was talking to myself.

I still couldn't reach the phone—why did I put it there? I dragged myself upright and hopped around to sit on the bed. I scooted back till I could reach the phone.

"Finally."

I hit talk and dialed 911. Didn't ring. Try again.

Hit talk. Listen for—wait, no dial tone? The phone lit up to show a stupid little cyberbirdie snoozing. No power? But—

I grabbed the cradle. No cord dangled from it. Useless. When did that get unplugged?

I cursed a blue streak under my breath and fell back on the bed.

"Calm the hell down." I needed to get a grip.

I took a few deep breaths. Letting my imagination run wild. I shouldn't have watched *Rear Window*. Was I really that suggestible?

Better catch the wheelchair before it runs away. My inelegant landing on the bed had shoved it out of easy reach. Fortunately I could reach the grabber from where I lay.

I sat up, laughing at myself, then nearly choked.

I was looking straight out my glass storm door to the parking lot. Somehow the cops' warning didn't seem so over-the-top now.

Sobered, I pulled the wheelchair closer, locked the one brake I could reach, and fell into the chair. Keeping my grabber close at hand, I started for the front door.

Before I could aim the chair through the narrow corridor between the bed and the bookcase, I heard a door shut out back. Curiosity won out. I backed up and returned to the windows.

The man was heading back toward the woods, carrying a shovel. Compared to inside the house, the night was fairly bright. A full moon? Maybe, but it was rising on the front side of the house, so deep shadows still obscured the backyards.

He crept into the woods. I could see some movement through the small patches of light coming through the trees from the houses beyond. Later—no idea how long—he reappeared. The moon must have risen over the roofline because I could see his face clearly. Definitely the man in the picture. Carlson. Not so pleasant-looking without a smile.

He bent over the thing he had dropped at the edge of the woods, shifted it, put it down, and stood up. Maybe stretching his back. He seemed to be scanning the townhouse windows.

Good thing he couldn't see me.

Snap! The timer light on the dining room table suddenly glared to life.

"Damn!" I scrambled to reach the lamp, managed to knock it over, breaking the bulb. At least it was dark again.

How long had the light been on? Seemed like forever. Maybe he didn't see me. Maybe he was bending down. Still, he would have looked up at the flash, surely.

I could hear my pulse hammering in my ears. Straining to see with my recently dazzled eyes.

Where was he? By the—the thing? In his yard?

Banging. My gate. He was trying to open my gate. It wouldn't open unless you knew the trick. It was out of alignment, you had to lift it off the latch.

The gate stopped creaking. Where was he now? It was too dark, the fence too high.

Hands, I saw hands! He was climbing over!

He pulled himself up and threw a leg over.

"Fall, please God, fall. Break a leg or something."

He half leapt, half fell into the yard. He stood, then ran to the back of my house. I couldn't see him, but I could hear him down below, trying my back door.

Did Bob forget to lock the back door after he raked the leaves yesterday? Like Shannon forgot to close the window shade?

The rattling stopped after a minute. Locked! Hallelujah.

He ran to my tool shed. Thank God for that heavy duty padlock. He couldn't get in and find something to break the glass in the back door or the windows. And his own shovel was on the other side of the fence.

Now what? I sat frozen to the spot watching him haul himself up onto the roof of the shed. Why?

He turned to face the house. Almost at my eye-level, he looked enormous, close, and dangerous.

The front door!

I whirled in the chair and sailed to the door. I threaded the needle perfectly, avoiding every dinged-up piece of wall, trim, and furniture that I'd already hit. I slammed the door shut and threw the bolt.

Now what? Turn the porch light on. Make it hard for him to stand there breaking down the door for all the world to see.

Get to a phone. Upstairs.

Wait. What if he came back with the shovel and broke in the back door?

"Think!" Slow him down. I rolled over and dragged the nearly full paper-recycling trolley over to the basement stairs and gave it a shove. It tipped over onto the small landing three steps down, cracking the drywall and spilling some slippery magazines down the long flight to the right.

Good. Now get upstairs.

First, weapons. I had the grabber. Big threat, but I'd need it to reach the phone. Apparently my decorating style was "put everything useful on the far side of the bed."

How about the trekking poles from my trip to Yellowstone? Damn, they were in the car. No wait, the one with the cracked handle was in the front closet; and it still had a vicious, ice-breaking tip.

Armed and locked in. My heart rate and breathing slowed a little while I twisted the trekking pole down to its shortest size to fit into the basket tied to the balcony rail for pulling things upstairs; wriggled the grabber through the banisters to pick up later; and locked the wheelchair before rising to drop my rump on the first landing.

I fell back onto my wheelchair in a panic. "The key."

Dear Lord, how many people knew about or used the key under the mat? Carlson might have seen someone use it. He wouldn't have to break in. He could just unlock the door.

I held my breath and listened. No sound came from the basement. Nothing from the back, either, but it was hard to hear much through my new, energy-efficient, tilt-to-clean windows. Not to mention over the pounding in my ears.

What's left? The gnome. Not much, but a start. If I could wedge it between the big and little wheels just right, the wheelchair might block the front door for a while.

Scooting to the powder room, I pulled out the walker, wasting a second to wish the door we'd taken off its hinges was on this level, not three steps down trapped behind the recycling bin. I backed the chair up tight to the front door and jammed on the brakes. I pulled both footrests up to horizontal, making it nearly impossible to move in the small space.

I reached back and flipped off the porch light. I wanted it as dark as possible inside. Carlson wouldn't know the layout like I did. My floor plan was different from all my neighbors.

But the light switches were right by the door. Damn.

Please be there. I felt around in the catch-all drawer in the credenza for a screwdriver. "Yes!"

I stood and twisted around, half kneeling on the wheelchair. Despite my shaky hands and the painted-over screws, I got the switch plate off in record time. I plunged the screwdriver into the electrical box and pried the hardware out, generating some sparks. Okay, no fire. And actually blowing a breaker might help.

Leaning heavily on the walker, I hopped over to the closet and pulled out brooms, mops, coats, anything that might make it harder to navigate in the front hall.

Don't get cocky. My good left leg ached from standing like a stork for so long. A few painful hops got me closer to the stairs, and I turned around.

I hadn't practiced hopping backwards, so I fell hard when my heel hit the stairs. At least I managed to stay on the landing. Three fewer steps to drag myself up. I kept a grip on the walker and pulled it up after me.

Before I could scoot around to the far side of the landing, I heard the storm door open. I jumped at the knock.

"Hello? Ma'am? It's the police. We need to speak to you."

Could it be? I lay back on the landing, rolled over onto my stomach, and peeked out the tiny gap where the shade didn't fall all the way to the bottom of the ten-foot-high bay window. The bay stuck out farther than the door, so I could see only the edge of the open storm door and a small patch of porch.

"Ma'am?"

I scanned the parking lot. Some kind of SUV was backed into one of 1778's spaces next to my own car. No patrol car in sight.

"Ma'am. We're waiting. Do you need assistance?"

What we? Unless two people were huddled on my postage stamp of a porch, he was alone.

"Ma'am? We got your call, we're coming in. Please get back from the door so we don't hurt you."

He was putting on an act for the neighbors! Pretending to be the cops. He must've found out they were in the neighborhood earlier.

The thud against the door made me sit straight up. I shoved myself to the far side of the landing and pulled the walker to the foot of the stairs. Now the hard part.

One, two, three, lift. My butt moved upward.

Slam. He hit the door again.

Startled, I slipped back to the landing.

Deep breath, again. One, two, three, lift.

Did it! Now the next step. One, two—

Slam. Ignore it. Lift.

Now I could grab the railings and use my arms to pull myself up instead of only pushing with my left leg.

Third step. It's too quiet. Don't think about it. I hooked the walker with my cast to carry it along.

Pull. Push. Fourth step. Lift the walker.

Push. Pull. Fifth step. What was that scraping sound? Had he found the key? I wiped my sweaty hands on my shirt.

Push. Pull. Sixth step.

The bolt! Jesus! Breathe.

Come on leg, push. Pull. Seventh step. How many more?

The door eased open an inch, then stopped.

One more step. Almost. Keep going. Don't look.

A footrest scraped against the woodwork downstairs.

The landing! Only three more steps to reach the second floor. The walker wobbled, almost slipped off my cast. Keeping my right toes curled up and my left hand gripping the very end of the railing, I leaned out and grabbed the walker with my right hand.

Breathing again, I shifted around the corner and set the walker fully on the landing.

This next step was hard. The balcony rail was too high, out of reach. Go! Lift!

Downstairs, the door and wheelchair were locked in noisy combat. Carlson didn't care what anyone heard now.

One more step to go. I glanced down. The door was open almost a foot now. I could just see an arm reaching around trying to dislodge the wheelchair.

I nudged the taped phone books, sending them sliding down to the landing, improvising an obstacle course. Carlson's combat downstairs with the wheelchair covered the sound. Now for Granny's chair.

I shifted back down the hallway just far enough to wrestle the heavy wooden armchair closer to the steps. I balanced it on one leg at the very edge of the top step, supported by the walker. With luck it would fall on him.

My assailant was winning the battle with the wheelchair. He could almost squeeze in. But he'd have to climb over that amazingly heavy credenza by the door.

I glanced at the rope hanging off the railing. No time to pull up the basket, which meant no weapon. I scooted down the hall, quietly opening every door that might have a lock on it, pushing in the locks, and pulling all the doors shut.

I could hear heavy breathing. He was getting in.

I made it back into the master bedroom and locked that door.

Now the phone. Damn! The grabber was still on the stairs.

The racket downstairs grew less metallic and more verbal. The swearing came from underneath me now, in the living room.

Can't make the floor squeak, he'll come upstairs too fast.

I needed to get on the bed. Reach for the phone.

Right knee, left leg, push. I fell halfway on the bed, face down.

Now turn. I sent the lamp crashing to the floor.

I listened, not breathing. Nothing at first, then footsteps. Damn.

I rolled over till I could reach the phone.

A dial tone! There was a God!

"911. What is your emergency?"

"A man has broken into my house! 1776 Liberty Lane!"

"Ma'am?" I could hear the disbelief in her voice.

"Really, it's a real address, please. The police were here this afternoon looking for my neighbor, Carlson. He's the one in the house. He saw me watching him drag something into the woods. Send help, please!"

"We're dispatching units now, ma'am. Please stay on the line with me."

"Oh God, he's coming up the stairs."

"Stay on the line."

The sound of wood rattling against wood—like a stick dragged along a picket fence—followed by thumping and bumping. He'd fallen down the stairs. Thanks to Granny's heavy chair. "My granny won't let you hurt me, jackass," I muttered to the back of the bedroom door.

"What, ma'am?"

"I think he fell," I told the operator, "but I hear him coming up again. I need to stay quiet."

"Just stay on the line."

No time. I looked around.

The bathroom? Just another hollow-core door and a dead end.

The windows?

Another crash. That was the guestroom door.

Yes, the windows! I dropped the handset on the bed.

"Ma'am? Are you there?"

Noise didn't matter now. I wrestled the floor lamp from between the bed and the side table. Using it as a crutch, I hopped to the windows, reaching for the cord that would raise the giant shade that covered the wall-to-wall, practically floor-to-ceiling panes. My left leg muscles were burning, and my thigh started to twitch.

I heard the linen closet door open then slam shut.

I gripped the lamp and managed two more hops; if only I could reach the window locks.

He was rattling the bathroom door. I heard the door splinter and tried to ignore it, concentrating on my task.

I needed both hands to do the next part. Lean against the window frame. Pull in on both slots, easy . . . easy.

The lower window fell slightly inward, testing my precarious balance. I turned my attention to the upper window. Fingers in the slots. Pull. Done!

My leg gave out, and I crumpled to the floor, followed by the two panes falling into the room. They stayed attached to the frame but banged together a few inches above my injured leg.

The bedroom door rattled.

I lay down on the floor holding the lamp, feeling oddly calm.

People laugh when action scenes are shot in slow motion. "Not enough script," they'll scoff, or "That's so fake."

But it's not. Ask anybody who's been in a car crash, for example. The crash happens in a few seconds, but they can tell you every tiny detail. In your mind, that few seconds is a ten-minute movie.

I don't recall hearing any noise when the door started to give. But everything else was sharp and clear. The tops of the trees. So many stars out my window. A nice view, I thought irrationally, even from the floor. And the fall smell—a hint of chill, a little wood smoke.

I heard the operator's voice twittering way up on the bed and felt something brush by my hand. Kato.

Then the door slammed open. "Where are you, bitch?"

Did he expect me to answer? Silly man.

He tried the light switch. Nothing. That bulb went out when I broke the lamp.

The bed shuddered. "Shit!" he yelled. He must have banged his shin on the footboard. Good. I hoped it hurt.

In the dim light I could see him feeling his way along the end of the bed.

Just a little bit farther. Come on. There!

I snapped on my lamp, aiming it right at his face.

Carlson lunged forward, but he hadn't reckoned on Kato and her claws. His hands flew to his face, and he screamed, sending Kato skittering off into the dark.

That's when I laughed. I couldn't help it. He turned to find me—a little too fast, I think. He tripped over my Day-Glo orange cast, losing his balance.

Couldn't let him fall on my poor right leg, so I shoved him out of the way with the lamp and my trusty left leg.

I heard the screen rip as he fell through the window.

Crack.

Thud.

Silence.

r　r　r

"He's dead?" I was exhausted and full of Percocet. I may have asked that before.

Sergeant Peters nodded. "Broken neck. He hit the patio head first." He and Officer Jeremiah had shown up at the emergency room; they'd come to take my official statement.

I vaguely remembered the police arriving and picking me up off the bedroom floor. When I told them that my leg hurt, they asked where Carlson went.

"Out the window." I giggled.

"Shock," somebody said.

"Sorry." I remember apologizing.

"Not your fault, ma'am. He must have tripped and fallen out the window." Funny, they didn't ask me why the window was open; only how to close it so Kato couldn't jump out.

Sergeant Peters coughed, bringing me back to the present.

A thought drifted to the surface. "What was in the woods?"

Neither man would meet my eye. "No need to discuss this now. We'll come back tomorrow."

I sat upright. "No! Now." My anger cut through the mental haze. "A man broke into my house and tried to kill me tonight. I want to know why. Why were you looking for him? What was he trying to hide?"

The nurse practitioner flipped through the curtain. "Are you all right?"

I nodded.

She turned to the cops. "Perhaps you gentlemen should leave now. We'll be moving Miss Ross to her room in a few minutes."

"They can stay till then, can't they?" I smiled meekly at my angel of mercy.

"Of course, they can, hon. Just try to speak quietly."

"Sorry. I've had a rough night."

She smiled and left.

"Well?" Better get them to spill now. The adrenaline rush was ebbing.

"We, um, wanted to ask Mr. Carlson about a missing person," Sergeant Peters offered.

"This woman." Officer Jeremiah handed over another photograph. "You may have seen her picture on television."

"I have seen her," I said, trying not to lose my grip. "Not on TV. On moving day, she brought lunch to the crew. I think one of the movers was her boyfriend or brother or something. Very friendly, we chatted. About my azaleas. Her favorite, except for lilacs." I looked down at my pretty, new blue cast. Definitely losing focus. "Why was she on TV?"

Jeremiah eased the picture out of my fingers. As I watched it disappear into his breast pocket, the penny dropped. "She's the missing teacher, isn't she?"

Jeremiah refused to meet my eyes.

"In the woods? Oh, please tell me she's not dead."

He looked away.

I fell back on the gurney. "Why? Why would anyone hurt her? She likes lilacs." I let myself slip into the Percocet haze.

"We don't know, ma'am." Before I could doze off, they awkwardly made their goodbyes.

"Oops, sorry!" A cheerful orderly popped through the curtains as the policemen turned to leave. "Drive carefully."

The orderly reached for my chart. "Let's see, Ms Elizabeth Ross, I'm Andrew, and I'll be taking you on a scenic tour of our wonderful facilities. Our tour terminates in the lovely room on the sixth floor we've prepared especially for you. I know we can't compete with your usual accommodations at . . ." he checked the chart. "1776 Liberty Lane. How very patriotic."

"You can't beat the view." I smiled sleepily. Time to surrender to the narcotics. At least he made double-checking my information entertaining.

He twisted my wristband around. "Ms. Ross, may I call you Elizabeth?"

"Sure," I said as the darkness closed in. "Just don't call me Betsy."

Like I said, I bought the place for the view.

———

Bonner Menking is an estate-tax attorney working on a legal thriller about an estate-tax attorney who leads a far more exciting life than most of her peers. Bonner spent eight long months recovering from an ankle injury that was entirely her own fault. Her much less athletic cat, Mame, was blameless.

SAFE SEX, VAMPIRE STYLE

by Helen Schwartz

You're supposed to approach a murder investigation with an open mind. But I found myself with four hundred years of attitude riding on the outcome as Harry and I entered a long, tree-lined drive in Potomac, Maryland, one early afternoon in late March. On the outskirts of Washington, D.C., the Bouchards' baronial manor held pride of place on its multi-acre lot, flanked on one side by a hotel-sized adobe hacienda and on the other by a colonial only slightly smaller than the White House.

A gaggle of TV broadcast vans already lined the street when we arrived, kept at the property line by a wrought-iron fence and private security guards. TV cameras from three channels filmed us driving in. No hope of our giving any information, but a handsome man driving a red Jaguar convertible with a passenger who could pass for Farrah Fawcett in her prime makes for some nice footage.

The day before, the Washington police had called us in on an unusual complaint. Mrs. Bouchard and her daughter had reported an alleged vampire; now the crime had escalated to murder, and Mrs. Bouchard lay on her back in the rose bushes with a stake through her heart.

When a parent pulls a kid out of school in a fancy Maryland suburb and trots her over to a Washington Metropolitan Police station, you figure the kid is in trouble. How had it come to this?

The D.C. cops thought of Harry and me as their go-to vampire experts ever since we helped solve the murder of a blood-drained corpse. As a step-vampire, I hated this reputation spreading. Sure, vampires are popular on movies and TV, but most people don't want one in their neighborhood.

So what's a step-vampire? My mother was pregnant with me when she was turned. During my last months in the womb, I acquired certain vampire traits, though I don't need to suck blood to survive. I eat vegetarian by choice and hate the taste of dead blood. Living blood is a different story, a treat, and one I've learned to indulge in sparingly. I hide my keen senses and speedy bounding. Over the centuries, I've learned to change identities to cover my slow aging. Unlike vampires, who always look the same as the day they were turned, I do age—one year of physical development per decade. These days I could pass for forty. You do the math. I'm currently using the name Ruth Nobis and working as a private eye.

Harry True, my thirty-seven-year-old boss and boyfriend, knows my history. He doesn't often tell jokes, but his granite face verges on a smile whenever he says, "I like older women."

From his expression during the previous day's interview, I didn't think he liked Mrs. Bouchard very much. I'd observed the police interview through a two-way mirror. They used the nice interview room: the chairs and table weren't bolted down and the paint looked fresh, as though Martha Stewart had suggested Banana Chiffon. Like a police tea party, Harry and Detective Benedetti sat on one side of the table, Mrs. Bouchard and her daughter on the other.

"Yeah, a couple of times I saw him turn into a bat?" Ashley Bouchard ended her statement with the raised pitch of a question—standard operating procedure for young women of fourteen. At about five-foot-eight, filling out a B-cup bra, she could pass for seventeen. With a pert nose and occasional pimple clusters, she slouched in her chair as though to disappear, yet wore black lipstick and blue polish on nails bitten to the quick. She tongued her bubble gum into position, sucked a bubble inside her mouth, and popped it.

Benedetti, with years of interviewing experience, had kept his tone neutral and controlled, slowly gaining the girl's confidence, teasing out her story. "And how would you describe his appearance when he was in human form?"

Ashley raised her blue eyes, shadowed by massive applications of mascara and eyeliner, and explored the ceiling as she answered. "He's dark. You know, from India? Not black but dark-skinned? About five-foot-ten, about sixteen or seventeen. Skinny in a sexy way—jeans and a Grateful Dead T-shirt?" She lowered her eyes. "Really hot." No question mark this time.

"And when he sucked your neck, he actually broke the skin." It was a statement, not a question. Benedetti had it all on the police report in front of him.

"Yeah, me and Deepak used to hook up for about a pint's worth."

The woman sitting next to Ashley shivered, making the tasteful highlights shimmer in the windswept blonde hairdo suggestive of lunches at country clubs. She looked as if she wanted to smack her daughter—whether for bad grammar or bad taste was unclear. From the way she looked at Benedetti, I suspected why he didn't want me in the interview room. I'd bet Mrs. B didn't like females. She felt comfortable with male authority figures.

"Ashley, what would you do on a typical date?" Benedetti was letting the girl provide all the details.

"Do we have to go into all this?" Mrs. Bouchard sat up straighter and crossed her arms over the puckered sleeves of her Prada jacket.

"Yes, ma'am. We need to see if there's any grounds for a criminal charge."

And it had to come from Ashley, signed by the mother as guardian.

Ashley draped herself in the chair like someone trying out for the part of a throw rug. Her red jersey top, too tight, ended four inches above her navel, which glittered with a ruby on a small ring piercing her flesh.

"Me and Deepak usually met at the Zoo entrance? Then we'd go into the woods off the road and hook up." Ashley smirked as she looked sideways at her mother and wriggled lower in her chair.

Mrs. Bouchard squirmed in hers.

Benedetti waited a beat. "And hooking up means . . . ?"

"She made me come here, y'know." Ashley pouted at Benedetti. "My dad has a mistress and my mom's just jealous that she's not getting any."

Mrs. Bouchard opened her mouth to speak, then thought better of it.

"So hooking up means you had sexual relations?" Benedetti kept his tone matter-of-fact, his voice a monotone.

Ashley started nibbling at her fingers. "Not the way you're thinking. At first, we'd, y'know, kiss."

"Same as with other dates?" Benedetti paused. "Or different?"

"Pretty much the same except his teeth were kinda sharp. I had to be careful with my tongue. And then he'd feel me up."

Benedetti was on the verge of a question when Ashley said, "Yeah, just like the other guys, but he'd put his lips over his teeth when he started sucking my tits." She paused to bite a hangnail.

Benedetti waited without any visible impatience, writing notes on a pad. Ashley proceeded, describing Deepak's lack of interest in further downward progress in comparison to other boyfriends. I kept my eyes on the row of gold studs that outlined the curve of her ears. I feared I was blushing.

"And then he sucked my blood. Here," she said, pointing to her jugular vein. "The holes have healed, but there's still a couple of scars."

Benedetti leaned closer, examined the scars, then added a sentence to his notes.

"Before he hooked up with Shayna Shemesh, he used to do three or four of us each night. We even, you know, wrote up a schedule. Deepak was actually getting a little chubby until he met Shayna." Ashley's tone changed from self-satisfied pouting to poisonous malignancy. "I couldn't believe Deepak was hanging with her. She's gross, really fat." She paused for another bite of her thumb until it oozed blood. "And then he stopped hanging with us."

So Mrs. Bouchard wasn't the only one not getting any. Jealousy, rather than Benedetti's interrogation technique, had made the girl talk.

Benedetti flipped his pad shut. "I'll have your statement typed up, and we'll ask you and your mother to sign it."

"I've fucked lots of guys," Ashley added, apparently intent on making her mother squirm some more. "But me and Deepak never did it. When Deepak sucked my blood it was like, like . . ." She paused to review the ten words in her teen vocabulary. "Awesome. Like, super-sex!" A sly smile crept over Ashley's face as she stared at the coffee cup trembling in her mother's hand.

While the aggrieved daughter and mother waited to sign the statement, Benedetti consulted with Harry and me. "So whaddaya think?"

"What's the charge?" Harry asked.

"Exactly." Benedetti stroked his upper lip with an index finger and scratched the tip of his bulbous nose. "It's not statutory rape. It's not menacing. By breaking the skin, maybe it would be battery if it wasn't consensual, but where's the crime?"

I cleared my throat. Both men turned to look at me.

"If what he told Ashley is true," I said, "this vampire's never killed anyone. He's Indian so I'd guess he gets his moral code, including non-violence, from being a Buddhist or maybe a Jain. But he needs blood every day. That puts him in a really tough spot."

Benedetti coughed. His face impassive, his voice a monotone, he finally spoke. "Maybe I'm missing something, but here's a kid who can have the vampire version of sex as many times as he wants—giving and gaining super-pleasure, according to Ms Blue Nails. And he doesn't go against his moral upbringing because he doesn't kill anyone. So how is that a tough spot?"

Harry studied the ceiling, as if counting the holes in the acoustical tiles might keep him from smiling.

"In case you hadn't noticed," I said, "he's given up playing the field. He needs blood every day, but he can't keep taking it from Shayna, the girl he loves, or he'd kill her."

"Maybe he's just given up Ashley Bouchard," Harry said.

Benedetti snorted. "I'm not sure there's a prosecutable crime here, but do me a favor. Check the situation out and let me know what you think."

After we left the police station, all it took was a little web-surfing to find Shayna's address and home and cell phone numbers. Surprise, surprise—the girl lived right next to the Bouchards. As soon as Deepak's name came up, Shayna agreed to meet us later that afternoon at Walter Pierce Park, near the children's playground on Adams Mill Road. I wondered why she chose a location in the District until I checked it out on Google maps.

Just before 4:30 we parked, and we passed a fenced dog run, a basketball court, and a soccer field in the oddly shaped pocket park before we arrived at the children's playground. Because the park was on a bluff high above the valley of Rock Creek, most people didn't realize it bordered on the National Zoo.

Across from the playground, we saw a young woman sitting on a bench, her back to a fenced garden. She was watching schoolchildren play on swings and a jungle gym about twenty feet away. Ashley had led us to believe that Shayna was huge, but the girl was merely pleasingly plump. She wore a blue, down-filled vest over a white blouse and a pleated, plaid skirt. At first I took her for a student at a Catholic girls' school, but after a silent exchange of questioning glances, she got up and approached us, her vest showing the bulldog mascot of Potomac's Churchill High School.

She looked the same age as Ashley but about six inches shorter. Her black hair, cut in a Dutch-boy haircut, framed a face enhanced by only a touch of lipstick. Her striking violet eyes, flawless skin, and perfect features, reminded me of a child star from the 1940s.

Harry initiated the conversation. "We're assisting the police with an investigation into a young man identified as a friend of yours."

"Are you police officers?" Shayna looked back and forth between us.

"No, but we have some interest in vampires." I waited for her reaction.

She stumbled backward into the chain-link fence surrounding the garden, grasping the arbor trellis for support.

"I'm part vampire myself," I said, watching the fear on Shayna's face give way to an assessing distrust. "My mother was turned into a vampire after she became pregnant with me. That's why I can walk around in sunlight."

At a shout from the playground, Shayna turned to watch the children with the practiced eye of a babysitter.

"Someone's made a complaint against Deepak," I said to her back. "There's no evidence he's dangerous. You can help us make his problem go away." Shayna turned as if to reply, paused, then held my gaze as I motioned her back onto the bench. She sat, then scooted over so there would be enough room for us.

"What do you need to know?" she asked.

"Tell us about your relationship with Deepak," I suggested.

"I met Deepak last December when I was volunteering at Zoo Lights," she began. "You know, the money-raiser for the National Zoo? After the zoo buildings close, visitors pay to walk past animal silhouettes made from lights. I'd heard from the girls in my high school about a sexy Indian guy who hung around the zoo, but when I met Deepak, I never put that rumor together with him. He was really shy and polite. It took him forever to get up the nerve to talk to me." She grinned. "My job was to stand at the entrance and take tickets," she explained.

"And?" Harry prodded.

Shayna shrugged. "After school started in January, we began meeting in the evenings at the Potomac Library. It's open until nine on Monday, Tuesday, and Wednesday." Her face lit with a desperate sincerity. "Deepak would never hurt anyone. He's a Jain. That means he hates violence. When he came to the U.S. in 1960 as an exchange student, he wouldn't even eat meat! But on his way back to India, he got stuck at an airport during a storm. Another guy who seemed to be stranded turned him. Against his will. Deepak never wanted to be a vampire or to hurt anyone." She sat back, hands folded in her lap, smiling as if recalling something pleasant.

Just as she got to the good stuff, I thought. "So you two have been dating almost four months?"

"We are pledged to each other." It sounded biblical, not like some current euphemism—going steady, pinned, troth-plighted.

"So you date only him," I asked.

Shayna nodded. "I give my blood to him of my own free will."

No mention of any accompanying sexual ecstasy, I noted. "And what does it mean that he is pledged to *you*?" I continued before Harry could barge in with a tactless question of his own. Harry is devoid of tact.

"He doesn't see other girls," she said and blushed.

Harry stood still as a statue, with only his eyes moving from Shayna, then back to me.

"Where does he get the blood he needs, then? If he took it all from you, you'd be dead by now." I stopped and watched Shayna blush again. "Is that too nosy a question?"

"His friends at the zoo also give blood to him."

My eyebrows rose in surprise. "You mean the animals?"

Shayna nodded. "He can communicate with them, you know."

Out of the corner of my eye, I noticed a woman in a business suit enter the park and walk purposefully toward the playground. With a nervous glance toward the newcomer, Shayna said, "I have to go now."

Harry stood up. "Can you tell us where to find Deepak? I have some questions for him."

"I'll get back to you." Shayna hurried to catch up with the woman who had retrieved her child from the playground. They left the park together.

"Sounds a little like Romeo and Juliet," I commented to Harry. "Star-crossed lovers." We strolled back toward the Calvert Street exit. "Shayna means 'beautiful' in Yiddish, did you know that? And her last name is 'sun' in Hebrew. Pity, isn't it? A vampire can never see the sun without being destroyed."

We passed the basketball court where the pole and backboard made a shadow like a gallows on the walk as the sun sank low in the sky.

"Right," Harry said, looking at his watch. "It's 5:20. Let's get going."

"I thought you wanted to meet Deepak."

"So? We probably won't hear from Shayna till she gets straightened away on the kid she was babysitting."

"She wasn't babysitting," I said, to Harry's annoyance. "Didn't you see the sign about the garden?"

"Yeah. No entry to the community garden area. Park visitors should retrieve any tools they left behind."

"What's important is the *reason* it's closed. They're doing archeological research on the site of an old African-American cemetery. Shayna may have wanted us to believe she was babysitting, but I'll bet she chose that spot to be near where Deepak rests during daylight. This late in the day he was probably already awake and eavesdropping on our conversation, even if he couldn't move." I checked my watch. "The sun sets in about half an hour. If my hunch is right, we won't have long to wait. C'mon."

One nice thing about Harry is that he doesn't mind my being smart about some things and his being smart about others. We're a good team. I bound after the bad guys to bring them down. He shoots if they're too far away even for me.

Vampires must lie in decaying soil, I knew, so when Shayna had suggested we meet at the park, I'd checked it out online, looking for nearby cemeteries. Jains don't have cemeteries, but Deepak had to have learned about those traditional vampire haunts. Or maybe he figured out that graveyards are the only open spaces in cities where people are sparse and leave strangers alone. At any rate, once I learned that the Colored Union Benevolent Association graveyard lay near the park, I knew Shayna had chosen the meeting spot because of its proximity to Deepak.

As the light faded, we made our way back to the bench near the playground and sat down. I shivered and wrapped my arms around myself, snuggling into my jacket. Even the squirrels were cold, scampering up the oak trees to their nests. As the moon became more visible in the sky, a tall, dark-haired teenager strolled out the arbor entrance of the off-limits garden. He had the regal bearing and classic profile of an Indian prince, but wore fashionable jeans, a vest with an Apple iPhone peeking out of a pocket, and a Grateful Dead sweatshirt.

"Deepak, I presume." Standing to greet him, I looked into his huge brown eyes, shaded by long, thick eyelashes. "I'm Ruth Nobis. This is Harry True." I held out my hand. "Shayna Shemesh says you know how to suck blood from a partner but can stop before you kill her. And you've never killed anyone."

He threw his head back and laughed warmly, then reached forward to grasp my hand. I felt an instinctive liking for Deepak until I noticed his long canine teeth, the tips still visible when he smiled. My instinct that he was trustworthy fought with my centuries-old distrust of all vampires.

"I stop feeding when they faint," he confided. "It takes a lot of self-control, but I do it. Shayna taught me how to cut back the time." He grinned, baring his teeth unapologetically, as if glad he'd found someone he could talk to about his love for Shayna.

"Interesting," I said, looking at Harry.

"Excuse me, but I gotta go meet Shayna." Deepak started backing away. "You understand, right?" Deepak's solid outline grew blurry around the edges. A mini-whirlwind materialized at his feet and spiraled up his body, turning it from substance to specks.

r r r

The following day, before we had a chance to report back to Benedetti, the Major Crimes squad of nearby Montgomery County summoned us to the murder scene at the Bouchard home.

We pulled around the house and parked next to a four-car garage adjoining the tennis court. Yellow police tape defined the crime scene as a double row of rose bushes separating the Bouchard property from the mini-White House.

A flock of crime scene investigators hovered over the body of Mrs.

Bouchard, lying on her back. The chauffeur had discovered the corpse, a wooden stake driven through her chest, as he walked to the garage early that morning. Mr. Bouchard had called the police.

The suit squatting near the body got up as we approached.

My partner extended his hand. "Harry True." He nodded at me. "Ruth Nobis."

"Bart Thigden, Montgomery County Major Crimes Squad." He shook our hands. Thigden was a wiry man with a fifty-year-old face and a forty-year-old body, His cropped hair and ramrod posture suggested prior military experience.

I shuddered as a breeze came up and clouds covered the sun. I inched closer to the body and noticed two puncture wounds, spaced just right for a vampire's kiss. The wound looked red and raw on the white neck of the victim. I could think of no explanation for the marks other than a fanging by the teenaged vampire we had interviewed at the zoo the previous day.

I'd never felt anything but hatred and revulsion for the vampires I'd tangled with over the centuries: cruel, heartless, ruthless. But if Deepak was telling the truth—and my instincts said he was—he lived by a strict moral code. He had never killed any of his all-too-willing pubescent victims. But Mrs. Bouchard was, what? Forty? Had he killed her by sucking her blood? And if so, why drive a stake through her heart?

As the photographer moved away, I noticed a wide, dreamy smile on Mrs. Bouchard's face. I nudged Harry. "We're dealing with a vampire, all right," I whispered.

Shayna and Deepak were to have met at the library. What had happened between the time the library closed the previous night and when the chauffeur found Mrs. Bouchard's corpse the following morning? I looked at the estate next door. The mini-White House, where Shayna lived, had a four-car garage and an Olympic-size swimming pool, heated, sending steam drifting up.

High overhead, clouds were massing and turning dark. The crime-scene photographer took a few last pictures in the fading light, then packed up. "Somebody sure fanged her," Harry mumbled. "If not Deepak, then who?" As we watched, the stocky forensic investigator laid out a body bag. Standing nearby, Detective Thigden ground the palms of his hands into his eye sockets, then pulled both hands back over his close-cropped hair. "Time of death?"

"Rigor has set in, so I figure the murder could've happened any time between 7:30 last night and 4:00 this morning." The forensic investigator stood up. "The small muscles of the face are still rigid. Quite a smile, eh? From the body temp, I'd guess it was some time before midnight. The autopsy may narrow the estimate a little."

"Cause of death?" I asked.

The forensic investigator stared, his jaw at half mast. "Is there something you think I should look for besides instant death from a lethal stab wound to the heart?" He waved a pudgy finger at the stake.

"Yesterday she brought her daughter into D.C. to swear out a complaint against a vampire and now she has puncture wounds on her neck."

The forensic investigator drew back and glanced sideways at Thigden, as though to ask whether I was wacko.

"Vampire wannabes go around sucking blood and carrying wooden stakes as standard equipment," I informed him. "Is there any chance that loss of blood from the jugular could have killed her? That she was staked afterward simply to make it look like the cause of death?"

"Not a chance," the forensic investigator said. "Whether death is inflicted by a bullet or a stake or a heart attack, once the heart stops, the blood stops flowing. If she died from blood loss at the neck wound, there wouldn't be much blood around the stake, but the ground under her torso is muddy with it."

"So someone made the fang marks before stabbing her with the stake," I suggested.

The forensic investigator nodded.

"The murder weapon came from the garden," Thigden added. "Used to stake a rose bush."

So Mrs. Bouchard hadn't come outside prepared to hunt a vampire. The stake was a weapon of opportunity, not premeditation. I turned to Thigden. "Can you lift fingerprints from a wooden surface?" A vampire wouldn't leave fingerprints, but maybe the test would turn up other suspects.

"We'll damn well try."

The wind picked up, and the CSIs hurried to finish. Thigden started walking away from the scene. "What do you make of it?" he asked. "You think the bite marks show a vampire's involved?"

"Maybe a vampire," I said. "Maybe a very effective stage setting—the neck wounds, the weapon connected with vampire lore."

Thigden nodded thoughtfully.

"Her visit to the police yesterday," Harry told the older man. "I figure Mrs. B. thought vampires were a possibility."

"Maybe she came out to investigate a prowler," Thigden said. "Pulled up a stake from the rose garden as a weapon. He fought her off—perhaps including a bite. He got the stake away from her and then brought it down through the heart."

I gave Harry a skeptical look. "With that smile on her face?"

Thigden looked startled. Murder he could deal with, but not attractive vampires.

"Any other suspects?" I asked. "Yesterday the daughter let drop that the father had a mistress."

Thigden took a deep breath. "Something's fishy about the report. The housekeeper said Mr. Bouchard usually leaves the house at 8:30, but he didn't call 911 until eleven. By the time we got here, his lawyer had arrived and the doctor had just administered a sedative to the daughter. Won't be able to interview the girl for a while."

We all stopped at Harry's Jaguar. "If Bouchard did it," Harry said, "he would have had an alibi lined up. He wouldn't have taken two-and-a-half-hours to call the police."

Thigden shrugged but didn't disagree. "Could be the father's protecting the daughter. The housekeeper said the mother and daughter argued last night. Mrs. Bouchard threatened to send Ashley to boarding school in Switzerland with the nuns." Thigden furrowed his eyebrows. "The girl really swore out a complaint yesterday against a vampire?"

Harry nodded.

Thigden shook his head while we got into the car. "The housekeeper also said the girl was raving about a vampire killing her mother."

So Ashley claimed to have seen the murder? Was it Deepak? Or did we have another vampire on our hands?

▐ ▐ ▐

"Is there any play for us in this investigation?" I asked.

"Depends on who you think killed Mrs. Bouchard." Harry drove past the TV trucks and turned toward the town of Potomac.

"I hope it's not Deepak." I stopped, amazed that my long-standing distrust of vampires had all but disappeared after I'd met one who avoided killing. "Plus I'd like to keep vampires out of the news."

"And . . . ?" Harry asked, ever a miser with words.

"The fanging didn't kill Mrs. Bouchard; that sounds like Deepak. Someone stabbed her in the chest; that doesn't." I stopped, but Harry waited for more, so I went on. "Even if it's Deepak, there's little chance of proving it. I doubt a vampire would leave fingerprints on a wooden stake. And there's no chance of catching him, anyway. Not with his powers of shape-shifting."

You can tell a lot about a town by what's at the crossroads. Bars? Churches? In Potomac, it was real-estate brokers, banks, and strip malls, with a branch of Morgan Stanley for good measure. Harry pulled into the closest mall and parked in front of a French pastry shop.

"The stake through the heart sounds like an attack." He turned to me. "Ashley? Maybe even Shayna?"

"Yesterday Deepak said he was meeting Shayna at the library. He probably took her home."

"So you think after dropping Shayna off, Deepak stopped next door for a tryst with Mrs. Bouchard?"

"Maybe. And Shayna saw and attacked her."

Harry shook his head. "For jealous rage, my money's on Ashley. First she loses out to Shayna, and then Deepak gives the vampire's kiss to her mother? Not likely to improve mother-daughter relations."

Harry pulled out his cell phone, looked up a number, and punched it in. "Is Shayna home?" He paused. "Gracias." He pocketed the phone. "She's still at school."

"Boy, how cold-blooded would you have to be to kill Mrs. Bouchard and then go to school like nothing happened?" I asked. "Let's find her at school. See if she knows anything. They let out around two o'clock."

Harry checked his watch. "It's almost two now." He clicked his seatbelt and peeled out of the parking lot, taking the corner on two wheels.

"Turn right. Take Falls Road north," I shouted as Harry ignored the stop sign. "She's at Winston Churchill High School. I'll find it on the GPS."

Driving with Harry on a road with some spectacular twists felt like something they warn you against trying in car commercials. The sky was darkening ahead of us. The wind was up, and winter-bare trees as tall as telephone poles were bending.

I navigated Harry to the school just as students started pouring out the double doors of the main entrance of the modern, brick building. The entrance was flanked by two long, multi-story wings, each with a parking lot, alive with motion.

"You check out the student lot." I jerked my head to the left. "I'll check the buses. She may take a bus."

The wind yanked the car door out of my grasp, but I managed to shut it and push through the crowd toward the place where I saw the school buses lined up.

Bingo. Several yards ahead of me was Shayna Shemesh. Among the jeans and cutoffs, her knee-length skirt stood out.

"Shayna!" I called, but I heard no response in the chaos of shouting, high-fiving, laughing, and dancing to the music from a sea of iPod earbuds.

Then the rain began. Students started running, some putting books over their heads, some opening umbrellas. I caught up with Shayna and pulled her aside.

She looked pale, uncertain, wriggling in my grasp.

"Deepak said he was seeing you last night. Did he take you home?" I asked.

"Deepak didn't kill anyone."

I'd been naïve to think Shayna might not know about Mrs. Bouchard's murder. With text messaging and Twitter, even if the news media hadn't yet broadcast the story, she still would have heard it by now.

"Mrs. Bouchard was alive when he left her. Honest."

"Did you see what happened?" I asked.

Shayna tore her arm away. "My father's lawyer says I mustn't talk to anyone."

I reached out and pulled down the neck of her pink turtleneck. Two fresh puncture marks stood out where none had been the day before.

She turned and ran toward the line of buses.

Harry beeped from a nearby parking spot. The convertible's roof was unfolding and stretching over the seats, attracting lots of interest— in the car (from males) and the driver (from females). Harry secured the roof to the front windshield frame, and I weaved my way through the crowd and jumped in.

"What?" Harry put the car in reverse and edged out.

"She's lawyered up, but she did say Deepak didn't do it. And—" I paused for dramatic effect. "Shayna has two fresh puncture marks on her neck."

"So if Deepak fanged Mrs. B., it wasn't from hunger."

"You got it." I clicked my seatbelt. "Shayna will have to talk to the police. Maybe they can get something out of her."

With a thunderous crack, the skies opened. The windshield wipers beat frantically, a continuous *thwack-thwack-thwack*, fruitless against the downpour.

We headed for the exit, moving to the head of the bus queue. A dark blue Lincoln, with its hazard lights flashing and trunk open, blocked the exit. A girl dashed out to the car, herding Shayna before her. With her black, spikey hair, Ashley was unmistakable. Did she have a gun? She pushed Shayna into the trunk of the Lincoln, slammed it shut, hopped into the driver's seat, and floored it, burning rubber as she turned right on Tuckerman Lane.

"I didn't think Ashley was old enough . . ."

I never finished the sentence. Harry shifted into super drive, honking to warn more staid drivers to get out of his way. The blue Lincoln streaked ahead of us, doing at least fifty.

The rain came down in sheets, and the windshield wipers went crazy. Harry turned right at Tuckerman, trying to keep the blue Lincoln in sight through the downpour.

Harry shouted as he hunched over the wheel. "Where's she going?"

"She's going to kill Shayna! I bet she killed her mother out of jealousy, and now she's going for a second victim."

At Falls Road, the blue sedan began fishtailing on the slick pavement, then completed a left turn as the light turned yellow.

Harry followed, leaning on his horn, as the yellow light turned to red. A silver Volvo that had already inched forward in the rain swerved into the driveway of the volunteer fire department to avoid us and blasted his horn for a good ten seconds, its wail fading behind us.

The wipers were slicing across the windshield now at warp speed.

"Looks like she's heading home," I yelled. But why would Ashley rush toward home and the police unless she was innocent?

"Maybe." Harry controlled the occasional skid as we followed the fleeing car south. "What if Deepak killed Mrs. Bouchard and Ashley's using Shayna to lure him back to the scene?"

Could be, I thought. I had no hard proof of Deepak's innocence.

An old church with a graveyard marked the intersection at Democracy Boulevard. At the last minute, Ashley turned left, skidded, then regained traction and took off. Harry followed in time to see the blue Lincoln turn right into a suburban maze, a wealthy neighborhood with curbs and stone half-columns as mailboxes. We struggled to keep Ashley in sight. I wondered if she knew the subdivision or was relying on a GPS to avoid turning into a cul-de-sac.

A flash of lightning lit the sky, followed by an almost instantaneous crack of thunder. Just ahead, the trunk of a huge tree split; a tangle of limbs and branches fell in slow motion across the road, just missing the blue Lincoln sedan. Harry swerved left into a driveway to avoid the limbs, then careened over a manicured lawn that would never be the same. We bumped over the curb back onto the road.

Harry super-shifted back up to fourth and we slowly began to gain on Ashley. She took the next right, then an immediate left. Harry followed closely until we hit a speed bump.

I flew off the seat, my head crashing into the canvas roof of the convertible. Good thing I hadn't been talking or I might have bitten my tongue off. I could feel my teeth rattle in my head.

Harry must have been stunned, too, because the car slowed.

"Keep her in sight!" I yelled.

Harry ramped up the speed, then bore left at a fork in the road.

The rain had let up a bit, though it was still coming down steadily. The road ahead was dark. Had Ashley gone this way?

"She turned off her lights," Harry said. He drove down Falls Road and stopped where the road ended at MacArthur Boulevard.

"Left takes us into D.C.—in search of Deepak," I said. "If Ashley's out to get Shayna, turn right to Great Falls."

Harry looked at me.

"Go right," I said.

The Jaguar screeched into the turn, spraying gravel as we hit the unpaved road. We zoomed down the twisting, turning lane and soon came upon a welcome sign to the Chesapeake and Ohio Canal Park. We hadn't spotted Ashley, but a broken entry bar at the park entrance showed we were on the right trail.

"Turn left!" The Jag raced into the parking lot. Sure enough, near the walkway leading to the Falls, the abandoned Lincoln sprawled across three parking spaces in the almost empty lot. Ashley was just entering the brush and undergrowth near the walkway that protected the fragile topsoil. She was herding Shayna, whose hands were now tied behind her.

Harry slowed. I opened my door and jumped out of the car. The rain soaked me in seconds. In huge leaps you see only in dreams and Kung Fu movies, I used my step-vampire powers to bound effortlessly toward the walkway entrance. The sound of rushing water filled the air as the runoff from the rain and winter melt surged into the Potomac River.

Above a raging stream, the walkway crossed a deep ravine. Ashley straddled the wooden rails, struggling to push Shayna up and over, to drop her onto the sharp granite boulders and foaming water below. I slammed into Ashley. She lost her grip on Shayna and swayed out over the railing. Shayna fell to the planks of the walkway, screaming.

Ashley, off-balance, started a backward fall. I grabbed her by the waistband of her jeans and by her left leg and held on.

r r r

The police found fingerprints on the murder weapon—Ashley's, not Shayna's. Mr. Bouchard hired a big-name defense lawyer for his daughter. The Shemeshes wouldn't allow Shayna to give any interviews, though her pictures were all over the evening news when a leak to the press hinted that Mrs. Bouchard had tried to mediate a jealous rivalry between Ashley and Shayna. Nobody mentioned Deepak or a vampire. No interviews with the housekeeper, conveniently visiting her family in Peru.

The TV coverage lasted almost a week, with pictures of Shayna (filmed as she entered school) and Ashley (taken during her arrival at the police station). "Crime of passion! Daughter stakes mother!" screamed the headlines in the *National Inquirer.*

What with the girl ranting about a teenage vampire and how he made her do it, Ashley's lawyers were able to postpone her trial while she underwent a psychological evaluation. An eventual plea bargain—manslaughter while temporarily insane—saw Ashley committed to a private mental hospital. About two weeks after his daughter's sentence was announced, Mr. Bouchard remarried.

By then an agent had signed the beautiful Shayna—much slimmed through unhappiness and fasting—to a movie contract in the name of Rachel Hunnicutt.

We saw Deepak again only once, when Shayna invited us to the premiere of her first film. As the searchlights circled, advertising the location of the gala event, we spotted in the crowd outside the theater the young Indian, pudgy and sorrowful, gazing with longing at his lost love.

―――

Grant writer, software author, and recovering English professor Helen Schwartz was inspired to a career as a mystery writer when ordered by her condo association to get rid of her cat. She sublimated her desire to kill and started taking courses at the Writer's Center in Bethesda, Maryland. Her short story "On the Sixth Night of Hanukah" appeared in the holiday anthology Dying in a Winter Wonderland *(Wolfmont). She is working on a novel series about Ruth Nobis, a four hundred-year-old step-vampire raised by Orthodox Jews, who now runs a bed-and-breakfast on Capitol Hill. She hopes for publication of her first novel,* The Wrong Vampire, *while she continues work on her second,* Not Bloody Likely.

REMOTE DEATH

by Shelley Shearer

Fear isn't rational, Kat reminded herself as Gerald nodded in her direction. With her broken ankle encased in plaster and propped on pillows on her low, front-porch railing, Kat felt trapped and helpless. Something about her geriatric neighbor made her want to walk away backward, never letting him out of her sight. She reached for her crutches and placed them across her lap, finding the weight of them comforting.

"Mail?" He gestured toward her mailbox, his one-word sentences replacing pesky small talk.

"If you don't mind," she answered, minding very much indeed. She couldn't find a polite excuse to stop the president of the homeowners association from fetching her mail, even if he did make her skin crawl.

As she watched, her neighbor methodically made his way to the mailbox at the end of her walkway and removed her mail one piece at a time, not bothering to hide that he was reading it as he went along. On the outside, he appeared to be an average senior citizen helping out a neighbor, but Kat had a gut feeling about Gerald. He reminded her of a decayed tree with bugs crawling just beneath the bark.

He read one of her postcards as he walked toward her. She made a mental note to have her mail forwarded to work until she was up and about. Not that he would learn any deep dark secrets from her electronics catalogs or zany postcards from friends, but it felt invasive and one more reason to think about selling. Too bad the neighborhood was heading downhill fast, and the last real-estate agent she'd called said houses in the area were selling for far less than the already below-market price she'd paid two years ago. Kat couldn't afford that kind of loss. Until the economy improved, she was stuck.

Gerald walked up the steps onto her porch. "Decorating?" He motioned toward the box sitting next to her rocker, the box labeled Halloween Warehouse, Inc.

Kat mentally cursed herself for not throwing her afghan over the box when she saw him on the sidewalk, heading in the direction of her house.

"Oh no. No no no." She backed up the verbal negatives with a headshake, wanting to make sure he understood she had no interest in ever decorating anything in "his neighborhood." His smirk at her backpedaling riled her almost to the point of declaring her home trick-or-treat central this year, but she kept her peace. Once and only once had she tried decorating her house for a holiday. The year she'd moved in, she'd unloaded her storage bin and dusted off a yard full of wonderfully tacky Christmas decorations. She wanted to be *the* house, the one that families went out of their way to drive by.

There were several bizarre inflatable mishaps and a disaster with the elf carousel, she remembered, followed immediately by visits from Gerald, who mentioned that the association frowned on over-the-top displays. His message had been clear. Frosty went into the garage with all the other seasonal decorations. When not a single nylon spider web came out to grace the neighborhood's trees the following autumn, Kat left her Halloween decorations boxed and sealed.

"My nephew's school asked for some decorations for their fall festival next week," she explained. "Do you have anything you're tired of?" When would he hand over her mail and leave?

A nod. "Eyah."

She couldn't tell if he was agreeing he had stuff he was tired of, or if he was willing to donate items, but he didn't volunteer anything more. As Kat reached over and took the mail he still clutched, she noticed a wolf spider crawling across the railing toward her foot.

"Ew, could you swat that for me?" Kat asked, willing to tolerate Gerald if it meant not having a big, hairy spider crawl up her cast.

She looked up when he didn't answer. His eyes appeared to be glued to the advancing spider.

"Um, Gerald, the spider?"

The creature edged an inch closer to her toes. Kat shifted her cast. The movement startled the spider and it reared two front legs as if preparing to jump.

Gerald turned abruptly and scrambled down the stairs, reaching the sidewalk in the blink of an eye. "Have to go home now, get some repairs done, you know," he stammered, backing down her front walk. When he reached her mailbox, he turned and power walked to his house.

From Gerald that could be called babbling. Practically a speech. Interesting. Her creepy neighbor had a phobia. Kat allowed herself a brief guilty moment to enjoy the thought of Gerald having a heart attack over the spider. Why did he bring out the worst in her?

Her foot safely off the railing, she rolled up a magazine and whisked the spider off into the bushes.

❧ ❧ ❧

Her throbbing ankle kept Kat from sleep, but she'd take the pain in a second over the dulled creativity that pain pills caused. Besides, being awake at midnight gave her extra time to fine tune the Halloween surprise she was making for her nephew. The remote control had glitches, making her creatures jerk and stagger instead of moving realistically, they way she'd hoped. They were larger than their biological twins, too, but not so monstrous to be outside the realm of possibility. She didn't want a lot of frustrated eight-year-olds on her hands.

Kat stared at the creatures and tried to figure out what she had missed. They lacked that certain wow factor. Sometimes rummaging through her attic helped inspire her so Kat stuffed a flashlight in her pocket, grabbed her crutches, and hobbled up the stairs. When she bought the house, the previous owners had left her with a pile of boxes so high it would have given the fire marshal apoplexy. Kat hadn't the heart to trash someone else's memories so she'd made a point of sorting through the stuff, using whatever she could. In her rummaging, Kat had uncovered everything from grade-school report cards to a stuffed peacock. There were newspaper clippings, snapshots of the neighborhood. Obituaries of people the previous owners must have known.

Beneath some red Christmas bulbs, which would work perfectly as eyes, Kat spied a packet of clippings stuffed inside a stained envelope with something scrawled on it. She squinted. Odd. Why was Gerald's name on an envelope in her attic? She dumped the papers out on a small table in the corner, sat down in a creaky chair, and sorted through them idly.

Someone had cared enough to be fastidious in record keeping. Newspaper clippings, magazine articles, and photographs all had been meticulously labeled with names, dates, and supplementary notations. Intrigued, Kat spread them out in chronological order.

The first clipping came from the local paper commenting on Gerald's 1967 election as head of the homeowners association. In the next story, dated September 1967, a Hazel Beecham wrote that Arnie Simpson had planned to do a full haunted house for the trick-or-treaters that year. Arnie's obituary was paper-clipped to the back. Kat continued sorting, her stomach beginning to clench as their common thread became clear. Phil's unfortunate house fire, clipped to a Polaroid of his charred porch showing blackened pumpkins and ghosts. Maria's car accident attached to a note that said she had been appointed to head the Christmas decoration committee. Kat grabbed the pile of clippings and took them downstairs to read in better light.

Three hours later, her mind still racing, Kat's pain took her thoughts to a darker level. It all came back to Gerald. Gerald's obsession and his insatiable need for control. How many people had he hurt? Kat's unusable leg was the only thing that kept her from marching across the circle, barging into Gerald's house and, and what? Telling the senior citizen that he had to stop terrorizing the neighborhood? That he better let the neighbors put up their ghosts and goblins without fear of personal harm? She couldn't exactly call the police to report that the president of her HOA hated holiday decorations and ask them to arrest him. She had no real proof anyway, but she knew Gerald was the cause.

Kat glanced down at the clippings she had brought to her worktable. Was this why her house had been so cheap? Had the prior owners been too frightened to stay, willing to sell at any price? Would she find a newspaper article about them in the pile dated right before they left, describing some unfortunate accident resulting from an Easter bunny malfunction?

With the articles staring at her accusingly, Kat worked in earnest on her remotely controlled devices. Plastic wrappers and battery packs cluttered the table, but by 5 a.m. she'd finished. With a master remote poised, she controlled the creatures' slow crawl down the sidewalk and up onto Gerald's porch. They were in place just in time. She had one hour before Gerald's strict schedule put him on his front porch drinking coffee and watching his neighborhood wake up. The early morning darkness worked in her favor, casting shadows to hide within. She waited.

␥ ␥ ␥

The sirens woke her later that morning. Her brain foggy from insufficient sleep, it took a moment for Kat to identify the sound. She checked the clock on her bedside table, then scooted to the bedroom window in time to see EMTs roll a bagged body on a gurney toward a waiting ambulance. Yes!

A few hours earlier, after her robots had started crawling over and around him in his chair, Gerald had staggered back into his house. He hadn't been screaming hysterically, so she'd worried her plan hadn't worked. Nevertheless she'd quickly twisted a dial and called the creatures back home in case he overcame his fear and went after one of her toys.

No need to hurry now.

After the EMTs left, Kat settled on her porch and inspected Gerald's porch through the high-powered binoculars she planned to give her nephew for his birthday. Had her creatures left any trace behind? No.

It was only a test run, after all, but the tarantulas had operated perfectly, their hairy legs moving in the realistic manner she'd worked so hard to configure. Over to Gerald's house and back. Flawlessly.

Her nephew would love them for his party. And Halloween was only days away. Time to dust off Dracula and decorate.

––––––

Shelley Shearer works full time in accounting, but her free time is reserved for writing. A previous short story, "Inked to Death," appeared in Chesapeake Crimes 3, *and she is working on a novel. She lives in Northern Virginia with her husband, two sons, and a Great Pyrenees, constant sources of support and inspiration.*

OLD ROUTE EIGHT

by Lisa M. Tillman

The noise should have been awful, but the thud was surprisingly ordinary, like a big bag of mulch heaved to the ground. If I'd had the windows up and the heat blasting as I normally would at that time of year, I might never have heard it at all. But a clear, warm night is a rare treat at the shore in early October. It would have been criminal to waste it, so the windows on my Honda stayed down. I savored the crisp sea air that blew across Old Route 8 as I drove the ten miles home from Ridgeport to Hawley.

To say I'd traveled this road thousands of times before might be an underestimate. Born and raised in Hawley, not far from Fishers Creek, I've spent my entire life on the Eastern Shore. The house my husband and I share with our six-year-old daughter is less than a mile from the one where I grew up. I know the two lanes of Old Route 8 as well as I know anything. Sure, sometimes when I'm in a big hurry I'll take the new highway, but I prefer 8. The two-lane road is far less busy and much more scenic. It meanders along the coastline, weaving between coves and marshes, passing waterfront houses both grand and sad, most of them empty this time of year.

I heard the thud a few miles from Hawley, near where 8 meets Goff's Landing. Along the stretch of marsh that no one had managed to turn into a beach house, yet.

I swear I saw the bicycle for the first time when it bounced off the hood of my car. It cracked my windshield before flying into the marsh. I assume the cyclist followed, although I never actually saw him.

As soon as I realized what had happened, I slammed on the brakes. My hands shook as I pulled the van over to the side of the road; my knees wobbled as I jumped out. The darkness was all enveloping, the kind of pitch-blackness that makes your hand vanish inches from your face. *Who rides a bicycle on a dark road at night?*

The minivan's lights illuminated the empty road ahead of me. My gait unsteady, I felt my way around the side of the van and then stepped to the edge of the marsh. I could hear the soft lap of the water and feel the sea grass brush against my pants, but I couldn't see a thing. I staggered back to my car and searched the glove box for a flashlight. It would never occur to me to stash one there for an emergency, but I knew my husband, Paul, a grown up Boy Scout, definitely would. I found a penlight, its beam too small to dispel the dark night. I saw no sign of a bicycle.

"Hello?" I called. "Is anyone here? Are you all right?"

Only the crickets answered. Could I be seeing things? How much had I drunk? A few cocktails? Maybe more. If only I'd called Paul to pick me up.

We'd had a girls' night out, Kim and Haley and Dina and I. The first in such a long time no one could remember when we'd done it last. The four of us at Boardwalk Charley's in Ridgeport, drinking cosmos, just like the old days. Before jobs and husbands and kids and mortgages.

I reached for my phone to call for help, then stopped. My cell would never work out here. Too far from town for a signal. I'll go home and call. Maybe by then the cosmos would have run their course.

At home, shaky and ill, my head began to spin. I didn't know if it was from the accident or the drinks. I figured I'd rest for a moment. Let the booze clear out. Then I'd call the cops.

I fell asleep on the living room couch.

"Must have been quite a night," Paul said when he kissed me on his way out the door the following morning.

"What time is it?" I croaked, rubbing my eyes. The sunlight streaming through our picture window was painful.

"Almost 8:20. You better wake Janie if she's going to make the school bus."

I sat up and immediately wished I hadn't. My stomach lurched, and my head pounded. I'd fallen asleep in my clothes. How did I get home last night? I remembered why I didn't drink anymore.

Paul took pity on me and fetched coffee and Advil as I raced to help my daughter dress. Since we had only twenty minutes to make the bus, I toasted a strawberry Pop-Tart for her. I felt guilty about the crappy breakfast, but Janie was thrilled. As she ate, I threw on my workout clothes and pulled my hair into a ponytail for the walk to the school bus stop. I followed Janie out through the garage, still trying to piece together what had happened the night before. Then I saw my car and froze.

The windshield was cracked.

My knees buckled as the previous evening's events rushed into my mind: cosmos at Boardwalk Charley's, the drive home, the thud. I reached for the car to steady myself.

Oh my God. What had I done?

It required all my strength to smile and wave as Janie boarded the school bus, but as soon as it turned the corner I ran home as fast as my hangover would permit. For the first time since we bought our tiny house, I was happy it only had a one-car garage. At least Paul hadn't seen the windshield.

I called in sick to the dental office where I worked part time in the billing department. Then I jumped into my van and drove the route between my house and Boardwalk Charley's, twice. I couldn't see any evidence of the accident I thought I'd caused—no bicycle, no skid marks, no damaged sea grass—nothing. Old Route 8 looked as it always did. I rested my head on the steering wheel. The cool, hard plastic soothed my throbbing head. Could it be possible I'd dreamed the whole thing? Something had cracked my windshield.

On the way home, I pulled into Hawley Motors and made an appointment to have the windshield fixed the next day. My stomach twisted when the manager asked what had happened. I told him I didn't know.

"Most likely a rock," he said as he ran his hand across the cracked glass. "Another car probably kicked it up. Happens all the time. Rotten luck."

At home I swallowed more Advil and checked the paper. My hands shook as I turned the pages, and my hangover made it difficult to read. I searched the news online, too, but found no mention of an accident on Old Route 8. Nothing. No one reported missing. No one found.

The afternoon crept by slowly. My hangover eased, but I still felt horrible. I jumped every time the phone rang, and I started to sweat when a patrol car turned onto our street while I waited for Janie's bus. I promised myself I'd never drink again.

I know I could have called the police then and confessed what I feared had happened, but I never picked up the phone. There are a million excuses why. What would I have told them anyway? That I couldn't be sure if I'd hit someone because I'd had too much to drink? I was petrified they'd arrest me for driving while intoxicated, or leaving the scene of an accident, or killing someone with my car. Sure the accident had been unintentional, but my behavior ever since had been quite deliberate.

Sleep eluded me that night. When I shut my eyes I saw that damn bicycle bounce off my windshield over and over again. Every noise frightened me. I was convinced the police were coming to snatch me away from Janie and Paul.

Hawley's fixed the windshield the next day, and since I pay all the bills, Paul would never see the charge. He'd never know what I did. I hoped. Almost forty-eight hours had passed. How could I tell my husband that I might have hit someone with the car two nights before and left that person for dead on the side of Old Route 8? Oh, and by the way,

I was probably a little drunk when I did it.

Paul would never look at me the same again. He'd also insist on searching the marsh. But then what? What if we found a body? Would we bury it? Then Paul would be sucked into this, too. What would happen to us if we got caught? Who would take care of Janie if both of her parents were in prison?

So I couldn't tell Paul. I would endure the guilt alone.

The sounds of that night haunted me. Every door I closed echoed the thud. My heart raced when I heard crickets. Sleep became torture. I relived the accident night after night in my dreams. I'd wake at dawn and run to grab the newspaper from the driveway. I scoured every news source I could think of in search of any mention of the accident I thought I'd caused.

As the days turned into weeks, my initial panic faded, but the knowledge of what I might have done hung like a weight around my neck. By the time fall turned to winter, I no longer sprinted for the paper, but an uncomfortable sensation lingered. A mix of guilt and apprehension settled in my chest. Every time there was a knock at the door or the phone rang I thought *this is it*. Discovery, I feared, lurked just around the corner.

Almost a year later, I sensed I was about to get what I deserved. One of the dental hygienists came to work late. My face felt hot as she described the detour around Old Route 8 she had been required to take because the police had blocked off the road near Goff's Landing.

According to the news reports, a survey crew, employed by the builder of yet another beach house, had found bones and a bicycle in the marsh. I knew the police would be coming for me soon.

The panic returned. I jumped each time the office door opened. My pulse quickened when the phone rang.

"Did you hear about the skeleton they dug up near Old Route 8 this morning?" Paul asked as we shared a pizza with Janie that night.

My husband had no idea he sat across the table from the person who had sent the body into the marsh. I watched as my family ate and wondered how many more nights I would have with them.

The police finished their work on Old Route 8, and still no one came to arrest me. Work resumed on the house near where the body was found, yet I walked free. A few weeks later the authorities announced they'd used dental records to identify the cyclist. The dead man was John A. Palek, fifty-six. His last known address was a transient motel about twenty minutes from Hawley.

According to the news reports, Palek had been in and out of jail most of his life. His long criminal record included convictions for sexual assault and child abuse. No one had reported him missing, and they hadn't located his next of kin.

"Sounds like someone did the world a favor," Paul said as we watched the news before bed. "I hope they don't waste too much time looking for whoever hit the creep."

I nodded. My wait, it seemed, would continue.

———

Lisa M. Tillman's novel Blood Relations *(Hilliard and Harris) was nominated for the 2005 Agatha Award for Best First Novel. She is a veteran television writer and producer whose work has appeared on Court TV and The History Channel. Born and raised in New York, she is a graduate of New York University's Tisch School of the Arts. She now lives in Maryland.*

ABOUT THE EDITORS

Many people helped to make *Chesapeake Crimes: They Had It Comin'* reality, including our editorial staff: editorial board members Erin N. Bush, Megan G. Plyler, and Mary Augusta Thomas, and coordinating editors Donna Andrews, Barb Goffman, and Marcia Talley. The editorial board undertook the monumental task of reading all the stories submitted by members of the Chesapeake Chapter of Sisters in Crime and selecting the ones that would appear in this anthology. Once the stories were selected, all six editorial staffers helped contributors with revisions and editing, and the contributing editors then prepared the manuscript for submission to our publisher.

The editorial board members could not submit stories. Coordinating editors could, but they had to pass the same blind acceptance procedure as any other chapter member. Barb and Donna are very relieved that the editorial board didn't hate their stories, and Marcia, whose stories have appeared in the first three volumes of the series, wants it clearly understood that she didn't have time to write anything this time around.

Erin N. Bush is a licensed private investigator, a historian, and the new media director for a local magazine. She is hard at work on her first novel, a cozy set in her hometown on the outskirts of Pittsburgh. An avid amateur photographer and cook, she is attempting to instill in her protagonist her own passion for food and camera equipment. She lives in Northern Virginia with a menagerie of four kids, four cats, and a husband.

Megan G. Plyler is the author of "Keeping the Peace: Violent Justice, Crime, and Vigilantism in Tanzania," in *Violence and Non-Violence in Africa*, Routledge, 2007. She is a cultural anthropologist at the Iris Center at the University of Maryland, College Park. She currently is working on a project in Kenya on access to microfinance for the poor. When not engaged in research overseas, teaching, or serving on editorial boards, she can be found reading and writing mysteries.

Marcia Talley is the Agatha and Anthony award-winning author of *Without a Grave* and seven previous mystery novels featuring cancer survivor and sleuth Hannah Ives.

Marcia is author/editor of two star-studded collaborative novels, *Na-*

ked Came the Phoenix and *I'd Kill for That*, set in a fashionable health spa and an exclusive gated community, respectively. Her short stories appear in more than a dozen collections. A recent story, "Can You Hear Me Now?" is featured in *Two of the Deadliest: New Tales of Lust, Greed and Murder from Outstanding Women of Mystery*, edited by *New York Times* best-selling author Elizabeth George.

Marcia is president of Sisters in Crime, Inc., serves on the board of the Mid-Atlantic Chapter of the Mystery Writers of America, and is a member of the Authors Guild. She lives in Annapolis, Maryland, with a husband who loves to sail and a cat who doesn't.

Mary Augusta Thomas is the author of *An Odyssey in Print: Adventures in Smithsonian Libraries*, 2002, and editor of *Information Imagineering: Meeting at the Interface*, with Milton Wolfe and Pat Ensor, 1998. She makes her living as deputy director of the Smithsonian Institution Libraries, guiding the operation of twenty libraries located in each of the museums and research institutes of the Smithsonian. In her spare time, Mary Augusta serves on editorial advisory boards for two professional journals and reads mysteries.

Biographies for **Donna Andrews** and **Barb Goffman** appear with their stories.

4970589R0

Made in the USA
Lexington, KY
21 March 2010